D0545092

We hope you enjoy this b̶ renew it by the due date.

You can renew it at www.norfolk.gov.uk/libraries or by using our free library app.

Otherwise you can phone 0344 800 8020 - please have your library card and PIN ready.

You can sign up for email reminders too.

NORFOLK ITEM

30129 083 446 956

NORFOLK COUNTY COUNCIL
LIBRARY AND INFORMATION SERVICE

ALSO BY ADRIAN WRIGHT

Fiction
Maroon

Non-Fiction
No Laughing Matter
Foreign Country
A Pagan Adventure
The Innumerable Dance
A Tanner's Worth of Tune
West End Broadway

THE
VOICE
OF
DOOM

THE FRANCIS AND GORDON JONES MYSTERIES

ADRIAN WRIGHT

Matador
9 Priory Business Park,
Wistow Road, Kibworth Beauchamp,
Leicestershire. LE8 0RX
Tel: 0116 279 2299
Email: books@troubador.co.uk
Web: www.troubador.co.uk/matador
Twitter: @matadorbooks

ISBN 978 1785893 285
British Library Cataloguing in Publication Data.
A catalogue record for this book is available from the British Library.

Printed and bound by CPI Group (UK) Ltd, Croydon, CR0 4YY
Typeset in 11pt Adobe Garamond Pro by Troubador Publishing Ltd, Leicester, UK

Matador is an imprint of Troubador Publishing Ltd

For Margaret Jones

CONTENTS

Contents

FOREWORD

It was once the convention for almost every work of fiction to insist that its characters were not based on any person living or dead. The fact that this was often not so need not concern us. An author can only hope that his inventions will seem real to his readers. For me, teenagers Norman and Henry Bones, created by the writer Anthony C Wilson in a series of books and dramatized adventures for the BBC *Children's Hour* begun in the 1940s, were characters that worked themselves into my head and stayed there.

Over the years, the idea of writing an affectionate pastiche of Wilson's warmhearted, innocent and highly popular stories of an earlier age, came and went. And kept coming back. In a first attempt, I tried ageing Norman and Henry, bringing them back in old age, still stumbling about solving mysteries. It didn't work. Eventually, my tribute to Wilson and his enterprising boys took a different turn: I went back to the 1950s, and Norman and Henry Bones were reborn as Francis and Gordon Jones. Neither they, nor any of the repertory company of characters that play their parts in these stories, bear the faintest resemblance to Wilson's original Norman and Henry Bones or any of Wilson's supporting cast, but they were certainly the inspiration for the stories you hold in your hand. For me, as for many, Norman and Henry were heroes of a forgotten England.

In April 1960, the children of Britain left the nation in no doubt. During a poll conducted for Request Week on BBC *Children's Hour*, the audience's favourite was revealed as 'Norman and Henry Bones'. Norman, a perennial 16-year-old, and his cousin Henry aged 14, lived close to one another in the middle-class comfort of a Norfolk village. These enduring characters were teenagers before teenagers had been discovered. Today, the mention of Anthony Wilson's 'boy detectives' still brings a smile to the face of those who remember them.

The eldest of four children, Anthony Wilson was born to a tenant farmer at Westacre, near King's Lynn, in 1916. Childhood was an enchanted time from which this tall, shy bachelor with a winning smile never fully emerged – his sister Rachel remembered him as 'a bit of a Peter Pan, totally unsophisticated. He liked simple things, being among ordinary village people. If he met smart people he shut up like a clam.'

The early years bound him to a love of the Norfolk countryside, its changing seasons, plant life and animals. And radio.

Anthony grew up at the same time as the wireless, which would come to play so important a part in his life. He never forgot the thrill of his father bringing home a crystal wireless set and, headphones on, hearing Stuart Hibberd reading the news from 2LO. When a Westacre aunt acquired a valve wireless set, he and his brother Robin every evening made the two-mile journey to her house to hear *Children's Hour*. It was during these walks, guided in winter by a hurricane-lamp, that an air of mystery seemed all around Anthony – a shred of fog across a path, the muted cry of a bird, the sudden crack of branches.

There was happiness, too, at Feltonfleet, his preparatory school in Cobham. From here, Anthony went to Repton, where, at the age of 16, he was diagnosed as having a weak heart, and sent home. The future seemed uncertain, until he was invited to return as school secretary to Feltonfleet, where his outstanding abilities as a teacher were soon recognised.

One hot afternoon in May 1940, a 9-year-old boy tugged at the sleeve of his Harris Tweed jacket (Anthony always wore the same design, replacing it when the one he lived in became too shabby for words) and asked 'Please, sir, will you tell us a story?' Years later, Anthony recalled: 'There was no getting out of it. Stories are children's prerogatives; one must never refuse them. And so, without the slightest idea of what was coming next, I plunged into the fray: 'Well, once upon a time there was a boy who was very keen on detective work, and his name was Norman Bones.' Henry was invented a few adventures later.

The enthusiasm of the Feltonfleet boys for the Bones cousins encouraged Anthony to submit the idea to the BBC. Josephine Plummer, a producer for *Children's Hour*, was immediately enthusiastic, and the first play, 'A Mystery at Ditchmoor', was transmitted in July 1943, with Charles Hawtrey as Norman, and Peter Mullins, later replaced by Patricia Hayes, as Henry. So successful were the characters that more than 120 adventures followed, only coming to an end when *Children's Hour* was axed in 1961.

David Davis ('David' of *Children's Hour*) once said that Sherlock Holmes would have welcomed Norman and Henry Bones to Baker Street with a more than usually lavish spread of toast and muffins – poor old Dr Watson, no doubt, recognising a soulmate in the devoted Henry. Conan Doyle would certainly have approved of Anthony's crisply-plotted and atmospheric stories, most of them set in Norfolk, with their fascinating titles – 'The Phantom Telephone' down which the cunning Mr Hayward sent shivers; 'House of Shadows' in which Dr Scott-

Mason harboured foreign criminals; 'The Mystery of Tyford Towers' with its ghostly monk.

In 1955, the Wilson family moved to the White Lodge, Swaffham, and it was here, in the school holidays, that Anthony continued to work at his radio plays and the series of books, translated into several languages, that carried the boys on to a more substantial immortality than radio could offer.

Turning these pages, it is not only Anthony's storytelling that is so sure, but the new-minted appreciation of a boy's world, far away from the knowing cynicism of our own. His characters may be from stock, but they inhabit communities bound together in nature: the cosy scene around a vicarage hearth, promises of lemonade and gingerbread, thick velvet curtains drawn against the east wind and, beyond, a world of suspicion, strange noises, Germans with menacing eyes, a scrap of paper with a message, tantalizingly torn in half.

When his mother died in 1971, Anthony retired from Feltonfleet to a cottage on East Walton Common. His life had been dedicated to generations of boys. Throughout the years, he had tirelessly produced the school play – writing both words and music, building the props and transporting them in his bulging Morris Traveller. Now, he turned to painting wild flowers – there are nine volumes of his meticulous botanical sketches – to amateur theatricals and to conjuring. His writing was not forgotten. As late as 1984 he was trying to break into television, but the moment had passed.

The heart disease that had threatened him early in life caught up with him at last. In February 1986, aged 69, he died while staying with his sister in Swaffham. He was sitting at her kitchen table, painting some pussy willow.

Reading his stories today, they seem to be happening

in a gentler England, an England for which Anthony – and Norman and Henry – had an intrinsic sympathy. If nature had been allowed to take its course, Norman and Henry would now be in their eighties. That, of course, is unthinkable. It was Anthony Wilson's particular gift to encapsulate that intelligent, caring and reckless zest of boyhood. He was that rarest of things, a born teller of stories. I wish I had known him. I hope he might even have enjoyed these stories.

A PROBLEM AT ST MILDRED'S

*O*ur beginning is in dark and wet weather in March 1956, somewhere in the East of England. It is a night when wind curls singing into chimneys and dogs have been recommended to stay indoors. Rex, a Labrador retriever, knows this time of year. His master, who also wears a dog collar, steps over him to put another log on the tremblingly low fire. He was in his study at Branlingham Vicarage working on his sermon when his young visitor arrived. The bicycle on which the boy travelled leans against the porch. Mindful of the delicacy of receiving an unchaperoned adolescent boy into the vicarage, the man looks out left and right before closing the door and showing his guest into the sitting room. If this were Colonel Bayliss arriving for his weekly game of chess the Reverend Challis would have wasted no time in pouring two large whiskies, but the etiquette of the youth club intrudes, and the reverend offers his glowing visitor lemonade and a slice of ginger cake.

'It's good of you to come to the house, Francis. I didn't want to rouse the suspicions of anyone from the village by them seeing us together.'

Francis sips at the cordial and puts down a hand to nuzzle Rex's nose.

'Do you have a case for me, sir?' asks Francis.

'As a matter of fact, I have,' says the Reverend Challis. He stands, moves to one of the many items of oak furniture in the room and lifts a pipe to his mouth. Francis jumps up, finds a spill on the mantelpiece and stoops to light it among the embers of the fire. Mr Challis is unperturbed, for he prefers the older, fuller figure. Only that morning he had slipped a photograph of Sydney Greenstreet between the pages of the latest Billy Bunter story. Francis carries the lighted spill to the bowl of his host's pipe.

'Thank you, my boy,' says the reverend. 'There have been some strange things happening in the village, Francis. My suspicions have been aroused, but in my position there is precious little I can do without tittle-tattle breaking out all over.'

'I see your predicament, sir,' replies Francis. 'It wouldn't do at all for a man of the cloth to get involved personally in any sort of investigation.'

'Quite so. It would, at least, be irreligious. Then, naturally, I thought of you. I know how you enjoy nothing more than a little detective work.'

'I couldn't do it alone, sir.'

Mr Challis agreed unhesitatingly. He knew that Francis's cousin Gordon would also be involved. The boys were seldom apart, although sixteen-year-old Francis lived with his parents at Red Cherry House and fourteen-year-old Gordon lived in the next village of Strutton-by-the-Way with his old uncle at Bundler's Cottage. The boys had impressed Mr Challis at the village fête last summer, the way they had assisted the elderly and infirm on and off the roundabouts, made sure the children came to no harm, and helped peg down the tea-tent. Now, Mr Challis sat close to Francis on the settle, his voice suddenly husky.

'The fact is, Francis,' said Mr Challis, 'that I am not altogether what I seem.'

Francis sat forward, eager to hear what this most respected of men had to tell him.

'Before I became a vicar,' continued Mr Challis, 'I was involved in… certain activities. It eventually became necessary, because of developments in a far-off country with which our government had been experiencing difficulties, for me to leave that country and return to England, where I took on a new persona.'

'You're not a vicar at all?' asked Francis, unable for the moment to control his surprise.

'Have no fear, my boy. After leaving the country of which I was speaking I went through all the necessary channels, theological college, and so forth. I am quite entitled to give the sacraments.'

Francis was relieved to hear it. He didn't fancy telling Mrs Shewin's Elsie that she and Dan from the farm had been married two weeks ago by an impostor wearing his collar the wrong way round!

'I had hoped,' said Mr Challis, his voice even lower, 'that my former life was quite behind me, but I'm afraid that is not so… In the last few months I have realised that there are those who know about my, shall we say, patriotic work. They have found out where I am, Francis, and they know that I am still the guardian of national secrets.'

This was thrilling! Francis was seeing the reverend in quite a different light. Mr Challis was a spy!

'Clearly, it wouldn't do for me to do anything… unvicarly… but it is necessary for me to find out more about these people. They need to be watched, Francis. I need hardly say that much depends on their being uncovered and rooted out, and the intervention of anything so ostentatious as a man in police uniform would immediately alert their suspicions.'

'Sending them back to that country and then hatching even more devilish plans?' suggested Francis.

'Exactly.'

Mr Challis placed his hand on Francis's knee.

'I cannot say too much,' said Mr Challis, 'but your name has been mentioned in Downing Street.'

'And Gordon's?' asked Francis.

'Naturally,' said Mr Challis. 'We must not forget Gordon.'

'*Well*, I think it's a crying shame.'

Doris Jones slapped a wedge of pastry on the wooden table of the kitchen at Red Cherry House. Clouds of flour emphasised her displeasure.

'After all the help our Francis has been to the local constabulary. An outright disgrace, I call it.'

Two weeks after his son Francis had visited the Reverend Challis, Mr Jones was in the Windsor chair by the range, pretending to read the evening newspaper. With any luck, his wife's attention would be drawn back to the completion of the Bramley apple pie she was planning for supper.

'When you think,' said Mrs Jones. 'If it wasn't for Francis and Gordon, the Countess of Marsham-Peckforth would be reduced to wearing imitation pearls at the Hunt Ball; poor Mr Carpenter at the funeral parlour would have buried the wrong man in Hemley graveyard and no one the wiser; little Toby Mallingering would have been smuggled out of the country covered in Cherry Blossom Boot Polish and passed off as the Heir Apparent to the throne of Narpithiia. And the police none

4

the wiser, Constable Cudd plod-hopping about the village and getting promotion for reporting old Ben Thropper for not having a light on his bicycle.'

Mr Jones turned a page and made a business of concentrating on something of compelling interest.

'And now this latest development,' Mrs Jones snorted, giving the flour shifter a violent awakening. 'Francis is being exploited, that's what. Him and Gordon together, made to do the work of the police force and in the unpaid service of the British government.'

'Steady on, Doris. Anyone would think the boys were working for the Secret Service. Once or twice, they've just happened to be in the right place at the right time, and been able to give the police information.'

'I'm surprised at you, George Jones. The whole village sleeps easier in its bed because of those boys, our boys. And I don't like seeing our son so put down.'

There was no hope of ever reading that newspaper. Mr Jones folded it noisily, pushed it away from him and folded his arms.

'What are you on about, Doris? And you've got flour on your nose.'

'Do something useful,' said Doris Jones. 'We're plum out of custard powder, and Mrs Robinson doesn't shut up shop till six.' She smudged her nose clean with a movement of her elbow, and remembered her career as a part-time corsetiere. 'Don't forget to remind her she's got a fitting on Tuesday.'

Mr Jones didn't need telling twice. He was already putting on his bicycle clips. Salt of the earth, Mrs Jones thought but didn't say, and turned to shaping the edge of the pie. Mrs Robinson's circular stitched bra would be a challenge. If all went well, Mrs Jones would turn her into the village's Jayne Mansfield.

'*Mother's* making an apple pie,' said Francis. 'Always a bad sign, so I thought I'd come over to see you.'

It was never a hardship for Francis to cycle the three miles to where his cousin Gordon Jones lived with his uncle in Strutton-by-the-Way. Gordon's Uncle Billy had been in the Navy and kept Bundler's Cottage ship-shape. Great logs were burning in the hearth, a welcome sight on such a cold evening.

'Come in and get yourself warm, Francis,' said Uncle Billy. 'There's enough supper for three if you're stopping.'

'That's very kind of you, Uncle Billy, but mother will be expecting me home for supper.'

'Ah,' said Mr Jones, who knew his sister-in-law's ways. 'I expect this is one of Doris's baking days. I'll put the kettle on anyway.' Something about the keen expression on Francis's face told him that the boy wanted to talk with his nephew. 'You two make yourself comfy by the fire.'

As his uncle went through to the kitchen, fourteen-year-old Gordon packed away the Meccano set and looked up expectantly at his cousin. He ploughed his fingers through his tousled mop of red hair, pushed his spectacles more comfortably on to his nose, and made room on the hearthrug for Francis to sit beside him.

It had been too long since they had set out to solve a mystery, and there was something urgent about Francis's face that promised the start of a new adventure.

'It's a beastly night,' said Gordon, 'so you must have a good reason for coming.'

Francis lowered his voice.

'As a matter of fact,' he said, and told Gordon about the unexpected summons to the vicarage and the Reverend Challis's story.

As he listened, Gordon's face changed as many times as the English weather! At first his green eyes began to sparkle, his cheeks glowed with anticipation when he sensed that a new extraordinary occurrence was about to be revealed, and then all hope faded from his expression. He couldn't remember when he had last been so disappointed.

'Fancy the Reverend Challis leading you on like that,' he said. 'I expect you were hoping he was going to ask for our help.'

'Yes, I did, but it seems the mystery has already been solved, and we're not going to be able to do any detective work on it.'

'So, correct me if I'm wrong,' said Gordon. 'The Reverend Challis is a government agent and a vicar who has been keeping an eye on a foreign spy.'

'Exactly,' replied Francis. 'The spy was known to be working in East Anglia, wanting to infiltrate local power stations. The spy was masquerading as a member of the community, and eventually was tracked down to a most unlikely location.'

'I should say it is unlikely!' Gordon smiled. 'St Mildred's School for the Advancement of Deserving Girls is one of the most respected establishments in the neighbourhood. And the spy had infiltrated the school, had she?'

'Exactly,' said Francis. 'In fact, she was a local woman, recruited from the village, and had been employed at the school for several years to accompany the girls when they went off on fact-finding trips to nearby factories and industries.'

'And power stations, no doubt!' suggested Gordon.

'Fortunately, the Reverend Challis had his suspicions, and

the spy was removed from the school a few days ago, so the case is closed. The pity of it is that now the school has not enough staff to carry on taking the girls out to points of interest, and the Reverend Challis, being essentially a charitable man, thought we might be of help.'

'I don't fancy taking a lot of girls on an outing,' said Gordon. 'Imagine the noise on the coach!'

'That's not the idea. He would like the girls to feel they are part of the community, and thinks they should be involved in activities with other people in the area. His theory is that St Mildred's has become too isolated, too much of an all-female establishment. Perhaps, if there had been some male members of staff, the spying would never have stood a chance of happening at all. He thinks St Mildred's would benefit by having some sporting fixtures with our school, and he wants us to suggest it to her.'

'Girls versus boys, you mean?' asked Gordon. 'St Mildred's against St Basil's Grammar?'

'Especially as a new headmistress has just been appointed, to ensure that the school can start off on a new footing. The Reverend Challis said we would be acting as ambassadors.'

'Well, at least that makes a change from being boy detectives,' said Gordon. 'As a matter of fact, I think I may already have met the new headmistress. I was riding past the gates of St Mildred's on my way back from a brass-rubbing the other day when this little Austin 7 whizzed round the corner to turn into the school and nearly knocked me into the hedge. The woman driver was most concerned. Got out of the car and made sure I was in one piece. A small grey-haired woman in a russet suit.'

'Yes, that would have been Miss Frobisher,' replied Francis.

'Just as well you've met her before. You can introduce me to her when we call at the school tomorrow morning. We have an appointment for 10.30!'

St Mildred's School for the Advancement of Deserving Girls comprised a fine Georgian house standing in six acres of pastoral seclusion, with various additional structures erected in later years with impeccable taste. Francis and Gordon rode up to the school's gates five minutes before they were due to meet the headmistress.

'My goodness,' said Francis. 'You must have been cutting along this road at a rate, if you almost collided with Miss Frobisher's car. The road is so wide here; you must have been wandering all over the place. You should be more careful.'

'Yes, I must,' said Gordon.

The sun had come out, a welcome brightness after the recent dull days. Today the school was at half-term; the boarders had been sent home, and not a whisper of the croquet mallet or happy cry of the netball court could be heard as the boys wheeled their bicycles around the side of the main house, leaving them in cycle racks at the rear of the tuck shop. It was then that a terrible cry cracked the stillness.

'Stop that!'

The boys turned to where an elderly man in dirty corduroys tied up with string, a fisherman's smock, gumboots and a battered trilby was waving a pitchfork in their faces.

'Don't leave them there lawn-mowers there!' he shouted through blackened teeth.

'Lawn-mowers?' It was no wonder the boys spoke in unison, as well as disbelief!

'Can't trust young roustabouts nowadays,' the old man

9

muttered. 'Them there lawn-mowers is to be delivered to the potting sheds, per Miss Frobisher's orders.'

'I'm sorry, sir,' said Francis, who had earned one of his Scout medals for dealing tactfully with the elderly and feeble-minded. 'I think there's been a misunderstanding.'

'Don't use that tone with me,' said the old man, with another dangerous wave of the pitchfork. 'Whippersnappers, the lot o' you.'

While Gordon was trying to suppress boyish giggles, Francis smiled gently at the deluded member of St Mildred's staff.

'We have an appointment to see Miss Frobisher,' he said.

'Yes,' said Gordon, 'and we haven't brought her any lawn-mowers either!'

'We were just parking our bicycles,' said Francis.

'Well, bless my soul!' said the old man. 'My missus is always sayin' I need my eyes examined. I wondered why them there lawn-mowers had bells on them. This way, young gentlemen.'

The old man led them across a courtyard until they reached the imposing front entrance of the school, where a middle-aged woman, crisply dressed in a blue and white sailor boy jacket and skirt, appeared smilingly in the doorway.

'They ain't brought the lawn-mowers,' said the old man.

'Thank you. That will be all, Parsons.' She dismissed the employee with an exasperated gesture. 'You must be Francis and Gordon Jones,' she said, extending a hand in welcome. 'The Reverend Challis told me you would be calling. Do come in, please.'

She shook hands with her visitors, and stared at Gordon for a moment.

'Oh dear,' she said. 'I think we may have met before. I do

hope you have had no after effects from our little collision.'

Laughing, and stopping only to admire the vaulted wooden ceiling of the school's ample vestibule, the boys were led into the headmistress's study. A painted sign on its door read 'Miss Maude Frobisher, RAC.'

'It is so good of you to call,' said Miss Frobisher. She ushered the boys to two comfortable armchairs and then sat, ramrod-backed, in the swivel chair behind her desk. Once seated, her tone became confidential.

'As you will know, the school has only recently dealt with a most serious matter. National security was being threatened by one of the staff, using her position for espionage purposes. Only Scotland Yard, MI5, the Reverend Challis and yourselves share this knowledge with me. That person has now been removed by the school and will be dealt with by the relevant authorities. It was also decided to appoint a new headmistress. I am she. The school may be said to be in a state of recovery. Which, as you will understand, is why I have been brought in. A new broom, so to speak. Nothing, of course, must be spoken of this outside these four walls.'

'Of course not,' said Francis.

'We are still Boy Scouts,' said Gordon.

Miss Frobisher leaned even closer across the desk, speaking in almost a whisper.

'I know of your reputation as detectives. The Reverend Challis has told me that more than once you have assisted the police.'

Francis almost said Mum's the word, until he remembered her Bramley apple pie.

'It must have been a very trying time for you, Miss Frobisher.'

'Yes, indeed. To think that the school had been harbouring

a spy in its midst! It's just as well that the holiday has arrived, although it feels very lonely now that the girls have gone down for the half term. I had planned to have a few days with my sister on the Isle of Wight, but I'm afraid I have had to cancel.'

'Oh dear,' said Francis. 'Is there anything we can do to help?'

'How kind. No, nothing at all. One of the boarders was unable to return home for the holiday as she has a highly infectious condition. Matron had already booked a week's tour of the lesser cathedral cities, but fortunately I worked as a nurse in earlier years.'

'I do hope your patient improves soon,' said Francis.

'Oh yes. Nothing to worry about, but she has to be kept in complete isolation. Now, how may I help you?'

Francis suggested his idea that St Mildred's might agree to a sporting fixture with the boys of St Basil's.

'My goodness!' cried Miss Frobisher. 'Boys and girls meeting together in that way. I can see that you go in for modern thinking, Francis.'

'As a matter of fact, my cousin Gordon is really the sporting one. I'm sure you would find him willing to help in any way you may suggest.'

'It is certainly true that we pride ourselves on keeping our girls healthy at St Mildred's. Our netball team is one of the finest in the county, and hockey has quite overtaken maypole dancing as a highlight of our curriculum.'

Gordon smiled encouragingly, and looked towards a pile of racquets in the corner of the room.

'I can see by the quality of the racquets you have here that sport is taken seriously,' he said.

Miss Frobisher turned her eyes to where Gordon was looking.

'Oh yes,' she laughed. 'If the girls are to be successful tennis players, they must have the very best tools.'

Her face grew darker.

'I am most grateful to you for bringing this idea to us. Quite a brilliant stroke, to bring the girls' school and the boys' school closer together in such a way. My only concern is that perhaps we should carefully consider the sort of activities they would be engaging in. Dominoes, perhaps, or tiddly-winks, might prove less eyebrow-raising. I do have the spotless reputation of St Mildred's to consider. But I am most grateful to you, and will be in touch.'

'Well,' said Gordon as he and Francis wheeled their bicycles towards the school gates, 'somehow, I don't think our Miss Frobisher will be agreeing to a mud-wrestling match!'

A week went by without further communication from Miss Frobisher. Gordon had nursed dreams of having a chess tournament between St Basil's and St Mildred's, with the hosting school putting on a slap-up tea of sandwiches and cakes, but as the days passed Gordon put the scheme to the back of his mind. There was plenty to occupy him at Bundler's Cottage. He hinged some Samoan stamps into his collection, pasted some cuttings about a new steam locomotive into his scrapbook, made progress with the balsa-wood assembly kit of the Champion Junior Glider aeroplane that Uncle Billy had given him at Christmas, attended choir practice, re-organised his fossil cabinet, bought the latest Biggles adventure, listened to a thought-provoking edition of *The Brains Trust* on the wireless, constructed a wooden frame for his Arthur Mee Writing Certificate, read that week's *Eagle*, and sponged his school blazer.

At Red Cherry House, Francis's life went on much as usual, although he often stared from the windows at the still dismal weather, longing to be out on his bicycle in the clean English air. Each day he expected to hear that Gordon had exciting news about St Mildred's, but nothing happened.

Towards the end of the week, his father was sitting in the Windsor chair after lunch (or dinner as Mr Jones would insist on calling it). He was scanning the Hatch, Match and Despatch section of the newspaper, and Francis was bowed at the kitchen table bent over an algebraic problem that needed solving, when the banging of the front door interrupted the blissful quiet. Mrs Jones entered, her cheeks rudely pink as she had driven her Raleigh the two miles from Strutton-by-the-Way, where one of her customers lived.

'I've never known such a thing,' Mrs Jones said, even more rudely pink as she spread herself before the range. 'All that way. A complete waste of time. Good afternoon, says Mrs Robinson, and very grateful I'm sure but I won't be requiring that circular stitched bra I ordered from you after all. You could have knocked me down with a feather. She's bought one of those new bullet bras. Brought it out, bold as brass, to show me. I don't know what corsetry is coming to, really I don't.'

'You've been over-peddling, Doris,' said Mr Jones. 'I'll put the kettle on.'

With the tea poured, and a slice of her very own Victoria sponge brought to her, Mrs Jones visibly brightened.

'And I just remembered,' she said, 'there's that slim-line Arabian Doublet brassiere that should have been posted off yesterday.'

'I'll pop down to the post office and send it on its way,' said Francis.

'Oh, that would be good of you, dear. The nuns will be thinking it's got lost.'

Although it meant driving through the drizzling mist that seemed to have escaped from some desolate fen, Francis was glad to be in the open countryside, and it was pleasant to step into the village post office, the tinkle of the bell above its door somehow welcoming him to another, enclosed, world. Miss Simms, the pinch-faced postmistress, looked at him inquisitively.

'Why, Francis, what brings you out on a day like this?' Her eyes twinkled over her crescent spectacles. 'Are you here to investigate a mystery?'

'Unfortunately not,' said Francis. 'Mysteries are thin on the ground just at the moment. I've brought one of mother's parcels to post.'

Miss Simms busied herself with the necessary processes, which involved careful weighing, forensic examination of the label, selection of the appropriate stamps, severe licking of the adhesive gum, much noisy pummelling with rubber stamps, and curious scratching in ledger books.

'And didn't I see you the other day going up to St Mildred's?' asked Miss Simms between a fourpenny and twopenny stamp. 'I thought as much,' she said, before Francis had spoken. 'Such a delightful lady. A Miss Frobisher. She came in here, you know, several weeks ago, on the day she came to the school for her interview. She was just on her way there, and I said to Joyce, didn't I Joyce?'

Miss Simms's assistant managed to murmur agreement as she was stocktaking the Basildon Bond.

'A most genteel person,' continued Miss Simms, 'and I would have been quite flabbergasted had she not been appointed as the new headmistress. And such a friendly soul. She must have stood there chatting away for an hour or more – mustn't she Joyce? – before she had to hurry away to appear before the school board. And when you've finished with that gentleman's postal order, Joyce, you can get on with mopping out the telephone box with Jeyes Fluid.'

Rather than returning straight home to Red Cherry House, Francis decided to cycle the extra mile or so to Bundler's Cottage, where Gordon was just waving off his uncle, who sat cosily wrapped against the cold in the driving seat of his Ford Anglia.

'Uncle Billy looks as if he's off on a mission,' said Francis.

'Well, he is, in a way. You know he likes to take a drink sometimes at the Wedded Stoat? He meets up with some of his old service friends. One of them works with Uncle Billy at Northcrack Staithe power station as a night-watchman, and he's been telling Uncle Billy he's unhappy about going on with the job.'

'That's not surprising, is it?' asked Francis. 'We know that the power station was targeted by the spy from St Mildred's, so it must have been very worrying for a night-watchman. But the problem has been sorted. Somehow, you need to let Uncle Billy know, so that he can reassure his friend.'

'I'm not sure it's as simple as that,' said Gordon. 'I don't think it is all over. Apparently, the night-watchman heard strange noises in the power station last night just after midnight, when he was doing his hourly round. He was quite shaken up. That's why Uncle Billy's driven over to see him.'

'It's probably his imagination. Having once heard such things, he thinks he can hear them again. If you're not careful, you'll have us thinking there's some sort of mystery about the whole thing, when we know jolly well the mystery has been cleared up.'

'Do you think it might be a good idea to speak to the Reverend Challis again? Surely he will know what's going on?'

'Exactly what I've been thinking,' Francis replied. 'I called in at the vicarage yesterday. His housekeeper answered the door. Apparently, he's been called away on an urgent episcopal matter and she couldn't say when he would be back.'

'He's deserted us.' A slight shudder ran through Gordon. 'That means we're quite alone.'

Then, Francis noticed the almost completed model of the Junior Glider, and before long all thoughts of Uncle Billy's worried night-watchman friend were replaced by the boys' eager perusal of the Comet balsa wood catalogue.

'*Wake* up, Francis!'

Francis stirred in his sleep. He had been dreaming about a night-watchman in a lonely, desolated factory building (very like a power station), and had just got to the moment when the night-watchman opened a creaking door and came face to face with a giant cuckoo clock, when the sound of something at his bedroom window startled him awake. Surely that was someone throwing stones? He walked to the window and looked down. Through bleary eyes, he saw someone in the garden below, someone who looked rather like Gordon. And then he realised it *was* Gordon, astride his bike and wrapped in a woolly hat and scarf and thick jersey coat.

'Gordon! What on earth?'

'Come down,' said Gordon in a hoarse whisper. 'Quick as you can.'

'It's one o'clock in the morning,' said Francis. 'What's so urgent?'

'It's the end of half term tomorrow, that's what's urgent,'

replied Gordon with as much emphasis as he could manage without disturbing Mr and Mrs Jones. 'I've got your bike ready, and there's hot coffee in this Thermos.'

Not waiting to remove his pyjamas, Francis quickly pulled a polo-necked sweater over his head and clambered into his favourite fawn trousers and shoes. Pausing only to leave a note ('Gone detecting!') on his abandoned pillow, he tiptoed downstairs. Opening the front door as noiselessly as he could, he saw Gordon at the ready for off, his bicycle aslant and his left foot on the pedal. He had already retrieved Francis's bicycle from the garden shed. The two boys silently manoeuvred their way into the road before setting off at a brisk pace, but to where Francis had no clue. The night was as black as ink, with a low mist swirling across the hard ground, making it seem as if they were moving above a cloud. Only the occasional sound of a wild bird, and the whining complaint of the east wind travelled at their side. Francis was about to demand of Gordon where they were headed, when the gates of St Mildred's came into view. Gordon signalled to Francis to slow down, and dismounted.

'Let's get the bikes off the road before anyone spots us,' said Gordon. 'Leave them behind the wall.'

'You haven't told me what this is all about,' said Francis.

'No,' said Gordon, 'because I don't quite know myself.'

Francis was about to complain about being dragged out of his warm bed on such an inhospitable night. He was freezing cold, his face was damp, his feet were almost numb, and his eyes couldn't adapt to the sudden complete darkness of the school's grounds, for not a light could be seen. Somehow, however, although Gordon was two years younger, he knew that his cousin must have good reason for this midnight escapade. He supposed for a moment he had been a little jealous of the fact that on this occasion it was Gordon who seemed to be leading whatever mission it was they were on. Jealousy was a most unpleasant thing, he knew. It was then he caught a glimpse of the glistening excitement in Gordon's eyes, and gave himself up to whatever his young cousin was planning.

'I'm worried about Miss Frobisher,' said Gordon. Grasping a torch and beckoning for Francis to follow him, he set off across the lawn with Francis close behind. As they turned the corner of the main building towards the rear of the premises, the wind cut sharply across the playing fields, and towering trees shook massive branches at their faces. For a moment it took their breath away, but subsided almost as quickly as it had begun. Through smarting eyes, they saw a pinprick of light in one of the upper windows.

'What are we looking for?' whispered Francis.

'First on the list,' Gordon replied, 'is a drainpipe.'

Having found one, he tested its steadfastness. Against the slightly sheltering north-facing wall, Francis cupped his hands to make a stirrup for him to start his ascent. Gordon climbed up and up, only stopping when Francis shone the torch on him to show the way.

'Switch it off,' called Gordon. These were anxious moments for Francis, left standing on the ground while his cousin slowly disappeared heavenwards. As his vision cleared, Francis could see that the room from which that single light was shining had a balcony beyond its window. Just as well that Gordon, who was much the sportier of the two boys, was the one best equipped to be like Jack climbing the beanstalk! He had reached the underside of the balcony, and by gymnastic twists and turns wound his arms around its parapet, looking as much like a monkey as a boy. Francis could not imagine why Gordon was making such an effort.

At that moment Gordon himself wondered if this whole business was nothing more than a folly, but having reached the balcony he felt he had nothing to lose. He steadied himself, glad to feel the solid base beneath his feet. If Miss Frobisher or the ancient Mr Parsons discovered him outside one of the rooms at the top of the building he would certainly have some explaining to do. He was probably outside Miss Frobisher's bedroom. Imagine the stories that would get into the newspapers if he were found to be spying on her at this time of night. Indeed, the sight of a young boy outside the window of her third floor bedroom would very probably result in the elderly woman suffering serious medical repercussions.

As silently as he could, Gordon moved closer to the window. Now that he was on a level with them, he saw that the heavy velvet curtains had not been fully closed against the night, and the light, that from the ground had seemed little more than a glow, shone clearly from what appeared to be a strong bulb suspended from the middle of the room. By pressing his back against the part of the window obscured by the curtains, and turning his head sharply to one side, Gordon could see into one of its corners. He could see a bed, and by its side a small table on which stood various bottles of pills and potions. By altering his position, he could make out the bottom of the bed, on the bars of which a medical chart had been hung. His first feeling was one of relief. This wasn't Miss Frobisher's bedroom at all. It must be the medical bay where the sickly pupil was being cared for over the half term holiday.

Gordon felt a bitter disappointment. He had been wrong,

ridiculously wrong. He had wanted to show Francis that he was just as capable as his older cousin of solving a mystery. His theory that Miss Frobisher's patient was a figment of her imagination was in shreds, for there was the poor girl, apparently fast asleep in bed. The best thing was for him to get back down to Francis as fast as he could.

Just as he turned to make his descent, he took one last look into the room. A slight movement in the bed caught his eye. Surely… yes, the patient was stirring. Her head, which Gordon had not been able to see at all, cocooned as it was with pillows and blankets, slowly rose from the sheets. Although he couldn't make out the features, Gordon could see at once that all was not as it was supposed to be. He had met blonde girls, redheaded girls, girls with mousy hair, girls with locks as black as a raven… but never grey!

At that moment, he was aware of a great burst of light. Twisting, he saw that the velvet curtains had been pulled apart, and before he could begin his escape the French windows of the room were almost savagely wrenched open. The curtains blew angrily into the night, and framed between them was a madly dishevelled Miss Frobisher, her face bilious with fury.

'*You!*' she shouted.

There was no doubt of it; Gordon was trapped. For a split second, he looked once more, deeper this time, into the room, at the bed. It must have been the shock, but for one mad moment he could have sworn that its occupant was… it couldn't be… *another* Miss Frobisher.

Then everything went black, and Gordon jumped.

*

21

Those gathered around Gordon's bed at Bundler's Cottage glowed with pride. Although it had been made clear to Uncle Billy, and to Doris and George Jones, that the exact nature of Gordon's adventure was a matter of national security and could not be divulged, each felt the sense of occasion. In the same room were the Chief Constable of the county, the genuine Miss Maude Frobisher, and the Reverend Challis.

'On behalf of the Norfolk Constabulary,' the Chief Constable announced, 'I have to thank you, Gordon, and you, Francis, for bringing this problem at St Mildred's to a successful conclusion. If it hadn't been for your persistence and your willing co-operation with one another to solve the mystery, the county would have been faced with a security crisis of the first order. You have earned the gratitude of the whole force.'

'And I,' said Miss Frobisher, a kindly smile folding over her features, 'would have been, well…'

'Up the creek without a paddle?' suggested Uncle Billy.

The party laughed heartily.

'More probably I would have been disposed of,' said Miss Frobisher, introducing a morbid tone.

The Chief Constable turned to Gordon and, seated at the end of the bed, Francis.

'Now, boys, tell us how you came to realise that, far from having been stopped by the appointment of a new headmistress, the spy ring was still operating at the school?'

'It was Gordon who was responsible,' said Francis generously.

'At the beginning, of course, when Mr Challis told Francis about the case, it seemed that the whole matter had been cleared up, and Francis and I agreed to go to see the new headmistress in an effort to bring St Mildred's more into the community.'

'Miss Frobisher seemed a very pleasant person,' said Francis.

'Yes,' said Gordon, 'but even at that meeting there was something that didn't seem quite right. Remember the racquets in the corner of the room?'

'Oh, yes. She said something about the girls being very keen on tennis.'

'But that's just it. They weren't *tennis* racquets at all. They were *lacrosse racquets.* Any genuine headmistress would not have made such a mistake.'

'Why didn't I notice that?' asked Francis.

'Because I'm the one who does sports,' said Gordon. 'Although you might just win an egg and spoon race!'

Everyone laughed easily again, pleased that Gordon was so much recovered after his fall.

'And another thing. I've got my cycling proficiency certificate. It was only afterwards I realised that on that day when I almost collided with Miss Frobisher's car outside the gates of St Mildred's, it wasn't my fault at all.'

'I told you to be more careful, and not wander about on public roads,' said Francis.

'Yes, but the fact is, it was the car that was at fault, because when it came around that corner it was on the right hand side of the road.'

'So what?' said Uncle Billy.

'Miss Frobisher, or the woman who was pretending to be Miss Frobisher, had only picked up the car that morning from the local garage a few streets away. Don't you see, when she

23

came around that corner, she was driving on *the wrong side of the road*. And they do that in foreign countries.'

'What have I always said?' said Mrs Jones, pulling an ominous face.

'And afterwards, when she came up with that story about having been a nurse, I remembered that when she got out of the car and found me knocked to the ground, she asked if she should get medical assistance. It seemed a strange thing to say for someone who told me afterwards she was a qualified nurse.'

'Fascinating,' said the Chief Constable. 'This is text-book stuff.'

'And there was something odd about that day I went to the post office,' said Francis, 'to post that brassiere for mother.'

Mrs Jones cast a worried glance at the Reverend Challis, whose face did not flinch at the mention of modern corsetry.

'Miss Simms told me that on the day the new headmistress had come for her interview, she had called into the post office and spent an hour chatting.'

'Chatting!' The Chief Constable snorted. 'Obviously, pumping poor Miss Simms for local information, to give her more ammunition to succeed at the interview.'

'And probably finding out all sorts of stuff about employees at the Power Station!' said Uncle Billy.

'She was casing the joint,' said Mr Jones, and regretted it because the Chief Constable might think he consorted with the criminal class.

'Except that she wasn't attending for interview anyway. The real Miss Frobisher…'

The real Miss Frobisher beamed up at the Chief Constable.

'The real Miss Frobisher,' she said, lifting up her cup and saucer in salute, 'was trussed and bound as soon as she arrived to take up her duties. It was an extraordinary occurrence.

Imagine how I felt when a woman who looked exactly like me – wigs, make-up and a natural talent for mimicry – overcame me, took me up to the sick bay, and imprisoned me, while she took my place. If Gordon and Francis had not acted as they did that night, she would have been forced to take desperate measures. With the girls and staff returning to the school the following day, I would have had to be...'

'Disposed of,' said Mrs Jones. 'So you said.'

'What I don't understand,' said Mr Jones, 'is why the police did nothing about it. We're talking about a spy ring here, but everything was left in the hands of our boys.'

'That's not entirely true,' said the Chief Constable with a playful smile. He turned to the Reverend Challis. 'Is it, sir?'

An electric shock might have gone through everyone in the room. The Reverend Challis got to his feet and then stooped, his face gnarled, his eyes squinted.

'Don't you young whippersnappers leave them there lawn-mowers there!' he said.

Francis and Gordon were as amazed as everyone.

'Then, you were working at the school?' said Francis.

'Yes,' said the Reverend Challis, 'working undercover. We had our suspicions that the spy ring would try to continue operating, but I was unable to do much as the new Miss Frobisher would not let me into the premises.'

'If it hadn't been for you, sir,' said Gordon, 'I might have been in a really bad scrape.'

The Reverend Challis gave Gordon's shoulder a reassuring touch. 'I was keeping a look out from the workman's hut in the grounds when I saw you boys arrive. I was aware that because the school was returning the next day, the spy – for I strongly suspected she might be one – would have to act decisively that night.'

'When I might be spirited away?' asked the genuine Miss Frobisher.

'Exactly. But I had no hard evidence. And I suspected that Francis and Gordon might know much more than myself. So I followed you both across the lawn, and when I saw Gordon climbing the drainpipe, I was alarmed. This might be very dangerous. Being M15 trained, and running the Scouts, I was quite prepared. I ran back to the workman's hut and pulled out an old tarpaulin and hurried back to where the boys were. I was just in time to see Gordon reach the balcony, and just before he jumped I leapt out at Francis and got him to help me stretch the tarpaulin.'

'Thus breaking my fall,' said Gordon.

Miss Frobisher had provided the sherry. Mr Jones was alarmed to see how expertly she tossed back her head and emptied her glass in one. As she did so, he could have sworn the headmistress winked at him.

'No nibbles,' said the Chief Constable, looking around disconsolately.

'We don't hold with nibbles,' said a voice from the kitchen, and there was Mrs Jones, triumphantly bearing a magnificent Bramley apple pie. The party broke into spontaneous applause.

'Not too much of that pie for the boys, Mrs Jones,' said Miss Frobisher. 'They will need to be fighting fit for the grand sports tournament St Mildred's will be arranging, or our girls will win all the trophies! We will also be holding a celebration at St Mildred's. It is the very least we can do to thank you. And now, I would ask you all to lift your glasses to Francis and Gordon… the boy detectives!'

THE PEARL OF THALIA

'*M*ay one ask the contents of the parcel?' asked Miss Simms.

Mrs Jones didn't like the look of the village postmistress at the best of times, and when Mrs Jones was attempting to post a black satin basque to the Lord Mayor's wife under cover of a plain envelope was not the best of times.

'Essential apparel,' replied Mrs Jones. A phrase she perhaps had heard in the war, two words that would surely guarantee access to the British postal service.

'We have to be so careful nowadays,' said Miss Simms, stamping the parcel with such ferocity that Mrs Jones feared for her delicate rib-work. 'People try to sneak all sorts of things through letterboxes.'

Mrs Jones smiled benignly as she opened her purse.

'Morality has gone to the wall,' Miss Simms continued, her voice ringing through the shop. 'We hear nothing but, at Gospel Hall. No doubt we shall be advised of fresh horrors at tonight's tambourine practice.'

Miss Simms turned the parcel once again, jabbing at it with a finger. Mrs Jones's reputation as an inventive corsetiere had excited comment in the village. Disappointed that she could find no reasonable excuse to force her customer to reveal the parcel's dubious contents to the listening queue, Miss Simms moved to a surer plane.

'Take this new show that's coming to the Hippodrome, *Ladies Without*. Without what, you may ask. According to what I've heard, without a stitch of clothing. Nudity on stage! The temple of womanhood with the doors wide open.'

The post office was quiet as a grave, as the queue strained to hear every word. Mrs Jones was equally appalled. The Hippodrome was a draughty old building, and she was sure that 'ladies without' would catch their deaths of cold.

'Well I never,' said Mrs Jones, relieved at last to see her Parisian garment drop into the mail sack. 'Still, I suppose we have to move with the times.'

Miss Simms, grasping this godsent opportunity and turning purple, replied 'If they move, Mrs Jones, the show will be closed down. By the Watch Committee, of which I of course am honorary secretary.'

'You haven't booked then?' asked Mrs Jones.

'Certainly not,' said Miss Simms. 'I shall be attending the opening performance in an official capacity with my fellow committee members to ensure that there is no hint of impropriety.'

'This change is sixpence short,' said Mrs Jones.

Mrs Jones enjoyed the walk back to Red Cherry House, contemplating the making of a Bramley apple pie in her steamed-up kitchen as she listened to the wireless: perhaps Wilfred Pickles visiting a rissole factory in Rochdale, or one of those Paul Temple serials that Francis enjoyed. Of course, her son had what might be termed a professional interest in such matters, what with his being known as a boy detective, along with his cousin Gordon, and getting their names in the local papers and being photographed shaking hands with the Chief Constable of the county.

Most recently, there had been that strange business at St Mildred's School, and then the night when Francis and Gordon had stopped the express train to London and prevented a catastrophe that might have led to the loss of many lives, not to mention the extraordinary disappearance of Lady Morton's ancestral tuning fork.

A mother's intuition told Mrs Jones that Francis was never happier than when he and Gordon were hot on the trail of a mystery that to others seemed utterly mystifying. In the fallow periods between cases, Francis kept up his spirits by studying the methods of Sherlock Holmes, from which much could be learned. Today, however, Francis had set aside the adventures of 221B Baker Street and was seated at the kitchen table deeply engrossed in Professor Challenger's lost world. The likelihood of finding extinct dinosaurs in Branlingham might be remote, but Francis delighted in the clarity of Arthur Conan Doyle's imagination. Clear thinking, sharp observation and wide reading were the cornerstones of good detecting, as he often reminded Gordon, who preferred the open air to books, and Francis soaked up the ambrosia of Doyle's crystalline prose.

Mrs Jones had no sooner taken off her hat and gloves than her husband excitedly bustled into the kitchen waving his hand in the air.

'What a fuss!' she cried. 'Just as I'm setting off on an afternoon of making gooseberry jam and damson preserve, lemon curd, coconut tartlets, shortbreads, an assorted assortment of fancies, date surprises, and a leaf patterned Bramley pie with scalloped edging.'

'It's a telegram,' said Mr Jones.

Never before having received such a thing, Mrs Jones was

speechless for a few moments, sat down quietly, propped the worrying document against the milk jug and gazed at it from various angles.

'I think you should open it,' said Francis.

A cup of tea having restored her courage, Mrs Jones slit open the telegram before her spellbound audience.

'Well, I never! It's from our little Glenda,' said Mrs Jones.

'Who's Glenda?' asked Francis.

'Your cousin! My late sister's daughter. What a turn up. She's visiting Norfolk and wants to stay here for a few days.'

'No room at the inn,' said Mr Jones, 'if she's the Glenda I think you mean.'

'I think it's wonderful news, George. I haven't seen Glenda since she was a little slip of a thing at school, must be fifteen years ago. Such spots she had, and a big girl. Buck teeth and a terrible lisp. Those National Health spectacles too, you've never seen thicker glass. My sister would be so pleased to think Glenda and I had met up again. To think my niece has taken the trouble to look up her old auntie.'

'Ay, and taken her time, too,' said Mr Jones. 'So fond of you she couldn't wait to get in touch fifteen years later.'

'She's arriving Monday week,' said Mrs Jones with a note of finality.

Mr Jones had heard enough, and slunk back into the garden, where the woody warmth of his cramped shed offered instant consolation. He lit his pipe and picked up that week's edition of *Tit Bits*. It was an especially interesting edition. Not for the first time, he read an account of the forthcoming show at the Hippodrome, *Ladies Without*. The photographs were worth a look, too.

*

'A most unusual request,' said Lady Darting. '*Most* unexpected from a man of the cloth.'

Her gimlet eye fixed on the spindly form of the Reverend Challis. The meeting of the Watch Committee had wound mournfully on for two hours in the bitterly cold council chamber at the Town Hall.

'As if the sordid details pertaining to the gentlemen's public convenience in Station Road Back Passage were not disturbing enough,' said Miss Simms, 'now we have to consider this.'

'Perhaps we should allow Mr Challis to expand on his proposal,' said Lady Darting.

'With pleasure, madam chairman,' replied the reverend. 'As I explained, I have been approached by the theatrical management which is about to present a glamorous entertainment at the Hippodrome, entitled *Ladies Without*. This is, as I am sure you will already have heard, a variety show in which its female participants appear at certain moments naked on stage.'

'So there should be no misunderstanding, Mr Challis,' interjected Lady Darting, 'by naked, you mean…?'

'Naked as in denuded of any covering, madam chairman.'

'I have it noted,' replied Lady Darting. 'I have it on authority from my husband that such entertainments have been – in his words – pulling them in in London for some years.'

'So I believe. The general manager of the Hippodrome is loath to accept such displays, but these are difficult days for the theatre. Last week's *Peer Gynt on Ice* played to very few patrons. He referred to the problem of bums on seats.'

'An earthy profession at the best of times,' said Lady Darting. 'One cannot imagine that a community such as ours will welcome *Ladies Without*. We can I am sure depend on the high moral standards of our citizens to boycott such a salacious offering.'

'The week is completely sold out, madam chairman.'

A clacking of teeth and tut-tutting permeated the council chamber.

'Please continue, Mr Challis.'

'Lord Darting is quite correct in pointing out that such displays as this are highly popular in our capital city.'

'Popular among fleshpots, perhaps,' interrupted Miss Simms.

'And have been approved by the Lord Chamberlain, who insists that during scenes involving nudity none of the young ladies may move so much as a muscle. In investigating this matter, I have learned that the moments of nakedness are often presented as historical scenes from the classical past, Greek and so forth. 'The Fall of Carthage' and 'The Rape of the Sardines...'

'*Sabines!* roared Lady Darting.

'Are you suggesting that this so-called entertainment is educational, Mr Challis?' asked Colonel Chatter, his neck suddenly popping up from his Inverness cloak. 'No wonder our scholastic institutions are going to pot.'

'Well, I cannot recall any allusions to classical history during recent shows at the Hippodrome. Last week, for example, Ronnie Ronalde appeared to be blithely ignorant of the finer points of Ancient Greece.'

Lady Darting put away her papers and pulled on her gloves.

'Then I see no problem. After all, the Lord Chamberlain has sanctioned the performance.'

'But the Watch Committee has not,' said Miss Simms, slightly trembling.

'Small mindedness,' said Lady Darting. 'As an elderly

unmarried sub-postmistress who has only ever *heard* of London, you can hardly be expected to have experienced life to the full. Even as we speak, they will be queuing up at the brothels of Lower Cairo! Indeed, my husband has left his panama hat in two or three of them on more than one occasion.'

'Then I may assume the committee agrees to the management's request?' asked the Reverend Challis.

'*Two* altar boys?' asked Lady Darting.

'Purely to add verisimilitude to the scene involving vestal virgins, the chief of them of course Miss Bunty Rogers, a famed exponent of the art of the unclothed.'

'A stripper,' said Lady Darting. 'No need to mince words, reverend.'

'The boys will be faced away from the female performers, one boy holding a lyre and the other a Grecian urn. They will be chaperoned at all times. Mr Penderbury, the manager of the Hippodrome, assures me that the show is run along strict moral lines, as if the girls were in a convent.'

'Hardly a good place to take two boys, then.' Lady Darting gave a flashing smile to the assembled company. 'You will of course have to select your boys carefully, Mr Challis. Do you have two clean-living lads in mind? I know that as Branlingham Scoutmaster many such pass through your hands.'

'That will not be a problem' said the Reverend Challis.

The remaining days before the arrival of Glenda Clatten (Mrs Jones's sister having married a Mr Clatten) were busy ones. At Bundler's Cottage, Gordon assisted Uncle Billy with the annual spring clean, dusting, polishing, emptying cupboards and washing china until the little home quite sparkled. Life at Red Cherry House was just as hectic. Mrs Jones was in a welter

33

of pastry making, enjoying a festival of shortcrust activity, and ran up a pair of new curtains for the spare bedroom in which Glenda would be installed. The spring weather likewise had its effect on Mr Jones. He was much looking forward to an outing with some of his work colleagues, the precise details of which he seemed unwilling to divulge. He was certainly not looking forward to entertaining Glenda Clatten, whom he remembered as a most unprepossessing specimen with demented pigtails.

It was a thrilling time for Francis and Gordon. May was burgeoning, and the two boys were eager to make the most of it. It was the ideal season for excursions into the woods at Branlingham Minor, Francis alert with binoculars, and Gordon scouring the hedgerows for birds' nests. He was well informed of what to look out for in the countryside at such a time, having lately been given a copy of Enid Blyton's *Book of Nature*, much more fun than an adventure of Noddy. But even Noddy had never been invited to appear in what Mr Jones described in an unguarded moment as a nude show.

'Or,' the Reverend Challis had suggested when he visited Red Cherry House, 'naked as nature intended. Do not be alarmed, my friends. Adam and Eve in the Garden of Eden had to do without a branch of Debenham and Freebody. The star of *Ladies Without*, Miss Bunty Rogers, has appeared in the West End of London, and been described by one of our leading dramatic critics as a true artiste. Francis and Gordon will be chaperoned at all times, and never exposed to the nakedness of Miss Rogers or her colleagues. It is, I suggest to you, an opportunity not to be missed.'

Initially, Mrs Jones hadn't been easily convinced. Mr Jones wondered if there might be a part for a slightly more mature male. Agreement was reached when a modest fee for the boys was agreed. They had been enthusiastic from the beginning. To think that for one week only they would leave school in the afternoon and at night step into the magical world of the theatre.

As it happened, their first night at the Hippodrome coincided with the worrying arrival of Glenda, and Mrs Jones rose to the double occasion with enthusiasm. Mr Jones was due out that evening with some male acquaintances at what he described as a 'social', but made sure he was at home during the day to look over his unwelcome guest. Uncle Billy drove Gordon to Red Cherry House, from where he and Francis would be collected by the Reverend Challis and taken to the theatre. All were in place when, at eleven o'clock, the sound of an approaching car drew their attention.

'A taxi!' cried Mrs Jones. 'Fancy! A taxi! I do believe it'll be our little Glenda.' Scurrying to the front door, she opened it and let out a tremendous gasp.

'Hello, Aunt Doris. How lovely to see you, darling.'

The young woman standing on the doorstep looked as if she had stepped out of a fashion magazine. As a corsetiere, Mrs Jones instantly recognised the beautiful cut of her clothes, the cusp of her coat, the quality of her leather gloves, the sheen of her stockings. Gone were the spots, the National Health spectacles. The buck teeth were now exquisitely white and even. The grating lisp had vanished too. The voice might have been that of an angel, and the face resembled something Mrs Jones had seen only in advertisements for expensive cosmetics.

'I'll catch my death out here, darling' said the young woman, and laughed, a bell-like sound that seemed to Mr Jones to be the breath of a zephyr breeze. And then, when they were settled in the living room with cups of tea and slices of Mrs Jones's Madeira cake, came the thunderbolt.

'I just can't take it in,' confessed Mrs Jones. 'I'd never have believed it.' She burst into tears. Her niece opened her faux alligator handbag and took out a lace handkerchief that she squeezed gently into her aunt's hand. Glimpsing across, Francis noticed a copy of Milton's *Paradise Lost* nestling in a corner of the handbag.

'Oh, poor darling!' said Mrs Jones's niece.

Mr Jones had never met anyone who used the word darling almost every time she drew breath.

'Honestly, darling! I've got so used to being Bunty Rogers that I've quite forgotten I was once Glenda Clatten. It wouldn't have looked good in lights, would it darling?'

'And all these years you'd never been in touch,' said Mrs Jones.

'I know. And I've felt awful about it. When Mum went away, I was on my own, and eventually – well, I don't really want to go through it all, Aunt Doris – I started doing some modelling, and then I got a job abroad. It was there that I got into show business, and Bunty Rogers became a pin-up in Scandinavia.'

Mr Jones suppressed a wolf whistle.

'Scandinavia!' exclaimed Mrs Jones. 'Just fancy, George! Our Glenda in foreign parts.'

'When I came back to England, I was taken up by a management that specialised in girlie shows.'

There was a palpable silence in the room as her onlookers wondered what to say to this. Of course, Branlingham was vaguely aware of such things, but imagined they only took place in shady clubs in the back streets of Soho.

'And I knew that you and Mum didn't get on very well, so I suppose I'd rather drifted away from the family. But now

I'm back, my dears, and it's wonderful to know we're together. Even more wonderful to know that Francis and Gordon are in the show this week. So exciting, darlings, and you are such handsome boys. You must take me all over Branlingham tomorrow, and show me the churches where you do your brass-rubbings, and let me into the secrets of your detecting, and not spare me any of your adventures. I've read about your amazing cases in the newspapers, and always felt so proud of you, and now to think we are together as we should be. I can't tell you how happy I am to know two such gorgeous young men.'

The family gazed at the vision that was Bunty Rogers until it was almost time for her and the boys to get ready for the theatre. Mrs Jones was in a whirl of excitement, fascinated by every detail of Glenda's (or Bunty's, she supposed now) make-up. And that gorgeous blonde hair, arranged in rolled bangs, set off her oval face like a picture in a gallery.

'You'll come round for champagne after the show,' insisted Bunty. Mrs Jones could hardly refuse. Three hours earlier she had considered it her duty to go to the first night to see that Francis didn't disgrace himself (or her); now, she felt at the very heart of the theatrical profession, a proud guardian of this beautiful young woman with a figure in little need of one of her aunt's corsets.

When Bunty had gone to her bedroom for a brief rest, and Mrs Jones had taken off her slippers to air her feet, Francis and Gordon had some sorting out of family history to attend to.

'It's just like your Mum said,' exclaimed Gordon. 'It is a turn up for the book. Very strange, isn't it, that Glenda –'

'You mean Bunty,' interrupted Francis.

'That Glenda stroke Bunty should reappear after all these years.'

'Well,' said Francis, and he lowered his voice, crept to the kitchen and softly closed the door, 'it would probably upset Mum to talk about it too much. She didn't really get on with her sister.'

'Glenda's mother?'

'That's right. Auntie Grace. I never knew her,' said Francis, 'but there was a sort of family scandal when Glenda was still a small baby. Her mother left home and went off with another man.'

'What happened then?'

'So far as I know, Glenda stayed with her father, but he died a few years later and Glenda was taken in by some foster parents.'

'What a terrible chain of events,' said Gordon.

'Yes, but think how she's overcome it all,' said Francis. 'She's a star. Imagine that, Gordon. A star in the family!'

As arranged, the Reverend Challis arrived at Red Cherry House later that day in his Morris Minor to collect Francis and Gordon.

'Now, boys,' said the Reverend Challis, 'the world you are about to enter is one of fantasy and fleshy delight. The first is harmless and the second best avoided. However, I have it on good authority of the manager at the Hippodrome that all the saints in heaven would have no objection to your involvement. The world of theatre is a mysterious and beguiling one, to which I myself have on occasion succumbed.'

'We have appeared on stage before, you know,' said Francis. 'Gordon was one of the train of little Japanese ladies in *The Mikado* last term.'

'And you, Francis…' said the Reverend Challis, taking

his eyes off the road, 'how well I recall your bewitching Lady Macbeth. Your mad scene reverberated with me for many months. Unfortunately, you will be required to do very little in this production. Movement, indeed, is forbidden, although as clothed altar boys you will perhaps be allowed to glide across the stage. It will make for a simple but striking effect, in those fetching Grecian tunics. Now,' he said as he parked the Morris Minor in the crescent forecourt of Norwich Hippodrome, 'you are about to enter the temple of Thespis.'

After reporting to the stage door keeper, Francis and Gordon bid goodbye to their chauffeur and were escorted through long stone passages that went deep into the earth. All around was a musty smell of underground damp, mingled with what the boys thought an air of intense anticipation. Eventually they emerged through the pass door into the auditorium of the Hippodrome, a sea of faded red velvet seats, chandeliers, balconies, boxes, and, at either side of the proscenium arch, what Francis recognised as caryatids, although Gordon only saw plaster versions of naked ladies in Greek costumes.

Francis and Gordon had visited the Hippodrome on various occasions (usually the Christmas pantomime), but neither had ever seen it so disorganised, so noisy, so alive with potential excitement, despite the naked bulb that hung over the stage, and the great dust cloths and bits of forlorn scenery scattered here and there like monstrous confetti. They found two seats on the aisle in the stalls, and began to soak up an atmosphere that had echoes of their experiences in their school productions, but heightened a hundredfold! Acrobats were tumbling through a routine, sometimes vanishing into the wings before leaping back on stage into the arms of one of their colleagues, and narrowly avoiding some female dancers who were practising some steps.

'Hello, boys. A nice routine, that one,' said a voice behind Francis and Gordon. They turned and saw that their newly discovered cousin Bunty had taken a seat behind them.

'They are not bad dancers. Two of them only joined the show last week at Rotherham, so they are still learning. How are you boys looking forward to your professional debuts?'

'A little nervous, Miss Rogers,' confessed Gordon.

'Call me Bunty. We're family, remember.'

It was difficult to believe that this glamorous creature was indeed one of their circle. It was, Francis thought, as if a beautiful swan had landed on a pond of ugly ducklings. Bunty leaned forward and put her arms around the boys. Francis breathed in so much perfume and face powder that for a moment he thought he might choke.

'You'll be the envy of East Anglia,' she said. 'There are men who would give their eye teeth to be on stage with us girls, and you're getting paid for it!'

In the orchestra pit a portly, balding man was speaking to a florid-faced man in a loud check overcoat on stage. The red-faced one was leaning over and handed the portly one what looked like sheets of paper.

'This is the band call,' said Bunty. 'Dick Slocombe is the comedian for the week, so he's just giving Bert the music he needs for his play on and off.'

'Bert?' asked Gordon.

'Bert Brownhill, our musical director. Not quite Malcolm Sargent, but Malcolm wouldn't want to look at this show every night, would he?'

'The tumblers are brilliant,' said Francis, who had been watching the male acrobats with fascination.

'Yes,' said Bunty. 'Nice lads, too. The Dramono Troupe. They're from Roumania, and send all their earnings back home to their mother. Can't speak a word of English, bless them, but they have impeccable manners. Oh, and that's our soubrette, Mavis Day. She sings selections from *The Chocolate Soldier* in camiknickers. She's toured with Donald Wolfit, but she gave it up after getting bad notices for her Falstaff.'

'Welcome to the Hippodrome, Miss Rogers.'

The boys looked up to see a tall, distinguished man beside them, dressed in an astrakhan coat, wearing a homburg and holding a fat cigar.

'Charles Penderbury, manager of the Hippodrome. I trust you have everything you require? Dressing room satisfactory, everything disinfected and so forth? We pride ourselves here at the Hippodrome, you know, and all artistes are treated equally. You lady – how shall I put it? – you lady *entertainers* are treated just the same as the greats.' Mr Penderbury puffed out his chest. 'We were privileged to have Sybil Thorndike here only last week. Such class! But we don't make distinctions. We put her in the same dressing room as Phyllis Dixey.'

'Not at the same time, I trust?' asked Bunty.

'Ah, dear Dame Sybil!' said Mr Penderbury. 'Now that's what I call an artiste. A very different type to yourself, of course, but we treat every one alike here, you know.'

'That's just as well, Mr Penderbury,' said Bunty, 'because Sybil is coming down to Norwich tonight to see the show, and I shall need a comp.'

Mr Penderbury spluttered. Sparks cascaded from his cigar end.

'Dame Sybil coming to *this* show?' he chortled. 'Oh, that's a good 'un!'

'She's a great admirer of mine,' said Bunty. 'Unlike some people I could mention, she is a person of taste and refinement, and knows a fellow artiste when she meets them. And make sure she is shown to my dressing room after. Francis, I would appreciate your help with my cases. You can stay here and watch, Gordon. Delighted to have met you, Mr Penderbury. I trust my dressing room in this clapped out flea-pit of a theatre will be up to Dame standards.'

Taking Francis's hand, Bunty strode purposefully out through the pass door. After a few incomprehensible grunts, Mr Penderbury sidled away into the rear of the stalls.

Gordon was thrilled to be sitting alone in such a great theatre, watching the preparations for a spectacle in which he and Francis were to play an essential part. How different from the grammar school's *Mikado*, when the school matron had frankly been an embarrassment as Ko-Ko (one of the older boys had said she was more like bromide). Anyway, that had been done in the school hall; this was a genuine – what had the Reverend Challis called it? – temple of Thespis. More than once, Francis had tried to persuade him of the pleasures of learning Greek, although usually Gordon was much happier on a cross country run, or taking his stand at wicket, or reading the latest Harris Tweed adventure in the *Eagle*.

Francis had certainly had some influence on him, however. It was Francis who encouraged him to take out a subscription to *The Children's Newspaper*, from which Gordon had benefited enormously. The articles on foreign countries, on strange rural customs in England, of developments in the worlds of science, and accounts of his various sporting heroes, had inspired him week by week. Then, of course, there was his personal link with the newspaper; after all, he was the proud recipient of an Arthur Mee Good Handwriting Certificate, signed by the great man himself, the creator of *The Children's Newspaper*. A short time ago, the paper had published a piece about the Muses. Surely, Gordon thought as his eyes roamed over the arch that curved above the Hippodrome's stage, he recognised some of what he saw there.

He had never before looked at the proscenium so carefully, but now it fascinated him. Female figures dominated the arch, each one identified by name. There were six in all: Calliope, Melpomene, Terpsichore, Thalia (he remembered that *The Children's Newspaper* had shown the enormous cameo of Thalia crowning the proscenium of the Playhouse Theatre in London), Euterpe and Euphrosyne.

Of course, these were the Muses, all in some way appropriate to the theatre. Gordon had made a point of learning about the Muses, and being able to recognise each of them. Because it was difficult to differentiate between them, it had been a test of his mental abilities. There had been some complexity about the Muses and the Three Graces, and no end of exploration through the pages of *Brewer's Dictionary of Phrase and Fable* had sometimes led to even more confusion!

Now, he remembered certain facts by the images on the proscenium. There was Terpsichore, the muse of dance, holding her lyre, and there was Melpomene, the muse of tragedy, standing in a most distraught attitude, her hand dramatically held to her brow. Euterpe, the muse of Dionysiac music, was identifiable because she was playing a flute (and anyway, her name had been painted below). Gordon remembered, too, that Thalia, a muse who had taken a particular interest in poetry and comedy (what would she make of Dick Slocombe?), was also one of The Three Graces. Now, what had been their names?

That was when the advantages of learning poetry at school came in so handy! It was in Spencer's epic *Faerie Queene*.

'They are the daughters of sky-ruling Jove,
By him begot of faire Eurynome…
The first of them hight Euphrosyne,
Next fair Aglaia, last Thalia merry;
Sweet Goddesses all three, which me in mirth do cherry.'

Gordon was surprised he had ever managed to learn such stuff. It wouldn't do his reputation with the Fourth Form Soccer Eleven much good. Now, he might even consider learning Greek. The Greeks always had a word for it – the problem was that he couldn't understand any of them!

Ladies Without was twice nightly, at 6.15 and 8.45. Between the shows, Bunty insisted on giving the boys an eggs and bacon supper cooked by her elderly dresser, Florrie, one of the several women who travelled with the management's shows and looked after its stars. They had all got on famously throughout the day, and when the time came for Francis and Gordon to rehearse their moves on stage, Bunty was there to give them confidence.

'Your appearance is in the very last item of the show, just before the walk-down. It's a tableau of an epic painting by John Martin, the Victorian painter. Not that the audience will have a clue about that, of course. But I've conceived it very much

44

along the lines of his work. Have you been to the Tate Gallery? You should, darlings. When you come to London, I'll take you there and we'll marvel at those enormous canvases of apocalypse and death and have tea and scones and go for a boat ride on the Thames and eat ice-creams in that wonderful restaurant with its delicious Rex Whistler mural. You won't have lived until you've seen the Pre-Raphaelites, darling Rossetti and Burne-Jones and Ophelia drowning in the prettiest frock you'll ever see.

'Now, Francis will be in this alcove here, holding a pitcher, darling, with your hand on your hip, and looking out to the audience. You mustn't move, darling, and you mustn't look anywhere but straight in front of you, and you'll be in this alcove on the other side, Gordon darling, and everything else ditto. The curtain will go up, and the girls will all be in place on stage among the Gothic ruins. I must remember to check that the new girls Trixie and Nancy know where they are standing, and then I rise out of a giant Botticellian conch draped in a diaphanous concoction. Actually, darling, Cecil Beaton designed it for me: so sweet of him. And I stand and look, and then the Beaton slips off my shoulders, and the lighting changes and the curtains close.'

'And that's it?' asked Gordon.

'That's it, darlings,' said Bunty. 'But it's when I come up in the shell… oh, darlings, for me that's the most wonderful moment of the show.'

Francis and Gordon looked puzzled.

'Come with me,' she said, and holding their hands she sped them back to her dressing room, where Florrie was ironing Bunty's crinoline dress for the first half finale. Bunty asked her to take some props to the prompt corner. The old woman gathered them together, swept some costumes into her arms, and cheerily left the room.

The boys had never before felt enveloped in such a dusty warmth, the smell of Bunty's greasepaint (Leichner 5 and 8 and carmeline for the eyes, and Gala pillar-box lipstick), the lingering fog of face powder, the blinding light of the bulbs around the mirrors that threw reflections of glitter and dazzle across the room, her leather suitcases (embossed with her initials, B.G.R.), and the array of flimsy gauzes, shot silk, fishnet and organza that lay in wait for her hand to pluck. Bunty closed the door, and almost whispered, 'I have something very special to show you.'

From a secret compartment in her travelling case she produced a small velvet box, and slowly opened its lid. Francis and Gordon were stunned. There, shimmering with a radiant intensity, was a huge pearl set in a pendant. Whichever way it was turned, the pearl shone with a translucent majesty that held the boys in thrall. Its effect was hypnotic, as if the pearl were drawing whoever set eyes on it deep into its centre.

'What a magnificent jewel!' exclaimed Francis.

'I wear it at each performance,' explained Bunty, 'in the final tableau. It is the only thing I have that once belonged to my mother. All through her life, she never appreciated its beauty or guessed its worth. When she abandoned us, she thought nothing of leaving it behind. And I think she never discovered *this*.'

With an intricate movement of her fingers, Bunty dislodged the velvet bed in which the pearl resided, and withdrew a tiny piece of paper, browned with age.

'Another secret compartment!' whispered Gordon.

'Yes.'

She unfolded the tiny document and Francis and Gordon read the barely distinguishable words

'A sibling pearl?' asked Francis, his voice almost hoarse in wonder.

'What does it mean?' said Gordon.

'I've always thought it meant that there were others like it. This is our secret, boys. No one else has ever been told of it, or seen that message.'

'Do you know where the pearl came from, originally?' asked Gordon.

'I believe it is many hundreds of years old,' said Bunty. 'My father always told me that it had been acquired by my grandfather, Horace Clatten.'

'Of course!' said Gordon. 'Sir Horace Montgomery Clatten, the great explorer and adventurer. I read about him in *The Childrens' Newspaper*.'

'Fancy you knowing that,' exclaimed Francis. 'You're quite right. Sir Horace was also a great inventor and eccentric. He developed the automated bustle, you know.'

'There are stories that he unearthed ancient treasures in foreign lands. And, yes, I seem to remember… it's coming back to me… wasn't there an account of him discovering the jewels of a twelfth century Peruvian princess?'

'Then you do know something about my pearl!' said Bunty.

'Yes,' said Francis. His face bore an expression of profound concern. He thought that if Gordon knew something about it, it was very likely that other people did too!

*

The opening night of *Ladies Without* at Norwich Hippodrome was a highlight in the theatrical calendar, an event in which Mrs Jones found herself a prominent feature. Aunt to Miss Bunty Rogers, mother of Francis Jones about to take to the stage with his cousin Gordon, and treated like a queen from the moment of her arrival at the Hippodrome, with Charles Penderbury escorting her to the front row of the dress circle, where such a very pleasant, well spoken lady was already installed in the seat next to her.

'Call me Sybil, dear!' the woman cooed. She and Mrs Jones got on famously, and by the time the curtain rose Mrs Jones felt quite at home. And what a show it was! Such colour, with the girl dancers opening the proceedings in a flurry of pastel shades, their colour magically enhanced by the footlights. Then there was the comic, Dick Slocombe, who told some stories that would have made his mother blush. Mr Jones worked hard at suppressing hearty laughter. And then the girls were on again, introducing the singer Mavis Day, and then a group of acrobats who swung about all over the place, one of them climbing the rigging up to the very top of the proscenium arch.

Best of all, of course, was the first appearance of Bunty. The audience held its breath as she emerged from a total darkness, with nothing more than a giant ostrich fan to cover her necessities, and walked seductively down to the footlights. She seemed to take the whole audience into her confidence with the most beguiling turn of her eyes, and then in no more than a flash of time she switched the fan dramatically to one side, just as the lights – as if by some magician's trick – faded to black. The applause was sensational. Bunty had cast her spell over all, even the woman next to Mrs Jones, who whispered 'What a remarkable gal! Better than Duse!'

By the interval, when Mrs Jones and Sybil retired to the bar, the atmosphere was at fever pitch. Mr Penderbury bought Mrs Jones a small sherry and Sybil a shandy, and made an inordinate amount of fuss of both. By the time they resumed their seats, Sybil had ordered a new corset from Mrs Jones, and assured her that she herself had begun on stage in just such a modest capacity as Francis and Gordon.

And what a finale the boys' appearance made! It was all Mrs Jones could do not to burst with pride when the lights went up to reveal Francis standing in an alcove, and Gordon exactly the same on the other side of the stage. Draped across the stage were the young ladies of the company in various advanced states of undress, their private parts shadowed and all but indistinguishable in the craftily lit classical disorder. From the backcloth shone a sympathetic moon, as unmoving as the clouds that trailed in its wake, and as motionless as the girls on stage, all of whom were placed so as to emphasise the presence of the star of the evening. Stillness was everywhere, on stage, in the stalls, in the balcony, in the very breath of the audience. And then, from the centre of the stage, rising from the ruins of what looked like an abandoned world, a giant shell emerged from the bowels of the theatre, with a shuddering slowness that was thrilling to see.

'How Botticellian!' whispered Sybil. And then the very top of Bunty's head appeared, her golden tresses winding down and down until they reached her feet, framing her naked loveliness. And there, at her throat, a piercing light shone with immense clarity from the great pearl that hypnotised every onlooker. The orchestra was playing *In an Old Persian Market*. The shell came to a shuddering halt. The music reached a crescendo. The lights played for a moment or two with subtle changes, at last resting

49

in fullness on the exquisite form of Bunty, and then slowly faded, the pearl retaining its enthralling presence until the very last moment of the blackout. The applause of the audience was tremendous, but very gradually, through that enormous noise came another sound: the shock of screaming and hullabaloo on stage. The curtain rapidly fell, and the house lights came up.

'The pearl has gone!' said Francis, running to Gordon across the stage.

Gordon was careless enough to bump into one of the acrobats, one of the many who had emerged from the wings. The muscular young man almost pinned Gordon up against the scenery and hissed 'Watch it, sonny'. He gave Gordon a penetrating glance, as if he suspected him to be the source of the trouble, and then ran back into the wings.

At the centre of the mêlée was a distressed Bunty, being comforted by some of the still naked girls. Amidst the general confusion, Mr Penderbury was fetched from his office, and immediately had a telephone call put through to the local constabulary. A moment or two later, the Chief Constable of the county, who had been in the audience with the fellow members of the Watch Committee, strode purposefully on to the stage.

'What's all this about, Francis?' asked the Chief Constable.

'Miss Rogers has been robbed, sir. A pearl of great value was taken from her when the lights went down at the end of our scene.'

'That narrows the field for suspects. Presumably the culprit must be one of the company who was on stage with her?'

'It may be,' said Francis, 'but not necessarily so. The whole company, and the electricians and backstage staff, were in the wings ready for the walk down. In the blackout any one of them could have snatched the pearl.'

'Nobody is to leave,' commanded the Chief Constable. 'My men will conduct a thorough search.'

Amongst the general confusion, the acrobat had returned with a glass of water, which he held to Bunty's lips as she reclined against her shell.

The search was taken up by a posse of policemen, but two hours later they confessed themselves mystified.

'But it must be found!' exclaimed Francis in exasperation. 'Mysteries are meant to be solved. It's not only that the pearl is of inestimable worth. Someone has taken it, and robbed our relative of a thing of great sentimental value.'

'Well,' said the Chief Constable, 'in this case I think you are up against impossible odds. No trace of the pearl has been found, and there is no hint as to who might be responsible. It really is a case of the pearl being a needle in a haystack. We have to recognise that a theft has taken place, and that there is little hope of recovery.'

'Not if we can help it,' whispered Gordon under his breath.

Red Cherry House seemed a much less happy place the next day. Bunty was perhaps the least despondent of all, already seemingly having accepted that the pearl would never be traced. Mrs Jones was in such a state of despair that she postponed the morning's pastry making, while Mr Jones was kept busy making cups of tea and coffee to keep the household's spirits up. Lady Darting arrived in her chauffeur driven Rolls Royce to communicate the Watch Committee's commiserations on Miss Rogers's loss, sat beside Mrs Jones on the settee and ate four of her coconut tartlets with obvious relish. From the post office, Miss Simms sent word that she was shocked to the core, and that if there was anything she could do in the way of postage she would be only be too happy to oblige. Up in Francis's bedroom, he and Gordon were in conference.

'Well, you know what Sherlock Holmes would have suggested,' said Francis.

'No doubt he would have discovered the whereabouts of the pearl through the aroma of some rare Cuban tobacco,' said Gordon.

'No. Something much more sensible than that. When you cannot solve something through any other method, then the most obvious solution is the answer.'

'Very clever of him, I'm sure,' said Gordon, 'but I can't see how it helps us. Everyone and everything was searched after the show. Of course, a pearl is a very small object, so there's nothing to say it can't have been hidden somewhere discrete – under someone's tongue, even – with very little chance of it ever being found.'

'The Chief Constable thinks there's nothing to be done about it,' agreed Francis. 'The best we can do is to take Bunty's mind off it, and create a restful and tranquil atmosphere.'

'Admit defeat, you mean? Well, perhaps you're right.'

Gordon wasn't at all sure… If one of the company had been known to covet the pearl, or if the pearl had been the subject of great public interest… but Bunty had never told a soul about its true value… to anyone who didn't know, the pearl might just as well have come from the jewellery counter at Woolworth's. Except, of course, for that almost blinding light the pearl gave off as the lights faded around it. Surely, that fact was crucial to understanding what had happened: as Bunty had told he and Francis, she had never before told anyone about the provenance of the pearl.

Gordon reached for the dictionary. Closing its pages, he sat without speaking for several moments before he announced to

Francis that they were about to bicycle to the Records Office at the Town Hall.

'The fact that you've just discovered we are related to a famous explorer has awakened your interest in the family tree,' laughed Francis, as they wheeled out their machines and set off from Branlingham.

Fifteen minutes later, they were seated at a table in the Records Office where the custodian Mr Charlesworth set before them several enormous ledgers wherein they might trace their family history. Mr Charlesworth was delighted to meet the boys, realising that he might be playing a small part in some mystery in which they were involved. When they needed more information relating to other parts of the country, he was more than willing to help by telephoning his colleagues in the north of England.

It was mid-afternoon when the boys thanked him and rode back to Branlingham, to make ready for that evening's performances. They couldn't imagine how Bunty would get through the shows in such dreadful circumstances, or how the rest of the company would respond to the previous night's events. Francis told Gordon in no uncertain terms that they must remain professional, and not let their personal involvement with Bunty affect them. They must remember that they were worshippers at the temple of Thespis.

The final two performances of *Ladies Without* went on in a spirit of resignation and sadness. During the days that followed the dramatic disappearance of the pearl, the police made no progress in discovering it or coming up with any theory regarding its theft. The Chief Constable was further discouraged by the fact that Francis and Gordon were themselves unable to shed any light on the mystery. It had been a difficult week. They spent the last day with Bunty, escorting her to Norwich, where they had lunch at the Maid's Head Hotel and spent an interesting hour in the cathedral before walking down to sit by the river at Pull's Ferry. Here, they were treated to Bunty reading poetry to them in that voice that Mrs Jones had thought that of an angel. It was an enchanted time, for Bunty seemed to have a direct emotional link to the mind of T S Eliot.

Refreshed and revitalised and seeing the world through eyes that had glimpsed the wasteland, the happy trio strolled arm in arm back into the city centre, to ready themselves for the final performances of the show that all Norfolk had flocked to see. There was a sense of sadness in the air, for their newly discovered relative would leave Red Cherry House the following morning, and goodness knows when the boys would see her again.

When they reached the Hippodrome and were installed in their dressing room, professionalism took over and the boys remembered that they were now, as the Reverend Challis had reminded them only the previous evening (he had not missed a performance), trainee priests at the altar of Thespis. As always, Francis and Gordon watched the show from the wings, only ushered away when Bunty and the girls shed their costumes. At first house, Francis was heading towards his dressing room when he heard the stage manager say 'He's got the bird' as Dick Slocombe took his bow, and there was something a little more reticent in Bunty's manner as she arose in the shell, but otherwise all seemed just as usual. It was an odd moment, because a trick of the light momentarily made Gordon think he had just seen Bunty in the wings, when she was in fact already in position in the shell, in full view of the audience. After first house, as he and Francis were making their way to Bunty's dressing room, they overheard the musical director Bert's booming voice.

'I've not been doing this for forty year without knowing me business,' Bert Brownhill was telling one of the acrobats. 'It were all sorted at Band Call, and well you know it. There were no rallentando at Band Call, that I do know. We had to hold up for several bars when you was doing the act on Tuesday night first house. Me musicians were mucked about with. And now it's happened again tonight. You was up on that trapeze so long we had to put in another ten bars. That trumpet'll not be so obliging again.'

The acrobat shrugged his shoulders, said a few rude words and waved his arms at the musical director.

'Bloody foreigners!' said Mr Brownhill.

After Francis and Gordon had enjoyed their last bacon and eggs fry-up in Bunty's dressing room – Gordon referred to it as the Last Supper – the curtain went up on Norwich's one remaining chance to see Miss Rogers in all her glory. Despite the upsetting business of the pearl, the show went with a swing. After the interval, the audience gasped as the Dramona Troupe spun and hurtled through the air. The climax of their act was always thrilling. The lights dimmed. The acrobats stood stock still, as if rooted to the spot in a moment of pre-electric genius. The hectic throb of the pit band fixed on a trembling note. This was the moment when the unbelievable happened every night: as the lights played on those members of the troupe standing on stage, the lights around the top rigging of the various ropes and swings was dimmed, until suddenly a dazzling light was shone on one of the acrobats who, in the pitch darkness, had climbed the rigging and was now perilously sat on a wire at the very top of the proscenium arch. Then, announced by a thundering roll on the drums, he would as always jump from the wire onto a swing that was thrown towards him, spending what seemed an eternity in mid-air.

Yes… he made the jump… the audience inhaled in terror at the risk, as always, and applauded madly as he reached the ground and bowed… but then, the audience gasped again, for way above him, balanced on that wire from which the acrobat had just jumped, was Gordon Jones, and in his hand, shining into the eyes of all who looked on, he held something tiny and brilliant and mysterious beyond words!

'Well, there is no denying it!' exclaimed the Chief Constable. 'The boy detectives have done it again.'

The throng gathered in Bunty's dressing room after the final curtain applauded his words.

'The local constabulary was baffled,' continued the Chief Constable. 'Quite frankly, I think if it had not been for you boys…'

'No!' interrupted Francis. 'Boy in the singular, I think. This one is down to Gordon!'

Everyone laughed, and Bunty gave Francis a great kiss, and squeezed his hand, and then kissed Gordon and ruffled his red hair.

'Oh, darlings. You are and always will be a duo, and sometimes – even in a duet – one or other must have a little solo.'

Mrs Jones was deeply touched by such wit. Who'd have thought our Glenda would turn out like this!

'Anyway, I think you are the best one to offer an explanation,

Gordon,' said the Reverend Challis, whose admiration for the lad seemed to burst from his being.

'I owe it all to Francis,' Gordon began, and then Mr Jones perked up and said that sounded like one of those speeches American actors gave when they were given an Oscar.

'It was Francis who encouraged me to learn a little about Greek,' said Gordon, 'and nudged me to take out a subscription to *The Children's Newspaper*. And it's always been Francis who says it's important to read and find out stuff, when I'd rather be playing football or cricket.'

'But how did you work it all out, darling?' asked Bunty impatiently.

'It wasn't a stroke of genius, or a sudden blinding light. Rather, it was a lot of small things that gradually came together to make a picture. First, there was the pearl itself. The piece of paper that had accompanied it for goodness knows how many years described it as a 'sibling' pearl. In fact, it described it as 'a sibling pearl of great beauty', so I looked up the word sibling in the dictionary and I wondered if that was a sly way of suggesting that the other pearls of which it was a sibling were not as beautiful, or as valuable.'

'You have a wonderfully intellectual mind, darling' whispered Bunty.

'Bunty had kept the pearl a secret, only ever wearing it on stage at the very end of each performance. Nobody, so far as she knew, was aware of it, or guessed its great age and importance. So, when it was stolen, it seemed to me that only someone who knew about it would do such a thing. Someone who knew the story of the pearl, and knew that Bunty possessed it. Therefore, that person or persons must be on stage at the Hippodrome.

'Bunty's mother had abandoned her and left her with her

doting father when Bunty was little more than a baby. Bunty was told by her father that the pearl had been left behind when his wife deserted them. As is the way of so many domestic upheavals, people often leave things behind that afterwards they wish they had taken. We know that Bunty's was described as a 'sibling ' pearl. There were others. I suspected that there were two other pearls, which may well have been encased in velvet boxes describing them as such. Bunty's mother took the other two pearls and left the one claiming to be 'of great beauty' behind.

'And there I rather stumbled, and ran out of ideas,' said Gordon. 'Until I decided to do some research at the Public Records office, looking up marriage certificates and birth certificates. There I discovered that Bunty's mother, Rose Grace Clatten, had remarried a few years after leaving her husband and given birth to two daughters, Beryl Grace and Mavis Grace. When they turned twenty-one, she gave each of them one of the sibling pearls, telling them that they were of priceless worth. Eventually, the girls probably had them valued, and learned that they were little more than cheap paste. They returned to quiz their mother. It was then that the story of the three pearls emerged.'

'And the pearl that Rose Clatten had left behind for Bunty to inherit was the priceless one that her grandfather Sir Horace Clatten had found in Peru?' asked Francis.

'Exactly: the one that adorned the throat of a beautiful Peruvian princess many thousands of years ago. The other two pearls were worthless. All this was too much for Bunty's mother and the two girls, who resolved to get the other pearl back. Since the only time when the pearl was in public was on stage during Bunty's act, they realised they would have to get into her show.'

'Of course!' shouted Francis. 'Those two dancers, Trixie and Nancy! The girls that the company picked up *en route*. Your two half-sisters, Bunty.'

'Yes,' Gordon explained. 'I suspected as much when I saw Trixie and Nancy's travelling cases, both of which had their initials stamped on them, and the second initial on each was 'G'. G for Grace, the middle name that Bunty shared with them.'

'The Three Graces,' said Bunty. 'How very mythological!'

'The two girls were supposed to be experienced dancers, but they didn't seem able to pick up the routines. And tonight, I suddenly thought I caught a glimpse of Bunty in the wings, but I knew she couldn't be there because she was standing in her shell on stage. It was *Florrie* that I saw.'

'Florrie!' exclaimed the Reverend Challis.

'Yes. For just a moment, I thought I recognised her, but then I realised. It wasn't Bunty in the wings, it was her mother! The mother who had deserted her years before had got herself hired as a dresser. This was all very well, but I still had no proof or knowledge of what might have happened to the pearl. Then, I remembered that on the night of the disappearance one of the acrobats had bumped into me on stage in the confusion, and wasn't very pleasant about it.'

'Quite understandable in the circumstances,' said Mr Jones.

'Possibly,' said Gordon, 'but he wasn't very pleasant in *English*. The acrobats were all Roumanians, and couldn't speak a word of English, but this one sounded as if he came from the Old Kent Road. I think we may discover that he is the father of Trixie and Nancy. Of course, the acrobats couldn't have explained his appearance in the act to anyone because they can't speak English.'

'Your mind must be left to medical science,' said the Reverend Challis, rapt in admiration of Gordon's intelligence.

'But what still puzzled me was – what had happened to the priceless sibling pearl? That is where I owe a debt to you, Mr Brownhill.'

'To me?' The musical director seemed as puzzled as anyone in the room.

'Undoubtedly. I heard you complaining to one of the acrobats that they had messed up the timings for the orchestra on the Tuesday night at the end of their act. This seemed very odd. Timing is absolutely essential in that act, so why should it be so altered at one performance? I realised that it was at the point of the act when one of the acrobats reached the top of the proscenium, and in darkness. It happened first house Tuesday. That was the first opportunity the thief had to plant the pearl in the crown of Thalia on the proscenium.'

'But wait a minute,' said the Chief Constable. 'Everyone was questioned after the pearl went missing.'

'But not the Roumanians,' said Gordon. 'They couldn't understand English, and everyone assumed they had nothing to do with it. Anyway, the pearl was so tiny, how could it be found? It really was a case of a needle in a haystack.'

'And tonight?' asked Bunty.

'Tonight,' Francis explained, 'Gordon knew that during the second house the acrobat would take the pearl *out* of the crown of Thalia, and it would vanish for ever. So during the lighting changes Gordon ran on stage and under cover of darkness preceded the acrobat, Bunty's stepfather, up the ropes and retrieved the pearl.'

'And there it lies,' said Mrs Jones breathlessly. 'Imagine! Peruvian, and priceless, and all.'

'So ends the story of the Three Graces,' said Francis. 'Bunty, Trixie and Nancy, alias Thalia, Aglaia and Euphrosyne, the daughters of sky-ruling Jove.'

'I feel I got to know Thalia,' said Gordon. 'All those hours I spent sitting in the stalls at the Hippodrome, gazing up at her on the proscenium, admiring her crown. The crown that I first really noticed the day the show opened. And then, later in the week, I noticed it began to sort of, well, glow. And I began to wonder if, somehow or other…'

'The Pearl of Thalia,' said Francis in a tone of wonder.

Life went on just the same as before in Branlingham after Bunty Rogers was swept away to the railway station from Red Cherry House. The Jones family had never experienced so much kissing, and Mrs Jones dabbing her eyes, and Bunty calling everyone darling, and giving Francis and Gordon such hugs and entreaties and promises not to lose touch. They stood at the gate of the house and watched until her taxi vanished from view. Mrs Jones, determined to keep up everyone's spirits, had made a Bramley apple pie especially for the occasion, and the day turned out a good one, the boys recounting their week at the temple of Thespis, Mrs Jones counting her blessings that Dame Sybil, that lovely lady she'd sat next to on Bunty's first night, had already sent her a postcard and invited her to pop up to London to see her at the Old Vic. The Dame had also ordered one of Mrs Jones's most progressive corsets.

Lady Darting arrived to personally congratulate the boys on their work, and accepted a substantial slice of apple pie that she pronounced far superior to anything that had ever come out of her kitchens at the Hall.

That week's drama reverberated beyond Red Cherry House.

Two days later, at the post office, Miss Simms clasped Mrs Jones's new parcel with both hands. There was no mistaking the feel of it; it contained more Frenchified undergarments. Miss Simms glared at the label in disbelief. It was addressed to Dame Sybil Thorndike.

At the Hippodrome, Mr Penderbury was in the manager's office. He had sat a long time, staring at the little velvet box which had that very day been delivered by special messenger, and at whose centre shone the great pearl that had been the cause of so much bother. Once again, he unfolded the note he held in his hand and read

Dear Mr Penderbury
I should like you to place this in the crown of Thalia. I like to think that at last it has come home.
Yours sincerely
Bunty Rogers

THE EMBERS OF TRUTH

*F*or the first time in his life, Francis Jones looked into a mirror *thoughtfully*.

A boy of sixteen has little healthy reason to gaze at his reflection. He has yet to begin shaving if his complexion is fair, or quiffing his hair, or checking the colour of his eyes, and it is not the sort of thing he would want to be caught doing by his parents, but they were away from home, and Red Cherry House was unnaturally quiet. Freed from the clatter of Mrs Jones's baking, the house was settling down to a few days calm, and Francis was taking advantage by gazing into a mirror.

He was determined to make a critical appraisal of what he saw. From some angles it seemed a promising face, although the eyes, cat-like grey, looked back at him like pools of vagueness. The chin was neither weak nor prominent, almost ending in a point. The slightly rosy cheeks reminded him of young farm labourers in Victorian paintings he had seen at Norwich Castle Museum, boys flushed from their labour in the fields. His finely delineated eyebrows dominated everything below them, as if they had been drawn and cross-hatched by an HB pencil.

It wasn't a bad face, all in all. His main criticism was

that it had none of the features of an incipient Sherlock Holmes. Where were the hooded eyes, the strong nose and inquisitive nostril, the finely intellectual forehead that marked the unmistakable profile of Baker Street's most distinguished inhabitant? So immediately recognisable was Holmes's profile that, after his return from the Reichenbach Falls, he had commissioned a bust of himself to be placed in full view in the window of 221B, to convince any would-be assassin that he was sitting contemplatively in his study – a ruse in which he was assisted by his admirable landlady Mrs Hudson, who frequently crawled across the study floor to adjust the angle of the bust. Knowing Holmes as he did, Francis suspected that Mrs Hudson had to buy her own kneepads.

The local newspaper had recently described Francis as 'a Sherlock in the making', but what chance of that when adventures were so hard to come by? There had been the excitement of the mystery at St Mildred's School, and the extraordinary affair of the Deepthorpe Dirk, since when there had been little to excite Francis's longing for mystery. The weather was depressing, too. It had been a brilliant September, and October had burnished Branlingham's trees with rich ochre and gold until, overnight, November brought biting winds and driving showers.

Outside Red Cherry House, leaves danced through the village. A low mist made a carpet across the surrounding fields. In the quickening gloom of late afternoon, the lampposts pricked with light, but all that Francis could see as the daylight faded second on second was a figure standing under the arc of one of the lampposts; a man wearing a belted trench coat and a hat tilted over his face. Through the haze, Francis saw sparks fly from the man's cigarette. For an instant, Francis turned away to the mirror. When he turned back to look into the street, the man had vanished.

While Francis worried that he was so unlike Holmes, Gordon was grateful that his cousin hadn't turned into him. At least Francis didn't play the violin (gut-scratching, Gordon called it), didn't smoke a ridiculously designed pipe, take cocaine, shoot holes in the walls of Red Cherry House, or wear one of those ghastly hats with flaps over the ears! And, unlike Holmes, Francis was never (well, not completely) insufferable or condescending. On the other hand there was always the danger that Francis might become what Uncle Billy called 'above himself', and Gordon wanted to avoid that ever happening. He was too fond of his cousin to see him change into a character of fiction.

A recent newspaper article about Francis had been enough to turn any boy's head, and barely mentioned the role that Gordon played in their cases. Perhaps Francis felt a little threatened by the fact that it had been Gordon who was at the very heart of putting an end to the spy ring at the girls' school, and it had been Gordon who almost single-handed had retrieved the pearl of Thalia. Gordon knew there wasn't a jealous bone in his cousin's body, but it was only natural that Francis's reputation as the elder of the boy detectives might have been jolted a little, making him even more determined than ever to emulate the greatest detective of all. What was needed was something to take Francis out of himself, or put Francis back into himself, and at once the perfect idea occurred to Gordon. What better to take Francis's mind off Sherlock Holmes than organising a bonfire night for the village?

'Well, I think it's a silly idea,' said Francis. 'All that work and effort, and in the end it all goes up in smoke.' The only thing that might have pleased Francis was the challenge of some fresh mystery!

Nevertheless, Gordon was determined that Guy Fawkes would win over Sherlock Holmes, and now, with just a few lowering days to go before November the fifth, the boys were busy organising the inflammatory event on Branlingham Common. The local children had wheeled their homemade guys beyond their garden gates, and the men of straw lay sprawled in wheelbarrows or awkwardly propped up over fences. The women were busy preparing for the feast – jacket potatoes and sausages and hot punch and toffee apples – and the stack of wood for the bonfire grew taller and wider day by day. There was so much to be done. Every establishment in the village had to be visited for one reason or another: Mrs Reilly for the loan of crockery, Jim Daley to arrange for the appearance of Branlingham Brass Band, Cawson's Garage for the donation of paraffin, and Mr Grimchance's butchery for pork meat. Even Francis threw himself into making the event one that everyone in the village would enjoy.

Late one afternoon, when almost everything was in place, the boys felt they deserved a treat. What better than to call at the Bide–a–Wee Tea Rooms, where as always the proprietor Beryl Sanders warmly welcomed them. Hot tea, she insisted, and fresh scones with strawberry jam and lashings of simulated cream.

'Not that your mother would approve of my baking, Francis!', Beryl laughed. She was well aware of Mrs Jones's reputation as a baker on an industrial scale.

Soon, the boys were enjoying crab paste sandwiches and anchovies on toast and dainty iced cakes, enhanced by the chintz décor and willow pattern crockery that Beryl had bought half price at a fire sale. As the low sun slunk out of sight, they were contemplating a final solitary scone when Beryl emerged from the nether regions of the shop, and, after standing for some moments at a furtive angle to the window looking on to the street, crossed to their table.

'We are deciding how to deal with a final solitary scone,' explained Francis, fearful that their hostess might be about to offer fresh supplies, but Beryl seemed agitated.

'It's wrong of me to worry you,' she whispered, 'but you being boy detectives and all… There is a man outside, just standing there, under that lamppost. I can't explain it, but I think he is watching you.'

The boys turned to look into the street. Gordon saw nothing remarkable: only a man in a trench coat and a hat tilting over his face, so that it was all in shadow, except for the slow glow of a burning cigarette, but Francis recognised the man as the one he had seen outside Red Cherry House, just as still and silent and watchful as he had been before until, all at once, he vanished.

There was so much else to be done to get ready for Bonfire Night that the boys barely gave the man in the shadows another thought. The next morning, Gordon cycled to Red Cherry House from Strutton-by-the-Way, to discuss some of the finer points of the firework display. As he pushed his bicycle up the path towards the front door, he was a little alarmed to see Francis sitting stock still in the window, his profile proudly defined.

'You're doing the Sherlock thing again, aren't you?' asked Gordon, as he dropped into one of the armchairs by the fire.

'As a matter of fact, I was thinking that to make the bust

trick work, it would have been necessary for Holmes to have already sat at his window for several preceding days in just such a still way, so that when he substituted the bust it would not have come as such a surprise to the evildoers who had been observing his movements.'

'Busts indeed! You should be thinking about how many Roman candles, and if we should give a lecture about the horrific evolution of the Catherine Wheel, and if we should measure the distance to which we have to retire after lighting the blue paper, instead of all this Baker Street stuff. After all…'

A knock at the door stopped Gordon, and jolted Francis from his rigid position at the window.

'Answer that, will you Gordon?'

Really, there were times when Francis seemed to regard his young cousin as his very own Doctor Watson!

Their visitor stood diffidently on the doorstep: a gaunt, silver-haired woman of indeterminable height. Her shoulders were hunched, as if for too many years she had borne a great weight. She wore thick tweeds over an off-white blouse clasped at the neck by a grimy cameo, her costume partly disguised by a voluminous, well-worn ulster. Her strangely pale nose was made the more grotesque by wired spectacles, and a puce beret crowned her disorganised home perm.

'Francis Jones?' she asked.

It was a mouse-like voice, the sound rising up from a long way down in her body.

'No, I'm Gordon Jones. Do come in. This is my cousin, Francis. May I ask…?'

'Miss Dean. Miss Felicia Dean. Do forgive my unannounced arrival. It's just that… oh dear…'

'Perhaps a cup of tea for our visitor, Gordon. Won't you sit down, Miss Dean? Take a moment to collect yourself.'

'How kind,' murmured the agitated woman. 'How very kind. Oh dear oh dear.'

Francis suspected that whoever his visitor was, she was not a great conversationalist, but the arrival of a pot of Earl Grey seemed to lift her spirits.

'I don't know where to begin,' stammered Miss Dean. 'I simply knew that I had to see you, and here – oh dear oh dear oh dear – here I am.'

'And on a matter of some urgency,' said Francis, sitting back luxuriantly in the window seat and looking hard at the nervous woman.

'For whatever reason, it is obvious that you have made a great effort to seek me out. You left home this morning having had nothing substantial to eat, mistook the costume that would be most comfortable for your journey in a third class railway carriage, arrived there on foot through streets that were under repair, and have come to see me on a matter not altogether unconnected with your profession as a piano teacher of small children in Somerset.'

'Remarkable!' exclaimed Miss Dean. 'Quite astonishing! I read in the newspapers of your abilities, but to experience them at first hand… How can you possibly have deduced all this when I have only this moment stepped into the room?'

'It is merely a matter of observation,' said Francis (rather smugly, Gordon thought). 'Your voice is weak, betraying the fact that you breakfasted modestly. Your costume is not especially well coordinated, and your hat, notwithstanding a very nice felt one, is an inappropriate choice, suggesting that you were in a state of confusion when you dressed. My mother is an acclaimed corsetiere, and I have been brought up to notice such details.'

69

'But how did you know I travelled from home on a third class ticket?'

'In your agitated state you played the ticket through your fingers throughout long periods of the journey, and the ink has imprinted salient details on your damp palm. On your way to the railway station you walked into puddles, perhaps caused by road-works, that have left on your right shoe smears of a clay found only within a few miles radius of Frome.'

'The very town from which I departed this morning!' declared Miss Dean.

'And your saying that Miss Dean is a piano teacher?' asked Gordon, his eyes twinkling hard at his cousin.

'The delicacy of your fingers, Miss Dean,' explained Francis, 'the fact that you carry not a handbag but a music-case, the curvature of your hands, betraying long hours of labour at the pianoforte, and your obvious short-sightedness, suggest such an occupation, quite apart from the fact that you give off what may be called a musical air.'

Gordon knew this wasn't the moment to point out that peeping out from Miss Dean's capacious music-case for all the world to see was a tattered copy of *Little Nellie's Piano Tutor (Spinsters' Edition)* and the cover of *Five Extraordinarily Simple Pieces for Oh So Tiny Fingers translated from the French of Erik Satie*.

Miss Dean sighed and set down her cup and saucer, unleashing a sweetened cloud of floral toilet water with which she had liberally anointed herself.

'St Cecilia has been a demanding mistress, and pays poorly,' she confessed. 'I do not complain, you understand. As a Twelfth Day Assumptionist, I am contented with my lot. And this highly coloured beret was the first thing I found in the wardrobe.'

'And yet something is troubling you,' said Francis, thrusting himself to the edge of his seat and staring intently into his visitor's eyes as she dabbed at a lace handkerchief. 'Something has brought you to me.'

'You are my very last hope,' said Miss Dean. 'Yours was the first name I thought of to turn to for help, but I resisted, knowing your youth and the terrible responsibility that I would load onto you if I unburdened myself. The truth is,' – and now she lowered her voice as if fearful that eavesdroppers were straining at every word – '*nobody will believe me.*'

Gordon was just as fascinated as his cousin to learn exactly what was troubling the poor woman. She seemed to collect herself, and slumped back into her chair.

'Felicia is not my true name,' she said, 'but when I reached adulthood, I realised that to make my life bearable I could not be known by my given name. Would either of you boys wish to have been christened Shillingford?'

This time it was Francis's turn to look perplexed.

'Shillingford? Surely that is the name that Conan Doyle originally considered for his great detective!'

'Precisely. But I am jumping ahead, when I should explain from the beginning. My poor mother was Irish, born and brought up in the shantytown of Dublin slums as Kathleen O'Flaherty. Having no expectations of bettering herself, she was fortunate to be given the opportunity to leave Ireland, travelling by boat to England, where she settled in London in the 1880s. She married well, possibly – although such details are not clear – with a man well respected in the medical profession. So far as I am aware, she never again attempted to contact her family in Dublin, but became the respected wife of this professional gentleman. Kathleen's natural charm seems to have compensated for her lack of education. She was readily accepted by the smart social circles in which her husband, my father, moved. A woman of iron resolve, she read everything and transformed herself into a highly cultured person. She went on to write several three-volume novels that, alas, are no longer in print. Perhaps you have read *The Stilled Strings*, in which a deaf lady harpist is possessed by Satan? It was once considered essential reading for the better-class parlourmaid.

'My mother's was a happy marriage, and for some years the sun smiled on her union, of which I was the only product. Sadly, Papa's medical skills did not include the ability to self-diagnose and treat any ailments from which he personally suffered, and, still an attractive woman, my mother was left a widow. Throughout her relatively brief married life she had been the chatelaine of her well-ordered household established in a thoroughly respectable street adjacent to Regent's Park. She had always enjoyed an efficient management of her home, assisted by a small staff. It seemed for a time that her personal loss would be compensated by a future that was monetarily sound, but, very soon after losing my father, it emerged that he had made ill-advised investments, and the collapse of the East Bergholt branch of the Patagonian Consolidated Envelope Trust, in which he had been a prime mover, spelled financial ruin. There could be no thought of Kathleen keeping on her servants. She had to give up the marital home she had so lovingly made with my father.

'Nevertheless, Kathleen was a resourceful character. She decided there could be no question of returning to Ireland, and by then she was in a delicate state, as I was to be born a few months after my father's untimely demise. She made up her

72

mind that she would stay where she was, that she would adapt to her unfortunate circumstances. She moved into rooms at the very top of the house and set about letting the other floors. When I tell you that the house was 221B Baker Street, and that my mother's married name was Kathleen Hudson, you may at last begin to understand my predicament.'

Gordon thought he had never before seen Francis lost for words.

'Miss Dean', said Francis falteringly, 'are you telling us that you are the daughter of Sherlock Holmes's landlady?'

'Indeed, yes.'

'Gordon' said Francis, who had turned white, 'I think I'd like a cup of tea, too.'

Miss Dean passed a photograph to Gordon.

'This is my mother. A snap taken, I believe, by Dr Watson.'

The sepia image showed a pretty young woman, her hair swept back in a chignon. She wore a high-collared blouse and long skirt, and was smiling directly into the camera. It was a forthright look, hinting that she was indeed mistress of the establishment against which she posed. And, there was no doubt of it, she was standing in front of a door which bore the number 221B.

'This is all quite fascinating, Miss Dean,' said Gordon, 'but as Francis has said, aren't you forgetting that Mrs Hudson, Sherlock Holmes, Dr Watson and everyone associated with them are figments of the imagination?'

Miss Dean gave an exasperated gasp.

'That is as the world has understood it, and the inevitable scorn of a sceptical public prevented my mother from putting an end once and for all to such a falsehood. I, also, have been too shy to tell the world, wishing for a quiet life in Somerset, unwilling to face the ridicule that would befall me if I spoke the truth.'

'But what truth can there be in this?' asked Francis.

'Do not misunderstand me, Francis. I am no scholar, and can offer the disbelieving world no proof of the existence of Sherlock Holmes. Some things may forever be beyond understanding. The misinformed see my mother as an elderly, homely, dumpy person forever running up to Mr Holmes's apartments with a note or visitor or tray of crumpets but, as you may clearly see, my mother was a slender, cultivated, radiant creature.'

'But, Miss Dean… the photograph… surely it might have been taken anywhere,' said Gordon. 'There must be many other 221Bs all over the country. It may be an elaborate hoax. Remember the Cottingley fairies! Those little girls who said they saw fairies in the wood convinced the most intelligent of people that they really had seen such things.'

'They certainly did,' agreed Francis. 'In fact, Conan Doyle was one of them!'

'And then,' said Miss Dean, her eyes imploring the boys to remain with her explanation, 'there is this!'

She held out to them a common or garden exercise book, obviously aged, its green cover faded, its corners wrinkled, as if it were a Holy Grail.

'It is all there,' she said. 'The truth.'

Francis and Gordon, almost frozen from movement, felt as if they might never find the strength or will to open its pages. The room was silent as a tomb. Almost fearfully, Francis turned the cover and read

SHERLOCK HOLMES: THE TRUTH
as known to Kathleen Hudson

'Imagine my surprise,' said Miss Dean, 'when I discovered this document. Like my poor mother, I have been a little unlucky in life. On a Christmas Eve of a few years ago I was turned out of the third floor back lodgings in which I had made myself comfortable for the past forty-five years. Since then I have lived in a series of inexpensive residential hotels with hot water and cruet included. In sorting the possessions of my mother which I had inherited and which had lain undisturbed for decades, I found, tucked into the sheet music of one of my mother's favourite songs – (do you know 'I Cannot Pluck the Harp Tonight?'; a sweet melody) – this account of her knowledge of Sherlock Holmes.'

Francis was still staring at the little book, but managed to splutter 'Do you not think, Miss Dean…?'

'You doubt its veracity?' said the woman, her face drawn, her eyes desperate in their pleading. 'Then, my time has been wasted. I had hoped, vainly as I now see, that Francis Jones…'

'And Gordon Jones' put in Gordon.

'That Francis Jones and Gordon Jones,' and now she sat erect, the face suddenly hawk-like, 'that *the Boy Detectives*, would listen, and understand, and profit by what I have come to tell them.'

'Did you say *profit*?' asked Gordon, who had an entrepreneurial streak.

'The book is yours,' announced Miss Dean. 'I cannot do with it any longer. I pass it on to you to do as you wish with it.'

'You are casting the runes?' asked Francis, fixing his visitor with a gimlet eye. 'Passing on something that has become a demonic possession?'

'Steady on, Francis!' said Gordon. 'It's an exercise book!'

'Indeed it is,' said Miss Dean, not taking her eye off Francis, 'but what it contains will merit your attention. You will read for yourselves. Read it and read it well. I will return tomorrow afternoon, when you will perhaps – if I may use a musical reference – have changed your tune. But make no mistake: it is as the title promises, the truth about Sherlock Holmes.'

'I don't wish to be rude,' said Francis, and Gordon didn't think he'd ever heard Francis being quite so kindly and gentle-voiced, 'and it may be the truth, but the fact remains there can be no truth concerning a person who never lived.'

'Never lived!'

Miss Dean got to her feet, reseated her beret, and flung her ulster violently around her frail body.

'You obviously know much less about Mr Holmes than I imagined. When he retired from detective work, he left his rooms at Baker Street and moved to a nice little bungalow near Eastbourne, a location recommended because of its low crime rate. In his last years, he became a respected lepidopterist, presenting a paper to the Royal Society on the latent criminal tendencies of the Large Cabbage White. He died in his sleep in 1948, and was obituarised by Mr E V Knox in the *Strand Magazine*!'

'He may well have had obituaries written about him,' said Francis, 'but that was all part of the game, Miss Dean.'

'Game? Did you say *game*? I don't think that is quite the appropriate word. If it is a game,' and her eyes narrowed, her voice dwindling to little more than a whisper, 'it is a very dangerous one.'

She moved with surprising agility to the window and, standing a little to the side of the curtains, peered into the street.

'I am being followed,' she explained. 'A man in a trench coat, smoking, trying to hide his face beneath a hat.'

Francis and Gordon crept behind her and searched the street with their eyes, but the street was empty.

'What could he possibly have wanted?' asked Gordon.

'I do not know,' said Miss Dean. 'But he has been standing outside, watching me, ever since I found that book.'

Profit. Money. Lots of it. The *Daily Sketch* wants this story, lads. It'll set you up for life.'

The reporter flipped open his notebook, licked his pencil and gave Francis and Gordon an encouraging wink, followed by a card that read *Jack Robbins, Chief Reporter, Daily Sketch*.

The boys had hardly recovered from the previous day's visit by the supposed daughter of Mrs Hudson. After she returned to the Balmoral Guest House where she was staying, they spent the evening poring over the exercise book that Miss Dean claimed had been written by her mother. Its contents were staggering. If this was indeed the truth about Sherlock Holmes, the world had been grossly misled. In fifty pages of persuasive prose, his reputation was questioned, belittled and ultimately destroyed. This was an extraordinary surprise to Gordon, but to Francis, who had worshipped the man and hoped to emulate his achievements, it was devastating. He had never read such an indictment of bungling inefficiency, misdirection, psychological misunderstanding and pig-headed obstinacy.

According to this account, Holmes had allowed countless

murderers to escape capture, failed to stop the theft of several sets of European crown jewels, had been invited to resolve the Austro-Hungarian crisis and almost single-handedly been the cause of the collapse of the Habsburg Empire, was known to have embezzled funds from the Baker Street Irregular Pension Fund which he had in happier days set up, had nothing at all to do with the affair of the Hound of the Baskervilles, was the anonymous author of a voluminous study of halitosis and had serious body odour. Francis's idol, rather like the bust that Holmes had commissioned, had been smashed. What a selfish, incompetent, heartless failure Sherlock Holmes had been! Then, Francis thought, 'I have to pinch myself. This is ridiculous. It's the exercise book that isn't true.'

'But what,' Gordon had said, '*if it is?*'

On the doorstep, the reporter from the *Daily Sketch* apologised for turning up without warning. Jack Robbins was a scruffy young man in a soiled herringbone suit, a pencil tucked behind one ear and a Woodbine behind the other. He had the beginnings of a feeble blond moustache, rabbity teeth, and wore large dark glasses. He was also the very first man Francis had ever encountered who seemed to be wearing some sort of aftershave.

'Excuse the shades, lads,' he said. 'My Gloria Swanson impersonation! Just like what she wears in *Sunset Boulevard*. Been working on a story with a lot of flashlight pictures being took. Hurts your eyes. May I have a minute of your time, lads? This is your lucky day!'

And so it seemed. He explained that his newspaper was prepared to offer a generous sum of money for exclusive coverage of the discovery of the exercise book.

'Now see here, lads, I'll be absolutely honest with you. A woman came to us months ago, offering us that book, and we turned it down. Fancy me, honest Jack Robbins, turning down a story that would have sold millions of papers! Trouble was, it had hoax written all over it. Imagine what harm the newspaper's reputation would have suffered if we'd gone ahead and printed the story. I mean, Sherlock Holmes a real person! And not a very clever or nice one, after all! That would have upset a few apple carts, I can tell you.'

'Then why are you here?' asked Francis, hoping he could keep level-headed, and wishing his mother and father were not away from home.

'Well, that was then and this is now,' said the young man. 'It's one of them stories that won't go away, you know. A sleeper, we call it. Yeah, a sleeper that's woke up sharpish. We've had some experts looking into it, and it seems there's much more to this than meets the eye. We want to tell the world what's in that book.'

The boys were almost lost for words. Francis stared at the reporter. The reporter stared at Francis. Francis stared at Gordon. Gordon stared at Francis. Nobody spoke. The eerie stillness was only broken by a sharp knocking at the door, and a voice that the boys recognised as that of Miss Simms, the postmistress. Gordon opened the door.

'Good morning, Gordon. Is Francis in?'

'Yes. Come in, Miss Simms. This is Mr Robbins.'

Miss Simms peered suspiciously over her spectacles in the manner reserved for anyone who had not lived in Branlingham for at least forty years.

'Good afternoon. I really must not stop. There has been a telephone call, Francis, from the British Museum. I made a note of it all, here. I do wish your mother would consider having the telephone installed. Yes, a message from the secretary of Professor' (she pinched her eyes to read her handwriting)

'Faversham, to say that he wishes urgently to speak to you and that he will be calling on you tomorrow morning at 10.30.'

'Thank you, Miss Simms, but I don't understand. Why on earth should a professor from the British Museum be coming to Norfolk to speak to me?'

'My reaction entirely, Francis,' announced Miss Simms. 'I thought it might be a schoolboy prank, one of your friends entertained by the idea that I would have to walk all the way here to convey the message, and that you would think something important was about to happen! But I telephoned back.'

'I'm sorry?'

'I telephoned back. To the British Museum. I asked to speak to the secretary of Professor Faversham and they said hold on in a very London refined accent, and after a little buzzing a voice at the other end said "This is Professor Faversham's secretary. How may I help you?" And yes, the professor is indeed coming to see you tomorrow. At 10.30. And now I must fly. If only your mother would embrace modern technology…'

'Well, well,' said Jack Robbins, the moment Miss Simms had left. 'Things are hotting up for you, boys. What did I tell you? This thing is big. Oh, it's very big.'

'How did you know the book was here?' said Gordon, and then cursed himself by asking such a give-away question.

'We've kept an eye on the old girl,' said Robbins, and winked.

'Miss Dean?'

'I come down from London special yesterday and caught her getting off the train. Followed her to that guest house in Norwich. Funny thing is, a bit later, there was this man standing across the road watching the house. Fishy looking, he was. Trench coat, smoking a nub end. Thought for a minute he might have been another reporter, but he was just stuck there, watching and waiting.'

'Have you had people watching us as well?' asked Gordon.

'Blimey boys, we're not the KGB. Of course not. Against our principles, that is. All we're interested in is getting hold of that book. Know what this is?'

'From here, it looks very much like a cheque book,' said Francis.

'That's it. A cheque book. And the figure I'm prepared to write out has so many noughts on the end it'll make your eyes bounce. And your names will be known all over the world. Just one thing, boys, if we're going to do business together. Ever heard of a deadline? Tomorrow. Mid-day. Twelve on the nose. Yes, we get that exercise book and let the world know that Sherlock Holmes was nothing more than a fraud, and you are two little rich boys, or the deal's off. Other papers on their way, see, want the goodies. So no messing about. Tomorrow, mid-day, you could be rolling in it.'

By the time Jack Robbins left, Francis's head was reeling. Something about it all seemed so wrong, as if he were living through a dream in which nothing made sense. His world was falling around him. Sherlock Holmes was a real person, Mrs Hudson's daughter had just had a cup of tea at Red Cherry House, a reporter from a national newspaper was promising untold riches, a professor from the British Museum was coming to Norfolk, *Norfolk*, to see him, and he was being watched by a man who was probably part of a notorious gang that might strike at any moment.

Francis tried to hold on to the knowledge that he was a grammar school prefect, but it couldn't be true, thought Francis... Miss Dean... and the reporter... and the professor...

it must be some sort of joke. He walked to the telephone kiosk in the yard of the Wedded Stoat public house, and put through a call to the *Daily Sketch*. They were bound to tell him they had never heard of a reporter called Jack Robbins, and then Francis would know it was all moonshine, that Holmes existed only in the pages of Conan Doyle. Of course he did!

He was ashen-faced when he walked out of the telephone box. The voice on the telephone told him that Jack Robbins was on the staff. Robbins was the *Daily Sketch*'s ace reporter, and to the best of their knowledge had gone to Norfolk on a very special assignment.

When Robbins left Red Cherry House with the promise to return the following day, Gordon was ready to cycle back to Bundler's Cottage. He knew that at midday Uncle Billy was coming home from the power station at Northcrack Staithe where he worked, and Gordon wanted to be there when his uncle arrived. It was only natural that Gordon felt the lack of a mother and father, both of whom had died in an accident on their first foreign holiday after the war. Uncle Billy had put his arms around Gordon and said 'You'll be all right, chum, you'll see. Don't be frightened of the dark. We'll be together now.'

And there was something about Uncle Billy that made everything all right. He understood the terrible blow that Gordon had suffered, and never pretended to be his father. Let him be quiet when he needed to be. Let him talk when he wanted to, and encouraged him in every way when he saw that was what his nephew wanted. Gordon knew how lucky he was to have such a rock. It was the least he could do to get home and make sardines on toast for when his uncle came back to the cottage for a quick lunch before his long afternoon shift. And Francis had wrapped up two portions of his mother's latest Bramley apple pie and wedged them in Gordon's saddlebag. Gordon had made the tea and set the table before he heard his uncle at the door.

'Couldn't eat better out!' said Uncle Billy, beaming at the little spread on the kitchen table. 'Couldn't get as good in a café if you was to pay twice the price!'

There was nothing wrong with Uncle Billy's appetite, but he couldn't help but notice that Gordon didn't seem particularly interested in his food, and had a distracted air about him.

'What's up, chum?' asked Billy, wondering if he could ask for a pickled onion without insulting the chef.

It was a relief for Gordon to unburden himself, and out the story came, about how Francis had been going on and on about Sherlock Holmes after that article had appeared about them in the newspaper, and how the strange woman had said she was Mrs Hudson's daughter, and how of course she couldn't possibly be, and how a reporter from one of the big London dailies had offered the boys a fortune if they gave up the exercise book.

'Money, eh?' said Uncle Billy, who had been passed the jar of pickles. 'Lots of it, you say? You'd have no more worries then, would you, chum? Set you up for life, that would. No more making do at Bundler's Cottage.'

It was the first time Gordon had ever felt really annoyed with his uncle. The thought that Bundler's Cottage was making do! Hadn't Uncle Billy done everything he could to make him happy and comfortable? There was always a fire in the grate, and food in the larder, and the house as neat and trim as any of the ships that Uncle Billy had served on in his Navy days. So far as Gordon was concerned, he was living like a prince.

Money wasn't everything, and he jolly well hoped that Francis subscribed to that philosophy too.

'It's just that I think this business about the exercise book could be a bad thing to happen in Francis's life. He's so wound up in the whole Sherlock Holmes thing that sometimes I think he can't think straight.'

'Yes,' said Uncle Billy, who was carefully trying to entice an onion onto the prongs of his fork. 'It's a rum business, and no mistake. That boy's always got his head inside a book. Nothing wrong with that, mind. This Sherlock Holmes, now. Never read any of them stories myself. Heard them talked about. Didn't he have funny habits? Pipe smoking, and a pal called Dr Watson?'

'That's right,' said Gordon.

'And was it Sherlock Holmes as said, if you can't find the answer to a mystery when you've turned it over and over in your mind, the most obvious answer is the one that's been staring you in the face?'

'Yes, he did say something like that', said Gordon.

It was early morning of November the fifth when Uncle Billy dropped Gordon off at the bus stop at Strutton-by-the-Way crossroads. The number 79 to Norwich would take him to the top of Grapes Hill, only a short walk from where Miss Dean was staying at the Balmoral Guest House, in sight of the great Roman Catholic Cathedral of St John the Baptist.

The prim house was almost hidden behind a high brick wall. The front garden had been concreted over, although two pots, containing what may once have been hydrangeas, stood to attention below the portico. Two columns framed the porch, above which flickered a flyblown sign that read *Balmoral*. A neon sign above the door intermittently transmitted the message *Vacancies*. Gordon knocked at the door. He thought he was doing the right thing in trying to have a quiet word with Miss Dean, when he could explain how concerned he was about Francis's obsession with Sherlock Holmes, and find out why she wanted Francis to take over ownership of her mother's memoir.

'Are you collecting for the guy?' asked the woman. She wore a floral housecoat and slippers.

'Oh no,' said Gordon. 'It's just that…'

Now, how would Francis carry this off?

'I believe you have a Miss Dean staying here at present?'

'That's as may be. She may be, and she may not. Who wants to know?'

'It is connected with a case,' said Gordon, beginning to falter.

'A case? This is a respectable house. We've never been in the papers,' said the woman. 'There's been a man waiting outside here since she came. I've heard her talk about him. Waiting, and watching. What's going on, that's what I'd like to know.'

Gordon stood firm, and put his foot in the door (another of Francis's tricks).

'If she is here, I should like to speak to her,' he persisted.

'Wait here,' said the woman. She shuffled up the stairs on to a landing, where Gordon heard her knocking softly at a door and calling 'Are you in, Miss Dean… Miss Dean?' He looked up to the walls of the stairwell.

Making her way downstairs again, the woman unsmilingly said 'Not in. Out.'

'Do you know if she will be back soon?' asked Gordon, smiling as sweetly as he could. 'It's just that I've come a long way to see her, and I am sure it would be to her advantage.'

'I can't say, I'm sure. She's free to come and go as she pleases. This is why I stopped taking theatricals! If she'd left by this door I could tell you how long she's been gone, but she may have gone out by the back door. I hear it go now and then, only I can't see into the back from my room. But I'll tell her you've called, Mr…?'

'Gordon… on behalf of the Boy Detectives,' announced Gordon with supreme seriousness, and with one last blinding smile, he walked back into the street. It was half past nine, and Miss Dean might be out for the day.

The street was deserted but for an old gentleman, a tired trilby in one hand, an untidy umbrella and a battered little briefcase in the other. Although he was some way away, Gordon could see that his suit was shabby and shiny around the seat. Gordon wondered at the problems of old age. Think of the difficult lives that people like Miss Dean and that poor old man had inherited after the war. They seemed to belong to a world that was fast disappearing. At least the old gentleman seemed to have some money about him, for he hailed a taxi, gave instructions to the driver through the window, and stepped inside. Such a funny walk, too, like something from a silent film.

Gordon made for the bus stop that would take him back to Strutton. He'd had enough of Holmes to last a lifetime, and determined not to think about him and that troublesome memoir of Mrs Hudson's on the journey home. After all, there was a hundred and one things still to organise for the party on the Common. Would there be enough sausages? Should the bread rolls be soft or crusty (a great number of the villagers had false teeth)? Had the fireworks arrived?

*

The fifth of November dawned, but any thought of Guy Fawkes or bonfires or fireworks didn't enter Francis's head. At 10.35, he was looking from the window of Red Cherry House when a taxi drew up outside and an elderly gentleman emerged. There seemed to be a muddle over payment with the driver, who shouted out of the window 'Talk about an absent-minded professor' as he drove off. Having first wandered up the next door neighbour's path, the old gentleman eventually found his way to the Jones's front door.

'Master Francis Jones?'

'I'm Francis, yes. You must be Professor Faversham.'

The professor peered anxiously into the street, looking left and right.

'I am being watched,' he said, and stepped inside.

Francis supposed that years of study in musty libraries had done their worst for the professor. By the time he finished his work at the British Museum, all the clothes shops had probably shut, for the professor was clearly unacquainted with modern fashion. His suit was of the shabbiest; the seat of his trousers might have served as a mirror if the professor had been a contortionist. His trilby was historic. His salt and pepper hair and the dandruff on his sloping shoulders showed a distinct lack of attention to personal appearance.

'I will come directly to the point, Master Jones. I have made my way here from the British Museum. It is my first visit to Norfolk, and I have found it deeply depressing. You do not need to tell me what has been happening to you. I know everything of the exercise book. It is a volume that I originally reviled as a work of falsification and lies. But I am the most respected authority on Sherlock Holmes…'

'Indeed, yes,' said Gordon admiringly, 'I know your work.'

'The most respected authority… and of course when that pathetic creature…'

'Do you mean Miss Dean?'

'… that pathetic creature Miss Dean applied to me for assistance, I almost laughed her out of court.'

Now, the professor moved his face closer to Francis and waggled his finger at him.

'But I have been convinced otherwise. That truth must now be told, Master Jones, and you are the young man who must tell it. That truth must be brought into the light of day. You must let the world know that Holmes was a scoundrel and a charlatan. If you do not act today, I fear for your safety. That gang, that emissary of the gang that I know has been watching me day and night…'

'Me, too,' said Francis. 'I've been watched day and night, too.'

'Once you tell the world about Holmes, that gang will lose interest. They will no longer be able to get at what they want. But you must act. Don't even wait for that reporter from the *Daily Sketch*. He's in it for what he can get. Don't waste time. Go to the BBC without delay, go to your local newspaper, hire a sandwich board and march up and down the streets of England proclaiming the fact that Sherlock Holmes lived, and lived a life of disgrace, scandal and failure.'

The professor's message was clear, and repeated over and over again until Francis thought the man would have a seizure. In some strange way, the wilder the professor behaved, the calmer Francis became. The old gentleman had almost collapsed and was mopping his brow, when Francis smiled back at him, gave a sigh of relaxation, stretched his legs and placed his hands together, fingertips moving together and apart, very much as Holmes himself might have.

'It is extraordinary, isn't it, professor, if we assume that Sherlock Holmes, as you and I indeed know to be the truth, was a living person? Does it mean that all the people associated with him were just as real? Of course, we know now that Mrs Hudson, Mrs *Kathleen* Hudson, was flesh and blood. That exercise book is proof positive. I have actually had tea and biscuits with the daughter of Sherlock Holmes's landlady. The next thing that will be discovered is that Dr Watson and Inspector Lestrade were real, as will no doubt be proved by deeper delving into the records of the British Medical Association and Scotland Yard. Then, we may look beyond that close circle, and consider the many hundreds of people Holmes came across through his work as a detective.'

'Yes,' said the professor, 'I see your point. A very interesting observation!'

'When Sir Arthur wrote *The Adventure of Foulkes Rath*... a story you must know well, professor?'

'Naturally.'

'In that story of Sir Arthur's, it must follow that when he wrote of the suspected murder of Percy Longton by his uncle Colonel Addleton... you recall it?'

'A dreadful business, the Longton murder...'

'... in that case, all the characters mentioned must have been real people.'

'My goodness, Master Jones,' cried the professor. 'What a fascinating door this opens for scholarship. The implications are quite astounding.'

'Indeed they are,' said Francis, and snatched up a book from the table.

'And in *The Adventure of the Deptford Horror,*' he said, and held up the first page of the story so that the professor could clearly see it, 'which I always think is one of the less successful of Sir Arthur's stories…'

'That is a matter for discussion,' said the professor. He was peering inquisitively at Francis, whose brow was furrowed with excitement, and whose nose seemed to be twitching.

'It's got that terrific opening line,' said Francis, 'which of course we now realise must have been written by the *real* Dr Watson – *"I have remarked elsewhere that my friend, Sherlock Holmes, like all great artists, lived for his art's sake."* Tell me. Do you believe in great artists, Professor Faversham? Do you believe in great men, men of outstanding talents who having been given the gift of extraordinary intellect bend it not to good deeds but to evil?'

'You are a philosopher, Master Jones,' said the professor, who was now anxiously looking over his shoulder, and playing tensely with his umbrella and trilby. 'I wish I could listen longer to your theories. Your youthful enthusiasm is to be applauded, but I must go now, go while the coast is clear and while the man in the street is not watching.'

'No, Professor Faversham, I think we may safely assume that the man in the trench coat is not waiting in the street at the moment.'

But by now the professor was out of the door, walking a little hastily away from the house, in search of a taxi.

'*What* I don't understand is… was that person a man or a woman?' asked Gordon.

'That remains a mystery,' said Francis.

'Well, an aspect of the mystery,' said Gordon. 'To you, Francis Jones, belongs the glory!' He made an exaggerated bow to his cousin, who spluttered with laughter and relief that the

Mrs Hudson business had been resolved. Of course, Francis had never once considered accepting the newspaper reporter's offer, had never wanted to become rich overnight.

'By the way, if you will allow me my own little moment of Holmesian brilliance,' suggested Gordon. 'There may still be one missing part of the jigsaw.'

So the case was not over yet! Francis realised how indispensable Gordon was. How selfish he'd been in recent weeks, his head too deep in Conan Doyle's stories, until – and how ridiculous and foolish it seemed now – he had begun to feel the alien spirit of Sherlock Holmes seeping into his body. How considerate and long-suffering Gordon had been, always on hand and ready to accept Francis's silly pretensions. For goodness sake... they were a pair! They were the Boy Detectives!

'Gordon Jones,' said Francis, 'you'd make a great detective.'

'It will mean catching the no. 79 bus,' said Gordon.

Half an hour later, the boys were standing outside the Balmoral Guest House where the neon sign still flickered.

'Someone should fix that dodgy bulb,' said Francis. 'The place looks a bit grim. As in Brothers Grimm.'

Even before she had fully opened the door, they heard the woman's voice moaning. 'No vacancies. Can't people read? No... Oh... Oh it's you again. Brought your friend this time, have you?'

'Good afternoon,' said Gordon. 'I'm sorry to trouble you again, Miss... ?'

'Evans. Mrs.'

At first, Mrs Evans had only glimpsed Francis, but when she looked at him again, and squinted at him, and peered through widely opened eyes, she smiled with a beam that cancelled out the faulty light bulb. It seemed to Gordon to be a magical transformation.

'Of course,' she laughed, and turned to Gordon. 'I remember you saying you was one of the Boy Detectives. Soon as you'd gone off, I knew I'd seen your picture in the paper. Well, come in the two of you.'

The back parlour of the Balmoral was poorly furnished and dark, but a coal fire in the grate did its best to break through the dusty gloom. Mrs Evans bustled about with cups and saucers, and warmed the pot from a kettle that seemed to be permanently steaming. She couldn't have been more cheery.

'Not every day we have celebrities calling at the Balmoral,' she said, her ample rump filling up the Windsor chair and smiling broadly as if in disbelief at their presence. 'Does this mean you're working on a case?'

'Well,' said Gordon, 'as a matter of fact, you may be able to help us. Could we walk up your stairs?'

'Whatever for?'

'It's just that, when I called here before, and you went upstairs to see if one of your guests was in her room...'

'Oh, yes. Miss Dean, wasn't it? Funny little woman. As respectable as could be, I thought. How wrong can you be! Went off this morning, not three hours since, without paying. What a state the room was in, too. Hair grips and some glue on the dressing table, and there's a man's trench coat she's left in the wardrobe, too. Goodness knows when she planned to wear that. Not exactly fashionable, Miss Dean.'

'I couldn't help but see as you were going up the stairs that you have a lot of fascinating photographs lining the walls.'

'Oh, them!' said Mrs Evans dismissively. 'Been there years.'

'And I remember you said something like "That's why I

stopped taking theatricals", which set me thinking. So you used to be a theatrical digs?'

This started Mrs Evans off on a long recollection of the many stars who had, a very long time ago, perhaps when the Balmoral had been more appealing than it was now, stayed under her roof. She was delighted to give them a conducted tour of the photograph gallery that graced the stairwell. The portraits dated from several decades earlier, of guests who had left Mrs Evans a signed picture of themselves as a memento of their transient fame. A toothy woman in a poke bonnet and frilly dress had signed 'Long live the Balmoral! Love, Daisy Delmont'; next to it, a middle-aged man in evening dress in front of a backcloth was signed 'To Mrs Evans, landlady supreme! Affectionately Harold Sneddock, The Voice to Recall.'

'These were real music hall acts,' Mrs Evans said proudly. 'No one would remember them now. This one is Monsieur Gardonimi with one of his performing seals. Stank out the bathroom, and the seals weren't much better. That's Ronald Spinks, the Sophisticated Songster. And this one, well, it's the pride of my collection…'

The boys bent closer to the wall to overcome the inadequate lighting.

'My goodness,' said Francis. 'It's signed Charlie Chaplin.'

'Yes, that's him,' said Mrs Evans. 'A bit boring, but nice as pie. The bigger they are, the better they are, that's what I always found.'

'I noticed that one when I was here before,' said Gordon, 'just a glimpse of it. And I thought it looked like Charlie Chaplin. It's the classic Chaplin pose, isn't it? Funny thing is, when I was here before I saw this old gentleman in the street walking away in the opposite direction and, it was so odd, he was doing the Charlie Chaplin walk, you know, the thing with the legs and the umbrella and everything. And there's another photograph at the bottom of the stairs… one with brown spots all over it.'

'This one, you mean,' said Mrs Evans, leading the way down. 'Oh! This is a very special photograph. Handsome lad, wasn't he? Funnily enough, he was in Charlie Chaplin's troupe. Stayed here the same time as Charlie. Very smart young man, acrobat and juggler and goodness knows what else. Brainy, too. He used to entertain us after the shows when we all sat in the front room, and he'd do these things… illusions he called them… and you'd never believe what he could make happen. When you looked at him, it was as if you couldn't focus on him. Makes me sound daft, but you'd look away and then look back at him and it was as if he'd changed into someone else, someone else who'd just come into the room without you hearing them come in. Even after all these years I can see him now, he used to look at you, just look at you normal like, but his eyes, his eyes… He stayed here just that once, but I've never forgotten. And when he left, he came into the parlour, just where you boys are now, and he looked at me and he said "I will return." Such a way with him when he said it, and I went cold all over. Them eyes looking into mine, and him saying… "I will return."'

It was the eyes that caught the boys' attention, too. Francis saw in them the eager, penetrating stare of Professor Faversham, and the newspaper reporter who had offered fame and fortune. Gordon looked into the eyes and saw the watery gaze of poor, muddled Miss Dean. It didn't take much imagination to see those eyes looking out from beneath a tilted hat under the shadow of a lamppost, either.

'This is the only photograph that's not signed,' said Gordon.

'Is it not?' asked Mrs Evans, and looked closer to make sure. 'Just as well I remember his name. Fancy, after all these years. Shows what an impression he made on me. One thing I remember… He was in here sat down with me and a pot of tea one day, and I suddenly shot out of this chair. "Whatever's up, missus?" he says, and I said "Can't you smell that soup burning?" Horrible stink it was, and he stood up and opened that window and laughed, and said despite all the gifts he'd been given, all the marvellous stuff he could do, he'd never had much sense of smell. Funny, the things that come back to you when you've forgotten them for years. You'd think I'd be standing here going on about having known Charlie Chaplin, wouldn't you, but it wasn't him that got into your head, it was young Mr Moriarty.'

Branlingham's Bonfire Night was a great success. The day had been dismal and cloudy, but the night turned crisply cold, the clear blue-black sky peppered with stars. Francis's parents had returned home in time to help with the final arrangements, and Uncle Billy had appointed himself Controller of Fireworks. The enormous bonfire roared with pagan splendour long after the last rocket had wheeled up to heaven, and at the end of the night, when the crowds had faded away and the fire was reduced to a glowing intensity, Francis and Gordon stood before it, well wrapped up with scarves and gloves and bobble hats.

'If there's one thing to be learned from all this,' said Gordon, 'it's that nothing much good comes from mixing fact with fiction.'

'No,' said Francis, 'but sometimes it may not altogether be a bad thing.'

Gordon sighed and gave him a playful shove. He wondered sometimes if Francis would ever learn.

'When did you find out the truth?' asked Gordon.

'Perhaps I just stopped trying to be Sherlock Holmes and turned back into me,' replied Francis. 'It was so simple. It was the overlapping.'

'The what?'

'The overlapping. You may remember that Miss Dean smelt horribly of cheap floral perfume. When the reporter came, I noticed the same smell, much less strong. Miss Dean hadn't washed it completely away before turning into her Fleet Street character. Then, I think Miss Dean had already prepared herself for another visit when she decided it was time for the professor to make another appearance, and changed into the disguise without remembering to wash off the floral scent that Miss Dean was so fond of. '

'I see!' exclaimed Gordon. 'Mrs Evans remembered that Moriarty had a poor sense of smell.'

'Yes,' said Francis. 'Anatomically fascinating: what you might call an Achilles heel of the nasal passage. And don't forget the reporter, who had a Woodbine behind his ear. He didn't smell of Woodbines but of French cigarettes!'

'Of course!' shouted Gordon. 'The reporter had just been the man in the street, smoking under the lamppost.'

'And Gauloises didn't really go with heavy floral scent' explained Francis. 'As for the man in the street, we saw him, of course. The professor *told us he* had seen him. Miss Dean *told us she* had seen him. The reporter *told us he* had seen him. But *we* never saw the man in the street when we were with any of the others. And when you told me about the old man near the Balmoral Guest House I recognised the description perfectly fitted Professor Faversham, who certainly didn't have any sort of Charlie Chaplin walk. No, our visitor was doing that comical walk in the street because he was so pleased with himself and all his disguises, and didn't realise that you were watching him.'

'And yet you checked up that the newspaper reporter really was from the *Daily Sketch*, and that Professor Faversham really was on his way to see you.'

'Yes. Moriarty left hardly a stone unturned. He had got himself taken on at the newspaper as a reporter, probably months before. As for our expert from the British Museum, I think we shall be hearing in a few hours that the real Professor Faversham has been found, bound and gagged, his clothes and identity stolen for those few necessary hours when Moriarty needed to impersonate him. My belief is that the professor intended to warn me that something was very wrong, and Moriarty had to prevent that at all costs if he was to convince me that the exercise book was genuine. If he could do that, his wish, to once and for all destroy the reputation of Sherlock Holmes, would be fulfilled.

'But I still had to be sure. When Professor Faversham paid a call, I knew things were coming to a head. I was almost being forced against my will to expose poor old Holmes. It was like being caught in a whirlwind in which I had no way to turn. But let the next bit be a lesson to you, Gordon. Read as much as you can!'

'What do you mean?' asked Gordon.

'The Professor was supposed to be an expert, perhaps the world's greatest scholar, concerning Holmes. He must know everything, have read everything. So, I began a discussion with him about some of Conan Doyle's stories. I asked, what did he think of *The Adventure of Foulkes Rath*? He wasn't quite sure. No wonder! That, and the other stuff I mentioned, wasn't by

Sir Arthur! Only last year I got this birthday present from Mum and Dad: *The Exploits of Sherlock Holmes*, not by Conan Doyle, but his son Adrian. The book is quite new. And I'd muddled up the information about the stories as well. I reminded him that Colonel Addleton had been suspected of the murder of his nephew Percy Longton, when in fact it was the other way round. And the supposedly leading authority on Conan Doyle hadn't a clue!'

'Moriarty wasn't well read enough!' laughed Gordon.

'Well, if that doesn't prove what I tell you – read as much as you can!'

'Point taken. But what would have happened if it had all been true?'

'That's what worries me, ' said Francis, and his eyes looked deep into the diminishing fire. 'It would have ruined Sherlock Holmes, and probably ruined me. I ask myself, would I have told the story? Would I have kept it from the world?'

'Whatever you would have done,' said Gordon gently, 'it would have been right, because you're back to being you.'

They stood silently for a moment or two, each with his own thoughts, and then Francis snapped out of it.

'It's cold,' he said. 'Those chestnuts should be ready by now.'

They had been cooking slowly in the glowing shreds of the bonfire, where Francis had placed them carefully above a small green exercise book.

'Coo… these are delicious,' said Gordon, hopping one of the chestnuts around in his mouth.

'They should be,' said Francis. 'They have been roasted in the embers of truth.'

THE VOICE OF DOOM

*T*hat December, King Wenceslas was two thirds correct: the snow lay deep, crisp and very uneven. Along much of the Norwich road to Branlingham, it lay in drifts that made the way impassable. No Christmas card could have looked more seasonal than the church of St Barnabas at Knee, every one of its features – porch, lich-gate, steeple, gravestone – topped with glistening white, thick as an over-iced cake. The snow had fallen, silent and rich, four days before Christmas Eve. In early morning the villagers pulled open their curtains and gasped at the crystal wonderland that was spread before them beneath a brilliant sun. The weather forecast, unreliable as it was, didn't mention a thaw. Gordon Jones watched shrewmice making their nests in the ground away from the prevailing wind. This year they were digging deeper than usual; it would be a hard winter.

The days seemed quieter when snow was about. Branlingham closed in on itself, as if a spell had been cast. It was the week that old Mrs Crossley died and came back the very next day, as if she were about to apologise that there would now be no one left in the village to see to the laying-outs. It was the week that Branlighamers watched as an elderly Austin van, with 'Pearson Brothers Wireless Services' painted on its side, crawled up the icy hill from Norwich and stopped outside Red Cherry House.

It was obviously an important delivery, for Mr Pearson himself was at the wheel, and got out of the van wearing galoshes. Short and portly, he was puffing alarmingly by the time he stepped into the Jones's front parlour, gratefully depositing his heavy burden on a three-legged fumed oak table. Entirely aware of the gravity of the occasion, he almost bowed to the furniture, and made a wide display of his hands to display his gift.

'Now, Mrs Jones,' he said (and he sounded reverential, too), 'do you know about the Horizontal Hold?'

Doris Jones could barely catch her breath. Beside herself with excitement, she collapsed on the leatherette sofa and waited for the set to be switched on. Never in her wildest dreams had she imagined that they would be the first in the village to have their own television. Of course, Lady Darting at the Hall had made a great to-do of purchasing one from Harrods for the transmission of the Queen's Coronation, but the very next day Lord Darting had taken it into the garden and shot it.

'And here,' said Mr Pearson, peering into the back of the set, 'is your Vertical Hold.'

As the mysteries of the Ekco unfolded, Mr Jones joined Mr Pearson in staring at it from all angles and getting to know its knobs and eccentricities. Mrs Jones was anxious to get on with that evening's viewing. She had heard great things about the brilliant repartee of *What's My Line?*, and even in the afternoons, when there was nothing on, you could watch a potter's wheel going round, or a waterfall. She was looking forward to never a dull moment.

'And with the youngster,' said Mr Pearson, nodding vaguely in Francis's direction, 'the educational element comes into play. He'll be the best-informed young 'un in the village.'

Not naturally rebellious, Francis squirmed. He rather hoped Mr Pearson didn't recognise him. He was annoyed with himself, embarrassed in case the man had seen him standing outside his shop in Norwich, watching the silent images on the television sets in the window of Pearson Brothers Wireless Services. One day, Francis had stood there for an hour or more watching a play. Unable to hear a word of it, or to work out any of the people or situations, he had made up everything – characters, plot and dialogue – on the spot.

Anyway, he wasn't interested in the educational stuff that might now be pumped into the living room at Red Cherry House. The men in those programmes wore boring clothes and pointed to charts. The television promised other delights that Francis longed to discover: *I Love Lucy* and *Sgt Bilko*, and a series about Robin Hood that, with its Sherwood Forest setting, was especially welcome on rainy days when he and his cousin Gordon couldn't get out. He couldn't wait for *Pinky and Perky*, which turned out to be a hit with the whole Jones family. His mother laughed at the squeaky voices, and his father tapped his feet to the piglet's signature tune, 'We Belong Together', and Francis thought, 'Yes, just like Gordon and me!'

That first evening, the set was red hot by half past seven, with images constantly being flashed across the room, and Mr Jones regularly having to fiddle with the Horizontal Hold. By the time Francis went up to bed, people on the screen were skidding about as if they were in a cement mixer.

*

The following day was a Sunday, and if Francis had known there was to be a television set at Red Cherry House he would not have arranged that evening's outing with Gordon.

'Stay in and watch the silly thing if you want,' said Gordon dismissively. He was already tired of Francis's enthusiasm for the contraption. 'I didn't want to go tonight anyway. It was your stupid idea in the first place.'

But Francis had wanted to go, and still did, although Gordon said there were certain things that shouldn't be experimented with, and God was probably top of the list. Nevertheless, he supported Francis in his campaign to test-drive religion. Francis said it was no more than buying a new pair of trousers: you had to try a lot on before you found the right ones. It was the same with church, he said, and from the start he had rather grandly described their regular Sunday night visits as 'The Quest'. Although both boys considered themselves Church of England, in the past few months they had sat through all sorts of services in all sorts of meeting places, gospel halls and chapels, and once at a mission on the sands at Hemsby.

This week it was the turn of the little spiritualist church, little more than a corrugated hut, hidden demurely in a side street on the edge of the village. The day before it snowed, Gordon had checked its noticeboard, which read: 'Next Sunday at 6.15 pm. Guest Speaker: Mr Crimp (Romford). Private consultations available.'

Perhaps the weather had kept a massive congregation at home, for there were only a few subdued souls present as Francis and Gordon took their places on the wooden forms, a few rows from the platform at the front. The place was bitterly cold, with an ancient paraffin heater wheezing in a far-off corner, eventually joined by the nasal throb of a harmonium, played by an elderly man with ill-fitting false teeth that threatened to come awry whenever he attacked a high note. Gordon was not yet past the giggling age. Francis nudged him. After a ragged opening hymn, Francis was surprised to see the local post-mistress, Miss Simms, rise to address the congregation. Her smile was as wintry as the weather.

'Welcome to you all,' she said, but the look she gave Francis and Gordon suggested she hadn't meant to include them. Miss Simms was known to be the worst (or busiest) gossip in Branlingham, read messages on postcards, and carefully examined packages for illicit objects. Two hymns later, both the room and Miss Simms's face had grown even icier. She dimmed the gas lamp that was feebly illuminating the dais, put down her hymn-book and spoke in hushed tones.

'And now, we come to the highlight of our meeting. We are delighted', and here Miss Simms gave a budgerigar tweak of her head to the man sitting at her side, 'to welcome as our speaker this evening, Mr Reginald Crimp. Mr Crimp. Of Romford.'

With a girlish flourish, Miss Simms sat as Mr Crimp rose to his feet. He was a bean-poled, angular man, sharp-edged in his limbs. His suit wavered and shone around him. He wore a not quite white shirt, frayed at the cuffs, a butterfly collar fastened with a brass stud and a black tie here and there browned with age. His hair was thin, sleekly laid across his head with a middle parting. His slightly pursed mouth suggested he had accidentally swallowed a number of acid drops. Perhaps to take away the taste, he lifted a glass of red wine to his lips and drank deeply.

'Mrs Crimp,' he wailed. 'Mrs Crimp.'

For a man who seemed in danger of being blown over by a

breeze he had a deep, sonorous voice that fixed his audience at once. Those seeing him for the first time imagined he was not wasting a moment to get in touch with those on the other side, and by intoning the name of Mrs Crimp was already expecting his late wife (or mother) to come through from the spirit world, until a ruffling and scuffling below the dais revealed a small, indistinct woman in shades of grey, moving towards an ancient wind-up gramophone with an enormous acoustic horn attached to it. She proceeded to wind the machine up, an act that clearly took a great deal out of her.

A hand tapped Francis on the shoulder. The voice of Lady Darting whispered 'Old Crimp can't cross over without music. Says it opens up the channels. Last time we had to endure three movements of a Beethoven symphony before the first spook turned up.'

Mrs Crimp's turning of the handle required more and more effort until, when it suddenly reached its potential, the creaking stopped with such violence that she was almost thrown across the room. Her husband (or was it her son?) was slumped in his high-backed chair on the platform, and was fixing his eye on something ethereal. With the skill of a conjuror's assistant, Mrs Crimp turned her back on the audience and then switched back to face them holding a 78rpm record that she placed with great ceremony on the gramophone turntable.

'Don't suppose it'll be Elvis,' Gordon whispered. He'd heard 'Heartbreak Hotel' a few days before and wondered if it might change his life.

The stentorian sounds of Dame Clara Butt squashed that hope. The sound seemed to go through Reginald Crimp like an electric shock. His body shook. His head lolled in the crown of his high-backed chair. His eyes opened and rolled as if everything around him were foreign. Dame Clara responded with terrifying contralto booms. Francis and Gordon were as transfixed as everyone else in the room. It was obvious that something, somehow, was going to happen. Mr Crimp's body vibrated ever more violently. He suddenly sat bolt upright, his hands placed before him on the table.

'He's off,' whispered Lady Darting.

Then, cutting into the silence, came the treble voice of a young child.

'Hello.' It was a meek, piping sound. 'Please may I play in your garden?'

Lady Darting prodded Francis.

'It's Crimp's familiar,' she said. 'Little Laughing Annie. She's usually the first to come through.'

As if verifying this description, the childish voice broke into gales of laughter.

'I have lost my little doll,' said Laughing Annie, who by now had stopped laughing. Francis and Gordon were spellbound; it was extraordinary watching Mr Crimp's mouth move about and to hear the girl's voice coming from it.

'Of course,' cried Mrs Crimp. 'The poor dear! Of course you may play in our garden.'

This restored the child's spirits.

'I want to be with the pretty daffodils,' said Laughing Annie, bursting into peals of delighted chuckling. 'And the snapdragons.' Her sense of fun was obviously her salvation, for once again Mr Crimp rocked in his chair, convulsed with girlish laughter. Then, almost without warning, the merriment faded.

'She's going,' said Lady Darting. 'Poor little Annie. Had she lived I believe she would have become a florist.'

Now, Mr Crimp took on the look of a vengeful eagle.

'How!' said his new voice, even deeper than Dame Clara's, which had just stopped revolving on the gramophone.

'We are in luck,' said Lady Darting. 'It's not often Chief Running Water comes through. His tribe took to the hills many years ago.'

'Greetings to the White Man,' announced Chief Running Water. 'Hiawatha is with me tonight. Will you share a pipe of peace with us?'

Miss Simms was visibly shaken by the invitation. The Red Indian had such a manly voice, and the thought of an assignation in a cosy tepee made her knees tingle.

It seemed to everyone that Mr Crimp had actually turned into the distinguished Chief. His forehead grew nobler, his nose hooked, his eyes bulged, his fingers might as well have clenched a tomahawk.

'The eagle is flown but the cliff is crumbled,' the voice warned. 'I go now! I go now!'

'Well,' said Lady Darting as the voice faded, 'we were very lucky to hear him at all. Chief Running Water has a frightfully busy schedule in the Happy Hunting Ground.'

If Gordon was struggling to suppress an attack of giggling, it was cut off with dramatic force. Up until that moment, the boys might as well have been in a variety hall, but the terrible look that now overcame Mr Crimp's face sent a shiver through them both. The man's face changed colour quicker than a set of traffic lights. His eyes shrivelled. He clutched at his throat, struggled to rise from his chair and in a croaking gurgle called 'Mrs Crossley! Mrs Crossley!'

This might have been exciting news for the congregation, for everyone knew that old Mrs Crossley (the oldest woman in the village) had passed away the day before, and it seemed that she was wasting no time in coming back from the other side. But it was not to be. Mr Crimp's face went from traffic light red to lighthouse white, before he fell back in his chair. He remained still. Very still indeed. Mrs Crimp slowly approached him from below the dais and gave him a little shake, but to no avail. Her husband had already crossed over to that place from which he had always welcomed visitors. Mrs Crimp screamed.

'I hate spooks,' said Chief Inspector 'Tod' Slaughter, 'and I'm none too fond of pesky boys neither.'

His assistant Sergeant Cudd, whose job mainly consisted of pouring oil on his superior's troubled waters, smiled encouragingly.

'They're good lads,' Cudd said. 'And they've helped the force with a few cases. There was that funny business at the Hippodrome, and the spy ring at St Mildred's.'

'Murder's a different kettle of fish,' snorted Slaughter.

He was exhausted. It was his misfortune that he'd been on duty at Branlingham police sub-station on the night of the incident, and he didn't like murders. Old ladies with or without lost umbrellas, and nipping down to the Wedded Stoat to make sure they weren't serving after hours, but murders, no. There'd be trouble at home, too. The only time his wife ever took an interest in his work was when it involved something gruesome. She'd be in her element.

'And we've got another problem, sir,' said Cudd. He cast a despairing look at his superior. Only that morning, the Chief Inspector had told his wife that his sergeant was wet behind the ears.

'It's a cat,' Cudd explained.

Slaughter sighed. 'Cudd, you should know I don't do cats.'

'Oh no. I forgot, sir. You being a Chief Inspector and all.'

'Neither do I do dogs, escaped budgies, or tame mice that have slipped their moorings. Any animal weighing over a ton or likely to cause a breach of the peace, I'm your man.'

'Of course, sir. It's just that this lady telephoned to say her cat is up a tree.'

'Well, this is probably your first opportunity for some serious investigative work. Method, Cudd, method! Ask yourself some questions. How tall is the tree? How far is the cat up it? Does the value of the cat equate to the effort necessary to get the 'orrible thing down from it? What number do you ring to get the Fire Brigade?'

'The Fire Brigade?' Slaughter watched his sergeant's face as the penny dropped. 'Oh, I get your drift, sir. I'll get on to them, then.'

'Case all but solved, lad. Then all we have to do is solve this other little case of murder and we can put our feet up with a cup of cocoa.'

Wondering what number he needed to ring to summon a fire engine, Cudd wandered into the police station's anteroom. Slaughter closed the door behind him, hitched up his trousers around his increasingly elusive waist, and picked up the surgeon's report. There seemed no doubt about it. Reginald Septimus Crimp, aged 59, of Romford, had died in suspicious circumstances while presenting a séance at Branlingham Spiritualist Church. The man was probably a fake, but had apparently been getting in touch with dead people who might have taken such a fancy to him that they invited him to join them. The glass of Wincarnis wine from which he had been seen to sip just before he went into his trance had possibly contained a rare poison of South American origin. On discovering him to be dead, his wife, who had accompanied him from Romford, had gone into a nervous hysteria, and amid much confusion the church had been cleared and a local doctor summoned. Unconvinced that this was a natural death, the doctor called the police. All Slaughter had to do was to find out why anyone would have wanted to murder an elderly spiritualist who looked as though a puff of wind might have done the job for them.

Cudd reappeared from the anteroom.

'That cat, sir,' he reported. 'The lady wasn't fussed about having it back.'

'Still up the tree?'

'The Fire Brigade is on its way. They'll take it to the animal sanctuary at Drayton. I telephoned Phyllis. She'll probably take it home.'

'Phyllis?' asked Slaughter. Cudd almost blushed.

'The girl friend, sir. Case solved, anyway.'

'Well done, lad, but don't look to get promoted just yet. And you needn't always get so personally involved with a case, otherwise you and Phyllis will end up with an animal sanctuary of your own.'

'Point taken, sir. It's just that Phyllis is hopelessly attracted to helpless creatures.'

'So it seems,' said Slaughter.

Well known as she had been in Branlingham, Mrs Crossley had seldom been a welcome visitor to her neighbours. For as long as anyone in the village could remember, she had been the layer-out of the dead, carrying out her business untroubled through eighty years. As Branlingham's population decreased one by one, she crossed most of the doorsteps. Mrs Crossley had a reputation for returning to each house immediately after the funeral to collect the two pennies that had served their purpose in closing up the eyes of the dear departed. Rumour had it that she used the same two pennies for eighty years. They had the head of Queen Victoria on them.

It seemed unfair that such respect should not be given her at the moment of her own passing. She had been in such a happy mood that Saturday morning, and was looking forward to visiting the Spiritualist Church the following day to hear Mr Crimp, who usually managed to have a word or two with her late husband, Arthur Crossley, when he could spare the time from the Elysian field.

'Why are we here?' asked Gordon. He and Francis were outside Mrs Crossley's ramshackle cottage.

'We knew the deceased,' explained Francis. 'We are offering our condolences.'

Another of his cousin's long words, and Francis was looking particularly self important for ten o'clock on a snowy Monday morning. They knocked on the door and tapped at the window before the latch was turned and the door screeched open a few inches. A grey-haired man, heavy and stooped, and with more than a day's stubble, peered out at them.

'Mum's not in,' he said, and went to shut the door in their faces.

Francis smiled understandingly and hoped the man hadn't heard Gordon's smothered giggle. At least Gordon had the wit to wedge his foot in the door, a trick he had learned when vacuum salesmen called at Bundler's Cottage.

'We've brought some chocolates,' said Francis. 'To ease your grief.'

'You'd best come in, then.' The man's eyes didn't leave the box of Cadbury's Roses that glistened in the sharp morning sun. Squeezing through the narrow opening, the boys sidled into the dishevelled living room.

'They took her away,' said the man. 'Saturday.'

'How are you bearing up, Mr Crossley?' asked Francis.

'Words can't express it,' said Jim Crossley, although he was thinking of a strawberry crème. 'The place seems so empty. Not like home.'

Gordon thought it could never have seemed like much of a home: the place was so neglected and dirty. He attempted a sympathetic face.

'I'd hoped that Mum would have been spared for a few more years,' said Jim.

'She was 102,' said Gordon.

'And working right up to the end,' said Jim.

'How wonderful.'

'Mum laid out her last client on Friday. The day before she…'

Jim stumbled for a moment, and looked down at the Cadbury's Roses.

'The day before she was taken. That job took her two days. Very thorough, Mum was. She never cut corners, not all the years she was doing, you know, what she did.'

'Laying out,' suggested Gordon, with relish.

''Course, she didn't work as quick as she used. She took longer to make sure everything was just so, if you know what I mean. Yes, she took a lot longer to lay them out more recently. She'd stopped taking bookings in hot weather, if you understand me…'

Gordon shifted uneasily in an armchair with its springs gone.

'I hope she didn't suffer,' said Francis. How difficult it was to find words at such a time!

'Not really. It was quick as quick in the end. Everyone's been very kind.' He wanted to get on with opening the cellophane, and he knew he'd be all fingers and thumbs.

'Just the day before, she'd had a little miracle. People are so kind.'

'A miracle?' Francis's ears perked up. 'What sort of miracle?'

Jim lumbered his body to a corner of the room by the fireplace where rolled up newspaper and wood remained unlit in the grate.

'I covered it up as a mark of respect,' he said, 'but see for yourselves.' With the gesture of a weary magician at a variety show, he caught the edge of a floral tablecloth and whisked it to the floor, revealing a gleaming television set. Francis recognised it at once: it was exactly the same Ekco model that Mr Pearson had delivered to Red Cherry House.

'Little Sir Ekco, how do you do?' he almost whistled.

'So kind,' said Jim, his words breaking up. 'Mr Pearson who runs the wireless shop heard that Mum was slowing up a bit and had it sent round. Funny, really.'

'Why funny?' asked Francis.

'She was pleased as Punch when it arrived. It bucked her up no end. It's a tonic, that's what she said. Mr Pearson brought it that morning, and the minute he'd gone she kept it on all day, until they played God Save the Queen and the screen went blank.' He gazed at the television with reverence. 'And it was with her at the end, as you might say. We'd been watching *What's My Line?*, and Gilbert Harding said "What possible use are you to the general public?" to one of the contestants, and Mum took it personally. "More use than you'll ever be, that's for certain," she said, and I told her he wasn't talking to her, only she's a bit deaf, so the set was up too loud for her to hear what I was saying to her. I got up and went and made a pot of tea. I was in the kitchen bustling about with the biscuits – we get nice broken ones from the shop on the green – when I heard a voice say "I know who you are and I know what you have done! The game is up! You are of no discernible use to humanity!" And then Mum called out "Jim! Jim!", and I come back in here, and she pointed to the television and gave a little cry. And that was that.'

'How dreadful for you,' said Francis.

'Still, we must be grateful it was so quick,' said Jim. 'Mum wouldn't want to have suffered. I thought you was the people from the undertaker.'

'Us?' said Gordon.

'They're supposed to be coming round this morning to collect the money.'

'Golly! They're not expecting people to pay in advance now, are they?'

'The two pennies,' explained Jim. 'Mum always said as how they would come in handy. And now, if you'll excuse me, I think I ought to write to the British Broadcasting Corporation.'

'What for?' said Gordon, who had just tripped over two enormous packing cases that were standing near the front door.

'To let them know what happened. It only seems right, with the television set being on at the time. Isobel Barnett will be upset.'

*

'*I* demand to see a proper policeman,' said Mrs Crimp. It was no surprise that the man facing her across the desk in the interview room at Branlingham Police Station didn't convince her.

'Inspector Slaughter is a qualified member of the force,' said Sergeant Cudd in a voice that conveyed his understanding of her attitude. After all, 'Tod' Slaughter made little effort to make himself appealing to the public. Even now, he was fixing the blonde-headed woman with bright lipstick and a dress that had a slit almost to the thigh, with a fishy eye. She bore little resemblance to the woman Slaughter and Cudd had seen when they were called out to the scene of the crime. That woman had been grey-haired and frowsy, with nothing brassy about her. Inspector Slaughter scowled at her.

'You are Dawn Daphne Crimp, of 25b Gas Lane, Romford?'

'No,' replied the woman. 'I'm Gina Lollobrigida. What is all this?'

'Married to Reginald Septimus Crimp, of the same address?'

'Not a crime, is it? As up until last night, yes. I'm a widow now, and by rights I should be in weeds.'

Cudd coughed gently.

'We're sorry to hear of your loss, Mrs Crimp,' he said, remembering that 'Tod' Slaughter had been on leave when they'd had training in how to handle the public.

'We're faced with what we call suspicious circumstances,' Slaughter continued. 'On Saturday evening an elderly woman by the name of Gwen Crossley died through reasons yet to be decided.'

'At the age of 102,' added Cudd.

'Like I said,' continued Slaughter, 'unexpectedly, i.e. no cause of death has hitherto been established.' He was now in

Training Manual mode. 'The following day your husband died at a séance held at Branlingham Spiritualist Church, after calling out Mrs Crossley's name. In my book, that spells suspicion.'

'Not in my dictionary, it doesn't,' said Dawn Crimp.

'We have to look into it, see,' explained Cudd. 'We have to establish a cause of death.'

'*Two* causes. Which I believe may have been linked,' added Slaughter ominously.

'Well,' said Dawn Crimp, 'at the age of 102, I'd put my money on the old girl dying of boredom or exhaustion. And you might as well know before you find out. Reg and me wasn't married.'

Slaughter's eyes popped. His teeth made horrible sucking noises.

'Best get it off your chest, madam' said Cudd, noticing just a little too late how much her blouse protruded.

'So,' sighed Slaughter, as if he were hugely disappointed in his witness, '*not* married.' He wrote the fact down three times on a pad. 'Well, well. This may be pertinent to the case. To your knowledge, did Mr Crimp know Mrs Crossley?'

'Don't be ridiculous!'

'Then how do you explain him mentioning her name? Calling it out in front of everyone in the church?'

'And then dropping down dead?' added Cudd.

'Well, it's obvious, isn't it? She must have come through. Reg must have got into contact with her.'

For the first time Dawn Crimp's heavy make-up cracked. She seemed lost, her eyes seeing nothing but a dismal future. 'She must have come over from the other side.'

'Your husband,' began Slaughter, '… that is, Reginald Crimp, was a well-known figure in the spiritualist movement. Had he ever mentioned Mrs Crossley to you before?'

'Reg knew very few people. In his line of work, he kept himself to himself. And not many people ever came through. It's a long journey from the other side. Of course, Reg had his regulars who always showed up. They haunted him. Little Laughing Annie: she hardly ever missed. I'd have given her a good slap if I'd got near her, always that silly giggling, got on my nerves, but Reg didn't seem able to stop her from communicating. And then there was his Red Indian guide…'

'Odd, isn't it?' said Slaughter. 'Why is there always a Red Indian turns up at these do's? I mean, you don't come across many of them in the normal way of things. Lived in Romford, did he, this Red Indian?'

'I don't think you realise the sort of work that Reg was doing, Mr Slaughter. It was in the churches he went into up and down the country that he did his best work, that's where he was needed. Sometimes there would be queues of the dear departed wanting to come across to have a few words with someone they'd left behind on earth. Reggie brought so many of them over, and such joy to them as wanted to hear from their lost loved ones. There was usually an Uncle Herbert who'd been in the Great War, with a message about his gammy leg and how everyone shouldn't worry about him, or a long lost Auntie Ada popping back with a cheery word or two, and the look of pleasure and contentment on the faces of the people in the audience who'd got a message, it made Reg's work worthwhile.'

Dawn Crimp's face crumpled again. 'And now Reggie has gone, and all them people will be wanting to come over with no one to bring them.'

'That's as may be,' said Slaughter, spreading his thick hands before him as if he were awaiting the Last Supper. 'But that doesn't solve the problem, does it? There's nothing the police doctor could find wrong with Mr Crimp except he stopped breathing. He's dead, and the last thing he said was the name of a woman who died without good reason the day before.'

'Two days after celebrating her 102nd birthday,' put in Cudd.

'So,' said Slaughter, 'what do you have to say to that?'

Dawn Crimp crossed her knees and took Cudd off his balance.

'I want a taxi back to Romford' she said, 'and a complaint form.'

There might have been butterflies in Francis's stomach. He felt uneasy. The door to Pearson Brothers Wireless Services jammed when it was only a quarter open, almost forcing him back on to the pavement.

'Oh! That wretched door!' called a woman who appeared from the back of the premises.

The door buckled and sprang back into the shop. It was the first time Francis had stepped inside. Before, he had stood in the street to gaze at the television screens in the window, hoping to watch a play for which he could make up the characters, plot and dialogue. A moment before, he had stood at the entrance like a child full of wonder at the prospect of entering Father Christmas's Enchanted Grotto in Garlands Department Store. Perhaps, just like the child, he would cross the threshold hoping that what was inside confirmed the enchantment that standing outside promised.

In a way, the enchantment was there. The first thing he noticed was the smell. A sense of comforting warmth struck him at once. Could it be the television valves, heated up and doing their work? He was surprised to find that although the screens hummed with life, there was no sound coming from any of them. Dust was an essential component of the room. There were drizzles of it on the shelves, and on the telephone, not recently taken from its rest. Disorder was evident in the random piles of leads and electrical parts and cameras that were distributed haphazardly about the place.

'Are either of the Mr Pearsons in?' asked Francis.

'I'm sorry?' The woman gave a careful smile and quizzically lifted an eyebrow.

'I'm not sure which Mr Pearson I need to speak to.'

'Well, there's no choice, I'm afraid. There's only one, and he's out on a delivery.'

'Oh. It says "Pearson Brothers" above the shop.'

'He should get it changed, but he's never had the heart. There's only the one Mr Pearson. He lost his brother some years ago. He was only in his 50s. There's just Mr Raymond now. It fair broke his heart when Mr Colin died. Was it something I can help you with?'

'Thank you, but it was really Mr Pearson I needed to see. I believe he delivered a television set to a Mrs Crossley last week?'

'That's right. You know she's died, don't you? Raymond will want to get the set back. As a matter of fact, I had words with him.' The woman lifted her eyes heavenward in light-hearted frustration. 'As if he didn't have enough on his plate with the business, but that's how Mr Pearson is, always thinking of other people and how he might do them a good turn. I mean,' (and now the woman was relaxed enough to open up to such an intelligent, well-mannered and handsome young man as Francis) 'he can't really afford to have me working in the shop nowadays. Things haven't been easy for him, not since Mr Colin died, but Raymond's always got time for other people.'

'Does Mrs Raymond help in the shop?'

'Mr Pearson isn't married' said the woman. She was blushing, and for a moment she lowered her head. 'When those new TV sets arrived he got it into his head that old Mrs Crossley might like one. No charge, mind you. That's Raymond all over. A shame she never got much of a chance to enjoy it. Poor old girl hardly had time to read the instruction manual.'

'It was an Ekco, wasn't it?' asked Francis.

'That's right. We had six in last week. All gone. You'd think Mr Pearson would be pleased to be doing some decent business for a change, but he's been a bit out of sorts. Come to think of it, the last time I saw him really happy was at the Hallowe'en party for the local orphanage. He's done a lot for the Dog's Home, too.'

Francis thanked the woman and walked from the shop into the empty street that suddenly seemed less hospitable than before. What, after all, had he learned? That Mr Pearson was no longer a brother, and was kind to animals and old people, and that the woman whom he couldn't afford to have work in the shop was probably madly in love with him.

The next morning, Mr Pearson drove up to Red Cherry House, arriving at ten o'clock.

'Morning, Francis. Your Mum and Dad in?'

'No, they are both out, but Gordon is here.'

'Oh. Morning, Gordon. How's your uncle?'

'Uncle Billy's fine, thank you, Mr Pearson.'

'Right.' Pearson was in the sitting room, moving towards the television. 'Something wrong with the set, is there?'

Was it the boys' imagination, or did he have a slightly wild manner as he looked at the Ekco?

'Is it the picture, or what?'

'I think we're generally quite pleased with it, Mr Pearson,' said Francis. 'It's a pretty good picture. You can see things very clearly.'

'It's one of the best on the market. Made in Southend, you know. Very good quality. Can't always say as much for the programmes!'

By now, there were beads of sweat lining the man's forehead.

'You've sold quite a few of them, then?' asked Francis.

'Sold out, as a matter of fact. You're lucky to have got one. So, what's the problem?'

'I was hoping you might tell us.'

Pearson stared warily at Francis for a moment, then smiled uneasily. 'Well, let's switch on and see what we can do.'

'This might help,' said Gordon. He handed Pearson a copy of the *Radio Times*.

'How do you mean?'

'Well, it's a little odd,' said Francis. 'You see, I was hoping to watch Muffin the Mule the other afternoon. I checked the time in the listings and switched on to watch it. And I didn't.'

'Good judgement,' laughed Pearson, but his hands were sweating as he reached into the back of the set for the Horizontal Hold. 'It's rubbish. You can see the strings.'

'Oh no. I *wanted* to see Muffin the Mule.'

'He's a sad case,' explained Gordon.

'But I didn't,' said Francis.

Pearson's fingers stopped moving. He stood a little way from the set, and wiped his mouth with a handkerchief.

'The fact is, there's nothing wrong with that television, Mr Pearson,' said Francis. 'I'm afraid we brought you out here on false pretences.'

'I see. What's your game?'

'There's nothing wrong with it at all, except that *it isn't the right one.*'

There was a moment's silence before Pearson slowly put down his screwdriver. In the voice of a ghost, he whispered 'What do you mean?'

'You had six new Ekco televisions delivered to your shop. Identical models. But this is the one you took a special interest in. The one that you *meant* to send to Mrs Crossley.'

'Poor old dear,' said Pearson, 'sitting there all day with nothing to do but look at the walls of that damp hovel or stare at that no-good son of hers. I thought the television would give her a bit of enjoyment in her last years.'

'But your shop's in a bit of a muddle, isn't it, Mr Pearson? Your heart's in the right place, but you've never been very good at keeping things neat and organised, have you?'

'Since Colin died,' Pearson stammered. He sat down, and sighed. 'Not since Colin died.'

'Colin was the economic brains behind Pearson Brothers, wasn't he? Brilliant with figures and made sure that everything ran faultlessly with the business.'

'Yes. He was a clever lad, our Colin.' Pearson's eyes filled with tears.

'You do yourself an injustice,' said Francis. Gordon always thrilled to see his cousin at his most kindly. 'You were the one who was a genius with electronics. You didn't just sell televisions. You understood them. You understood them inside and out.'

'A fat lot of good it's done me,' said Pearson.

'You knew how they worked and you came to see what might be done with them. In fact, I think you may be on the brink of something quite extraordinary, something that will change the way people live. I think you may become a very rich man whose name will go down in history.'

'How's that?'

Pearson looked at Francis with wide eyes.

'Somehow... I don't know how... you implanted a film within the television, and at a certain moment when the set was switched on, the film would arrive on the screen, supplanting the programme that was being broadcast at that time. I was so looking forward to that programme. You see, according to the *Radio Times* listing, it was supposed to be *Muffin the Mule* – oh, and you're right about the strings, by the way: ridiculous! – but it wasn't. Instead of Annette Mills, it was a man in a dark cloak and a ghostly chalk white face, standing in a graveyard. I recognised it at once as the graveyard of St Barnabas at Knee. And then the man looked directly from the screen and said that he knew what had been going on, that the wrongdoing would be exposed, and that the time was up.'

'A Voice of Doom,' said Gordon dramatically.

'And it was meant for Mrs Crossley, wasn't it? It was intended to give her the fright of her life.'

Pearson's shoulders slumped. He seemed for a moment to almost slide from consciousness, but lifted his head and took a deep breath.

'It all started when Colin died. He was always the driving force of the business, a financial wizard in his way. Like me, he never got married. The firm was his life. Perhaps because he was a financial wizard, he didn't believe in banks. He looked after all our money. Kept it all at his house. Under the floorboards, behind radiators, under the mattress, in secret places that he was sure no one would ever discover. He'd always lived with Mum and Dad, see, and when they died he stayed on in the house. He said it was impregnable, safer than any strongroom, and he'd made sure the money was in places that nobody would ever dream of looking.'

'Except people who'd made a profession of it,' suggested Francis.

'When Colin died, he left instructions that he wanted to be looked after like Mum and Dad had been.'

'You mean he wanted Mrs Crossley to lay him out?'

'Yes. She'd prepared Dad ten years before, and then Mum, of course.'

'So Mrs Crossley had been in the house before?' asked Gordon.

'Yes. Old Ma Crossley and that rat-faced son of hers. He always helped her out. It was like a ritual that everyone in the village had to observe when someone died. You sent someone round to the Crossley's cottage and they'd begin manoeuvres. She insisted on complete privacy while she was doing the laying-out. Respect for the dead, she called it, and it wasn't a quick do. She said it had to be done thoroughly. It was like a mysterious rite, a passing over of the spirit she used to call it. And for that to happen she and Jim had to be the only ones in the house.'

'And that's what happened when Colin died?'

'Yes. The Crossleys must have been alone in the house for hours. Well, I had to do what Colin wanted, didn't I? And when I went back to the house after they'd left, I looked for the money.'

Francis leaned forward excitedly in his chair, his hands clasped tightly between his knees.

'They'd found it,' Pearson hissed. 'All of it. There was ten and sixpence on top of the living room sideboard. Nothing else. A sort of tip, I suppose. Like a plague of locusts, the Crossleys had stripped the place of every bit of money we'd ever saved.'

'Why on earth didn't you go to the police?' asked Gordon.

'There was no evidence. What could the police have done? The word of a failed business man whose shop wasn't making any money against the word of a very old woman who was one of the most respected in the community, and known to generations of families. Anyway, I did decide to go to the police after a few days. They went to the cottage. All they found were two bewildered people, not the brightest on the planet, who lived as poor as church mice, used the same tea bag for three days of brewing up a pot, and sitting there perishing cold because they had no means of heating.'

'But something happened, didn't it?' asked Francis.

'Yes. A few weeks ago. I was in Norwich. I'd gone into one of the big electrical goods stores to see what the competition was doing, and as I came out I noticed Jim Crossley across the street. Nothing surprising in that, but when I looked at the place he'd just come out of, I saw it was a property management agency. I thought it was a bit odd. I couldn't imagine why Jim would want to go there. But I had a feeling in the pit of my stomach, you know, that sort of feeling when you know you're about to find out something that will alter everything.

'I waited until Jim Crossley vanished round the corner, then I crossed the street and went into the building. "Sorry to trouble you," I said, "but my brother Jim has just been in. He's so forgetful now. He was supposed to have asked you several things, and I'm wondering whether he remembered to check them all with you. It's embarrassing, but we have to keep such an eye on him nowadays."

'The woman looked at me suspiciously, but there must have been something convincing about how I looked and sounded, because after a second or two she gave me such a sympathetic smile, and said how lucky he was to have such a caring family. Still, she only said "Yes, he asked his usual questions." It was a wild guess that I suddenly knew I had to make, and I said "He's always worried about his properties", and she smiled and said "Understandably. But he's got nothing to worry about." And then… I knew.'

'That was when you should have gone to the police,' said Francis. 'They could have followed it up from there.'

Pearson banged his fist on the television table. The Ekco shook.

'No! It was too late. Colin was dead. Nothing I did would have brought him back. And what if the police had gone in and done them? It would have been months before they'd even finished their investigations. After all, once it had got out that they'd swindled us, other families who the Crossleys had laid out would have started bringing claims against them. And I didn't altogether blame Jim. He was always not quite right in the head, something a bit odd about him, and he was a mother's boy. No, it was old Ma Crossley to blame for it all. She was the inspiration. That funny little old woman who everyone thought was something between a witch and a saint.'

'An old woman,' murmured Francis. 'That was the problem,

wasn't it? She was very old, and you couldn't wait for justice to take its time?'

'She was older than Methuselah,' confirmed Gordon.

Pearson seemed to come back into the room, his eyes fiercely staring at the boys.

'I swear I never meant to do her any real harm. I just wanted to frighten her. To let her know that I knew the truth, so she'd know before she met her maker.'

'So,' said Francis, 'you painted your face white and put on a cloak you'd borrowed from the party you gave the orphans at Hallowe'en?'

'It looked very convincing,' said Gordon.

'You saw it too?' asked Pearson.

'Oh yes, Gordon has seen your film. He may grow up, if he ever does, to be as clever as you are with machines. He even got your film to replay.'

Pearson gave Gordon a look of deep appreciation.

'You're a bright spark and no mistake,' he said. 'We could do with someone like you in the shop to help Susie.'

'I think you should patent your film device,' Gordon replied.

'What chance of that, now?' said Pearson. 'When this story gets out, it will all be over for me. They'll put me inside for causing Ma Crossley's death.'

'Why should it come out?' said Francis. 'The truth is that in the disorganisation of your business you mixed up the set meant for Mrs Crossley with the one you earmarked for us. Mrs Crossley never saw your film. She never heard the Voice of Doom. She wasn't a terribly bright woman. By her very nature she was a woman who believed in superstitions. Crafty and devious and money-grabbing, yes, but her understanding of the modern world was lamentable. She probably imagined that the people she saw on the television screen were squatting inside the set. So, when Gilbert Harding looked directly at her and said "I know who you are and I know what you have done! The game is up! You are of no discernible use to humanity!" she didn't realise he was being rude to one of the contestants on the programme. She thought he'd found out about her life of crime. It wasn't you that killed Mrs Crossley. It was Gilbert Harding.'

That evening, Mr Jones called the Bingo for the pensioners down at the Wedded Stoat. Mrs Jones was giving a recital of mad scenes from French operas at the village hall, having had her hair professionally distressed at Madame Pfob's salon in the Royal Arcade. Francis and Gordon sat alone at Red Cherry House. A fire bristled cheerfully in the grate, and outside the carpet of snow was turning to slush. The boys stared at the blank television screen.

'I think I prefer it when it's off,' said Francis.

'Oh, I don't know,' said Gordon. 'I think I'd like the variety shows.'

'In that case, you must look out for the Great Comprendo and his assistant Rosita.'

'Who?'

'That should be The Great Comprendo and Mrs Crimp. That was the act Mrs Crimp was doing before she met up with Mr Crimp. It was a mind-reading act, in which she was noted for her skill at throwing voices.'

'So!' said Gordon triumphantly. 'Then Crimp *was* a fake after all! How did you find that out?'

'Some of my more arcane reading involves old volumes of the *Stage Yearbook*, where variety turns advertise their acts.'

'Little Laughing Annie... that Red Indian... they were all Mrs Crimp's voices! What a fake old Crimp was!'

'Oh, no,' said Francis. 'I'm afraid you have missed the point. You see, when Mr Crimp called out Mrs Crossley's name, she had actually come through. For the very first time in his life he got in touch with someone who had died. Wouldn't it have been fascinating to hear what she had to say? Would it have been a confession, I wonder? We will never know. All we can be certain of is that Reginald Crimp was so staggered at what happened that he dropped dead from shock, just as Mrs Crossley had.'

'Goodness!' cried Gordon. 'What a very unusual case this has been.'

'And not quite over yet,' said Francis. 'I've been in touch with Inspector Slaughter. I think he'll find that there are two enormous packing cases at the Crossley's cottage that are worth looking into...'

'Of course. I almost fell over them when we were leaving.'

'... and that property management shop will be having a visit from our boys in blue. Furthermore, I fancy that Mr Pearson will be getting some support and encouragement from a bright young lad' (and now he winked at his cousin) 'who is intent on helping him patent his invention – how to put a film into a television set. And when Mr Pearson realises that things are looking up, he may catch the eye of his shop assistant, Susie. A wife is always an asset in a business.'

'He won't have to pay her, you mean?' said Gordon.

Francis looked scornfully at his cousin.

'Yes, it's been a strange business. You know, I think it helped that I'd stood outside Pearson's shop and watched stuff on television screens without being able to hear what was being said. This case has been very much about that, if you think about it. There was Mrs Crimp throwing her voice and pretending to be people she wasn't, and poor Mr Pearson painting his face and pretending to be the Voice of Doom…'

'Great title for the case!' exclaimed Gordon.

'… and us seeing him and hearing the Voice of Doom when he'd only intended it for Mrs Crossley.'

'So, what does it all go to prove?' asked Gordon.

'It proves,' said Francis, 'that you can always find something interesting to watch on television.'

THE BENSONIAN DIFFERENTIATOR

*D*id camels have eyelashes?

The alarm clock by the bed stared silently at Mabel Mayfield. It was a quarter past three in the morning, and the worry had woken her. Mabel Mayfield should have known. She had had her monies worth out of camels, had dealt with them for years, but had she ever come face to face with a camel, and, if so, had it fluttered its eyelashes at her?

In the miasma of her evaporating dream, Mabel recognised the lush lashes not as those of a camel but of Lady Ursula Malpractice, lashes surrounding eyes that wept ladylike tears as she was swept off her feet in the chaos of the crowded casbah. The camel onto which she had been thrown was from the stable of the impossibly handsome Prince Hamil, whose features had used up many of the words Mabel kept in the notebook that proved so useful when writing purple passages (and all Mabel's passages were purple).

Prince Hamil was swarthy, splendidly muscular, haughty and deep voiced, ripplingly masculine, his hands sinews of steel, his chest godlike, his legs the colour of brilliantly tawny sand by moonlight, his nostrils flared with the insidious longing of a sexually frustrated tiger, his voluptuously full mouth twisted with lascivious disdain. His eyes had a strangely hypnotic, magnetic appeal, and as for his eyelashes… eyelashes that now fluttered on the edge of Mabel Mayfield's come-and-go dreaming… eyelashes that fluttered in synchronisation with those of his camel…

The ragged conclusion of the chapter that Mabel had completed a few hours earlier straddled her mind, with Lady Ursula denouncing Prince Hamil's ungentlemanly intentions as he threw her on to the luxurious scatter cushions of his tent (one of the cushions looked very much like one Mabel had seen on the W.I. craft stall). Lady Ursula did not know how to cope with the impending fate that she had been warned was worse than death. Her education at Roedean suddenly seemed inadequate. Wasn't there something about leaning back and thinking of England?

Mabel snapped out of the dream just in time to save her heroine's virtue. Her success as a romantic novelist was based on the belief that everything stopped at the bedroom door.

In her bedroom at Red Cherry House, Doris Jones set aside the Mabel Mayfield novel she had been reading, wishing that her eyelashes were as alluring as those of Lady Ursula. The assistant at Branlingham Branch Library, Blodwyn Williams, had told Mrs Jones that Mabel was noted for her meticulous research, and was one of Gerald Rusgrove Mills and Charles Boon's best sellers. *The Frustrated Sheikh* was in the top league of the authoress's achievements, but tonight Doris Jones couldn't concentrate on the book, and had abandoned the story just as its perilously underdressed hero was about to be draped in ropes of pearls. It couldn't be helped. There was a lot on Mrs Jones's mind.

A few months before, she had been known in the village for the dexterity of her pastry making, and her creation of imaginative corsets. Now, how her life had changed! Not only was she on the friendliest of terms with Dame Sybil Thorndike, but with Branlingham's titled grand dame, Georgina, Lady Darting.

It started the day when her ladyship called at Red Cherry House in her chauffeur driven Rolls, and gave aristocratic approval to Mrs Jones's coconut whirls. As President of the local W. I. (although, in the manner of the Queen, she rarely attended) Lady Darting had insisted that Mrs Jones should at once be inducted into the organisation. What was more, during the meeting at which her ladyship had been present, Mrs Jones's voice rang out with such fervour during the singing of 'Jerusalem', that Lady Darting announced that Branlingham W.I. had discovered a diva. Indeed, Mrs Jones had been obliged at that very meeting to give a solo reprise of the song.

It was nothing now for George Jones to hear his wife practising scales as he approached the garden gate. There was so much teeming through her mind nowadays; only that week, she had embarked on a correspondence course on Mongolian throat singing, and bed seemed the perfect place to practise it. The guttural sounds so unnerved Mr Jones that he put two legs into one leg of his pyjama bottoms. With little hope of getting to sleep, he picked up Doris's bedside book. The well-constructed Lady Ursula had bosoms that did nothing but swell, heave, pout, protrude, shiver, shudder and tremble… and as for her eyelashes… No wonder that sheikh was frustrated! Who on earth wrote such stuff?

In his bedroom across the landing, Francis Jones stirred awake. It might have been the wind in the trees that he heard, but he was conscious enough to recognise the sound of his newly Mongolian mother. He sighed, and turned his head against the pillow. Tomorrow was going to be an interesting day. He needed to be up and doing early. He and Gordon had an important appointment to keep.

There was something unworldly about the drive to Northcrack Staithe that Saturday morning. A sleek, grey Bentley collected Francis from Red Cherry House and Gordon from Bundler's Cottage, and purred its way to Northcrack Hall, where they were greeted by an attractive young woman who was anxiously looking out from the great oak door.

'Good morning,' she said. 'I'm so glad you've come. I'm Janet Smedley, Sir John's secretary. Sir John is in the library. This way.'

Northcrack Hall was a fine old house, built to Victorian baronial standards, with here and there a turret or two, and what looked like a tower reaching up in its midst. The interior of the Bentley had been hushed, velvet-soft on the ear. The boys recognised much the same qualities when they entered the Hall. They passed a mediaeval man in armour standing silent guard, and Francis looked with quick fascination at the heavily varnished paintings lining the walls.

The library was imposing but welcoming, with a happy fire in the grate taking the edge off the sharp spring morning. Standing with his back to the marbled fireplace was a gleaming and impeccably dressed man, his well-cut hair streaked with silver, and his friendly face retaining a touch of youthfulness. He moved forward and held out his hand to the young visitors.

'Francis and Gordon! I have heard so much about you. What a pleasure to meet you at last.'

'Thank you, sir,' said Francis. 'What a magnificent house.'

'It's not bad, is it?' said Sir John Richardson. 'Perhaps you would like a tour later? You will be interested in climbing up into the old tower, I'm sure.'

'That would be super,' replied Gordon.

Sir John closed the door as Janet left the room. Directing the boys to an elegant sofa, he sat in a club chair beside the fire, and considered them carefully.

'I want you to know that I have complete faith in you both,' he began. He took a pipe from an adjacent table and tapped it against the grate. 'The Chief Constable has told me of your achievements, and very impressive they are, too. Of course, you understand that everything said in this room and beyond must go no further. Top secret, that's the order of the day.'

This was exciting! The boys felt that unmistakable thrill that came with the beginning of any case, the sensation of being plunged into an affair that would lead who knew where.

'I am not a Branlingham boy,' explained Sir John, hoping to break the ice.

'Come to that, neither am I,' laughed Gordon. 'Strutton-by-the-Way, born and bred. But Francis is true Branlingham stock.'

'Very commendable,' said Sir John. 'I'm a foreigner in these parts. I came to Northcrack Hall only two years ago, when I left London. For all the locals know, I am a Londoner who decided to live a quieter life in the remote reaches of Norfolk, but I came here for a purpose.'

Sir John's voice grew darker, and the lines on his forehead knotted in concentration. 'Come with me. There is something I have to show you.'

The boys had no idea where they were being taken. Gordon

hoped it was to explore the tower, which looked like the keeper of a hundred years of spooky secrets, but Francis, whose sense of smell was stronger than his cousin's, detected a strangely clinical atmosphere in the library that reminded him of the chemistry laboratory at St Basil's.

Sir John led them across the hall and stood outside a door in a secluded passage that seemed not to belong to the old house. The door was made not of oak, but of steel. Sir John, his eyes twinkling with amusement at the bemused expression on his visitors' faces, was about to open it when Janet Smedley reappeared.

'You mustn't forget the security forms, Sir John,' she cried. The uncomfortable manner she had shown when they first arrived was still apparent.

'I should have been marched to the Tower of London if I'd forgotten them!' laughed Sir John. 'Would you boys sign, here and here? It's standard procedure. What's the form called, Janet?'

'The Official Secrets Disclaimer 88 XB. It must be signed if you go beyond that door.'

Sir John's voice took on a dramatic slowness.

'You are about to cross the threshold into another world, a world that very few are aware of. You have been selected not only because of the reputation you have gained as the Boy Detectives, but because the Youth of Britain will inherit the world that lies in wait behind this eighteen-inch-thick steel aperture, and because Gordon came top in Physics last term. You are ambassadors for your generation.'

The boys felt immensely proud! Gordon thought the man's speech would have been much enhanced by an orchestral backing of Eric Coates's 'Youth of Britain' march, which his

Uncle Billy was always playing very loudly on the gramophone at Bundler's Cottage.

Sir John took a tiny torch-like cylinder from his pocket and pointed it at the steel door. He might have been Dan Dare, for the door opened slowly, with a deathly silence, as a sequence of flashing lights shone out within the metal. The boys looked on in astonishment at the sight beyond. It seemed to be a corridor of extraordinary length, with a raised platform running along one side, below which lay a railway track that went on into infinity.

'You are two quite remarkable boys,' exclaimed Sir John, as he stared along the platform towards the tunnel, from which the faintest rumbling could be heard. 'Your names have been chosen from a select list, and only yesterday were approved by the Home Secretary. We live in a highly dangerous world, which at any moment may be threatened by the decision to launch an atomic bomb. Of course, the government has done all in its power to safeguard its citizens should such a devastating event occur, but they have been spared any details of what we call the Doomsday Scenario. However, this is neither the time nor place to split hairs about the splitting of the atom!'

Sir John waited for a chuckle that didn't come.

'In the event of a nuclear attack, the Prime Minister has decided that at least two young people will be brought to safety here. Our facility is impregnable and top secret. You are about to enter a world that I fervently hope you will never have cause to enter again.'

'Only two young people, and it's us,' whispered Francis.

'Perhaps it'll be a sort of Noah's Ark,' Gordon whispered back. 'Two of everything.'

A sharp gust of cold air rushed towards them as a train

came hurtling through the tunnel. It was the tiniest train the boys had even seen, smaller than the one in the model village they had seen at Clacton, but the speed of it was terrifying. It was going at the speed of sound, but just as they closed their eyes they heard the mechanism of the train switch off as if by magic and... it seemed impossible... the train went from supersonic to stationary within a few seconds.

Sir John opened one of the carriage doors and beckoned Francis and Gordon inside the spotless vehicle that looked as if it had just arrived from Mars. The décor was space age, like a futuristic cartoon cutaway in the *Eagle*. The boys stepped into the train and slid onto a cool steel bench. The sides of the train had glassless windows. The passengers had barely settled themselves when a figure bent his head into the carriage.

'Tickets please!'

Sir John handed over three tickets that the man clipped with a machine that might have been borrowed from a Blackpool tram. It was only when he winked at Francis and Gordon that the boys recognised the attendant in the smart uniform and peaked cap. It was Uncle Billy! They knew that he worked at Northcrack Staithe, but were astounded to find him here.

'Hold tight!' cried Uncle Billy, and blew his whistle before scurrying back to the driver's cabin.

'Fancy!' said Gordon. 'I never imagined Uncle Billy as the Fat Controller!'

The train set off again at alarming speed and shot back into the tunnel, but the smoothness of the motion made it seem as if they were floating through air. Francis checked his watch, hoping to make a mathematical calculation as to how fast they were travelling. The boys had lost all sense of time and place when at last the train emerged from the tunnel into an open concourse where it abruptly came to a halt.

'Thank you for travelling with us today,' cried Uncle Billy. 'Please remember to take all your belongings with you on leaving the carriage. All change!' He touched his cap and gave a cheery wave to Francis and Gordon as Sir John led them towards another steel door along the platform.

'It is essential that the aura of calm and unhurried scientific contemplation in which our team thrives should not be disturbed,' he explained. 'Beyond this door are two men on whom rests the safety of Great Britain and very possibly the Empire itself. I am especially keen that you should meet Rodney Fellows, one of our most brilliant young scientists, who will be escorting you around the facility. Then, of course, I hope you may be able to speak with the great Professor Drakananoff.'

Francis's ears perked up.

'Drakananoff? Do you mean the famous Russian scientist?'

'Indeed; the most eminent of his generation.'

'And rather more than that,' said Gordon. 'He's a Grandmaster at chess. He's the envy of our chess club at school.'

'Quite so. The USSR's loss is Great Britain's gain,' Sir John smiled. 'He may seem a little odd to you. Like many with abnormally advanced brains, Professor Drakananoff inclines to the eccentric. A man of few words. Indeed, saying boo to a goose would be anathema to him, and would probably be said in a foreign language. His unique mind beats on in magnificent quietude. So, take deep breaths. You are about to encounter a scene of total scientific serenity and deep, contemplative genius.'

Sir John shone his torch at the great door. It opened with extraordinary smoothness, but inside the room...

The visitors looked on with disbelief. The laboratory was in chaos. The work-benches were littered with chards of glass and broken instruments; phials and coloured liquids were strewn across the floor, and a harsh chemical stink clotted the air. On the banks of screens that lined the walls, flashing lights accompanied the sharp ringing of alarm bells. In the midst of this Armageddon was a man who looked everything one might have expected of a Russian scientist, but his eyes were a little too wild, his hair a little too deranged (as if he had put his finger into an electric socket, thought Gordon), his limbs jerking uncontrollably around his sweating body. His quivering lips struggled to form words. And then he cried 'Help me!'

In Russian.

Sir John and the boys had struggled to get Drakananoff onto the train for the return journey to Northcrack Staithe. Now, on the lawn of the Hall, two white-coated men were trying to persuade the gibbering professor into an ambulance.

'Most unfortunate that you should have come on such a difficult day,' said Sir John. 'I am sure the professor is just a little overworked. He seems to have been locked up in the laboratory since last evening. These temperamental geniuses do tend to have a funny turn now and again.'

Sir John didn't sound convinced, and solemnly shook the boys' hands.

'And such a pity that Rodney Fellows has not turned up this morning. Unlike him not to do so... Next time, perhaps... We'll meet again,' he said, and Gordon thought he might be breaking into a Vera Lynn song. The unfortunate man seemed distracted as he walked from the room, turned and said 'My secretary will be in touch', and was gone.

Francis and Gordon hurried to the window. One of the white-coated men had his knee in the professor's back, and the other had him in a half Nelson. Still swearing in an unknown language, the distressed scientist was bundled into the back of the ambulance, which sped away down the drive. The boys turned to see Janet Smedley standing in the doorway, twisting her hands nervously as she peered into the hall.

'Is something wrong?' asked Francis.

'What is happening?' asked Janet.

The boys looked to one another, wondering how to react to this troubled young woman, and alarmed at the distracted look in her eyes, which had already filled with tears.

'There must be something,' she said. 'I need to know. I don't know what to do.'

When she almost collapsed onto the sofa, Gordon moved swiftly to the mahogany desk and poured a generous shot of whisky from a crystal decanter into a glass.

'Medicinal,' he explained. 'Drink it.'

They ignored the unladylike gulps that followed, but the Macallan had the immediate effect of restoring Janet's calm.

'I'm sure there's nothing we could tell you that you don't already know,' said Francis.

'You're wrong' she replied. 'I've never been beyond that door. I've never been aboard the Fantasy Express… that's what we call the train. I haven't a clue where it goes to, except that it's miles and miles away.'

The glass shook slightly in her hand as she drained the last of the musky liquid from her glass.

'I know that you will not divulge anything of national importance. You are, after all, grammar school boys, but the name Rodney Fellows… it *was* mentioned, wasn't it? I know it was.'

'Well,' stammered Francis. 'Rodney…?'

'Yes, of course it was.' She smiled. To Gordon, it was as if the sun had suddenly come out. 'Rodney is assistant to Professor Drakananoff. Rodney is absolutely splendid, in every way.'

She lowered her eyes, and turned the empty glass in her hands. 'I live with him.'

'He is your husband?' asked Gordon.

The pause was one that seemed perfectly timed for the mid 1950s. Janet drew herself together. Strength, resolution, and a regained confidence shone from her.

'No. We are not married. We live together.'

This was the first time that either of the boys had come up against a challenge to the accepted rules of respectability, although Francis had recently caught a whiff of winds of change, reading about a new play called *Look Back in Anger*. Of course, they had glimpsed a very different sort of morality through their association with the Queen of Striptease Bunty Rogers, but she inhabited an unreal, theatrical world. For the moment, the boys remained silent, waiting for more disclosures.

'Rodney and I are in love, but we've kept it a secret from Sir John and the station, because we thought it might compromise his position here. But something has gone wrong. He was due to have a few days off next week. We'd booked a weekend at Great Yarmouth, where he spent much of his childhood. There was someone he particularly wanted to see there. We were planning to leave for the holiday this afternoon after Rodney finished work, but he didn't come home last night, and I haven't seen him or heard from him since. He was supposed to be at the laboratory with the professor until twelve o'clock this morning. I have no idea where he can be.

'But there's something else, and I'm frightened. You see, Rodney and I shared everything. He told me things they don't even tell people who get to ride on the Fantasy Express. And a few months ago he began to do something that is strictly forbidden. He began bringing his work home, locking himself in his room for hours on end. It was like an obsession. Nothing else seemed to matter to him, and then a few days ago… it was as if he couldn't keep it to himself any more…'

'And he unburdened himself?' asked Francis. 'Well, that would be the natural thing to do.'

'Oh, it was awful. It poured out of him. And all at once I understood everything. You see, I think I know what had been happening at the station. And I am so scared…'

Mornings were busy at Branlingham Branch Library. The daffodils circling the Nissen huts that made up the complex of wartime buildings gave them an unexpected appeal. Inside Hut No. 1, Blodwyn Williams took a damaging bite from a Wagon Wheel just as a cloud blotted out the sun. Blodwyn looked up. The shadow belonged to the giant, crow-like form of Lady Darting, towering above Blodwyn and slapping a book onto the library counter.

'This book is filthy,' announced Lady Darting.

Blodwyn wasn't surprised. She and the librarian Mr Quantock had remarked many times that Lady Darting read dirty books.

'I think it's one you requested from our Restricted Section,' said Blodwyn. 'If they're restricted, you'd expect them to be filthy.'

'A rasher of bacon between Chapters Three and Four, HP sauce on page 243, and a rubberised item on the Table of Contents.'

'Oh,' said Blodwyn. '*That* kind of filthy. I'll mention it to Mr Quantock. He'll withdraw that book. He's punctilious. Gets a fit if you so much as make a smudge with the date stamps. Very fussy over details, Mr Quantock is.'

'Ah, yes!' snorted Lady Darting, assuming the face that could terrify an entire committee. 'Mr Quantock, our so-called librarian. I wish to speak with him.'

Blodwyn glanced nervously around the room. 'I'm afraid Mr Quantock is busy at the moment, Lady Darting.'

'Nonsense! The man is a public servant. I know how to deal with servants. My father frequently horsewhipped them. Kindly inform him that I am here.'

'Excuse me,' said a timid voice at Lady Darting's back. Miss Simms wore a brocaded helmet dotted with macramé daisies that made her look like a troubled hamster in a meadow.

'Good morning, your ladyship.'

'Morning,' snapped Lady Darting. 'I did not take you for a reader, Miss Simms. One would imagine that your postal duties left little time for intellectual pursuit.'

Overcome by having the word 'intellectual' appended to her name, the local postmistress lost all inhibition.

'Oh yes. The literary ocean is one into which I frequently dip my toes. Chaucer, Shakespeare, Balzac, Rabelais...'

'Balzac and Rabelais!' exclaimed Lady Darting. 'I very much hope that literature of that type is not being made available to the working classes.'

'Or one of the Brontës for light relief,' said Miss Simms, hoping to recover ground. 'Oh yes. I lean to the classics.'

'Here's the classic you asked for last week, Miss Simms,' said Blodwyn, stamping a book and holding it out. 'The new Mabel Mayfield. *The Hopeful Virgin*. You've read all her others, haven't you?'

Miss Simms faded from view behind some bookshelves, at one stroke avoiding the scorn of Lady Darting and the arrival of Doris Jones, who had breathlessly parked her bicycle in the rack outside the hut.

'Ah! Mrs Jones,' announced Lady Darting with a great display of teeth. 'Our very own Branlingham Nightingale!'

'Good morning, ladyship. Fancy seeing you here,' said Mrs Jones. 'I've come for that book you recommended me. Morning, Blodwyn.'

Blodwyn half looked up and half smiled. Mrs Jones decided that pigtails didn't look good on an overweight forty-year-old wearing a utility issue boiler suit and enduring the birth of a moustache.

'Yes, it's come in,' said Blodwyn. '*Teach Yourself Coloratura*.'

'I am sure it will repay study,' said Lady Darting, 'although yours is such a natural talent. Your lily needs no gilding.'

'Thanking you, I'm sure.' Mrs Jones almost dropped a curtsey to Branlingham's nobility before turning to Blodwyn. 'I was wondering if you had a book about gargling exercises. That Mongolian throat singing plays havoc with your vocal chords.'

'Frankly, I doubt it,' said Blodwyn, betraying no sign of any interest. 'Of course, in the valleys we had a much wider stock of choral related material. We're more cultured in the valleys, see. I'll check with Mr Quantock, if you wish. Won't be a jiffy.'

She lumbered from her chair and eased herself into Mr Quantock's office, taking great care to open the door just far enough for her to squeeze into his room, and closing the door behind her.

'Of course,' whispered Lady Darting (whose whispers were not of the quiet variety), 'that woman is carrying on with the librarian.'

'Really?' said Mrs Jones. It was the first she had heard of it.

'No doubt of it. The man is a Tin God. Jeremy Quantock M.A., indeed! Struts about the place as if he were Cock o' the North, and hides in his office when he should be dealing with ratepayers' literary requests.'

The office door opened and Blodwyn squeezed out through a gap that was even narrower than the one she had gone in by.

'No go, I'm afraid,' she drawled. 'No demand, Mr Quantock says.'

'Really!' cried Lady Darting. 'The incompetence of the man. The stock here is appalling.'

'Excuse me, your ladyship,' said Blodwyn, her cheeks flushing bright red. 'I look after the stock here, and I was taught by masters. Morgan the Organ taught me music, and Mr Pritchard taught me everything I know about indexing, and...'

'Irrelevant!' exclaimed Lady Darting. 'It is high time you realised that there is more to literature than that drunken sot Dylan Thomas and *How Green Was My Valley*. And what of this rumour that *Lady Chatterley's Lover* is to be issued in unexpurgated form? My husband is most keen to get his hands on it.'

'It's just a rumour,' said Blodwyn, hoping to fit in another bite of her Wagon Wheel. 'I think he'll have to wait a few more years for that one.'

'Then kindly tell the publishers to get a move on,' said Lady Darting. 'Lord Darting will be 87 in February.'

Breathing a sigh of relief as Lady Darting swept majestically into the car park where the Rolls was already panting, Blodwyn picked up yet another Mabel Mayfield romance and flicked idly through its pages. She couldn't imagine why people clamoured for them, and Branlingham Branch Library had more than a fair share of her titles. Really, the rubbish that people read...

But there was already too much on Blodwyn's mind. She supposed she ought to speak to someone. Tomorrow, perhaps, if she was still worried. Tomorrow...

On the Sunday morning, the day after their trip on the Fantasy Express, and the removal of Professor Drakananoff to a rest home, Francis and Gordon once more found themselves delivered to the door of Northcrack Hall by Bentley. The Chief Constable had called at Red Cherry House late the previous evening, straining to give the impression of light-heartedness as Mrs Jones insisted he sit down to a slice of her Bakewell tart, but his heart was heavy and his voice doom-laden as he asked Francis and Gordon to attend a meeting at the Hall the following morning. Now, in the early daylight, the great house took on a sinister aspect, the vapour of last night's fog clinging to its hem.

A bleary-eyed Janet Smedley showed them into the sitting-room. The Chief Constable and Sir John Richardson were in conversation by the French windows. With them was a tall, reedy man in a pinstriped suit. He peered unsmilingly through thick horn-rimmed spectacles at the young visitors.

'Good morning, boys. You know the Chief Constable, of course,' said Sir John, hurrying forward. 'This gentleman is Mr Ponsonby, from M15. We are to refer to him as X.' (Both boys had already registered him in their minds as Pinstripe.) Sir John moved effortlessly to his seat behind the mahogany desk. 'Institute Permanent Priority B2, Janet.'

Janet drew in her breath sharply. There had been the rare occasions when Sir John declared a Peremptory Priority B4 and even Prime Priority Plus Purple B3, but no prior situation had ever needed a Permanent Priority B2.

'Has the girl got full clearance?' asked Pinstripe as Janet left the room.

'Certainly,' said Sir John. 'Janet has been with me for years.'

'The use of Christian names suggests laxness,' said Pinstripe, whose face could become disagreeable with ease. 'There has already been catastrophe enough, and the presence of adolescents is absurd. This is top secret business, not Bob a Job week.'

The Chief Constable bristled.

'May I remind you that Francis and Gordon are the Boy Detectives. They are here with the full knowledge of Her Majesty's Government.'

'Ah,' said Pinstripe, turning his full attention on the boys for the first time. His teeth gleamed through what was intended as a smile, but his dentures had worked slightly loose, and his voice whistled. 'My apologies. I know of your work, of course. The retrieval of the pearl of Thalia! Brilliantly done!'

He bowed slightly from the waist, which had the odd effect of making the stripes of his pinstripe seem even straighter and longer, and switched on his heels towards Sir John.

'Well,' said Sir John, leaning back in his chair and tapping

147

his fingers on the desk, 'as you may know, Northcrack Staithe Power Station was officially opened in 1952 by…'

'You are not a guide book,' snapped Pinstripe. 'The bald facts will suffice.'

Sir John's face tightened.

'The historical context is not irrelevant to the current crisis, and make no mistake, gentlemen, a crisis we most certainly have. The public think that our work at Northcrack Staithe is no different from that at any power station in the land, but for the past year we have been at the forefront of atomic research. For this reason, the station was linked to an underground facility some thirty miles away on the Suffolk coast. The public know nothing of this. Work essential to national security is done there.'

'Work on the atom bomb,' said Pinstripe, rocking on his heels and sucking air into his roomy gums.

'It was therefore essential that we acquired the services of Professor Sergei Drakananoff. As you know, there was much press coverage when he defected from the USSR, but, with the assistance of our colleagues at M15' (Pinstripe's stripes seemed to salute) 'we brought him into the Northcrack Staithe fold. So far as the public is concerned, after the initial furore over his defection, Drakananoff vanished from the news, but he has been heading up our team here. Last week, he informed me (through a translator, obviously) that he was on the brink of completing his work on a weapon the like of which cannot be imagined. That weapon is one to make our enemies tremble.

'He gave no more details. Even his assistant, Rodney Fellows, was not completely "in the know". As we have seen, these plans have come to a shuddering end. The professor's mind is broken. Beyond a few words in his native tongue – mostly "Niet" – no sense can be made of his crazed ramblings.'

'Poor chap,' sighed the Chief Constable. 'Presumably everything is being done for him?'

'Yes,' said Sir John. 'The British government is financing his psychiatric care, and the Russians are sending a baby rattle.'

'Do we know what has happened to the professor's notes?' asked Francis. 'He must have accumulated a vast amount of information.'

'A most intelligent interjection,' said Pinstripe, leaning his stripes towards the sofa and dislodging some teeth.

'They have vanished,' said Sir John. Beads of sweat broke on his forehead. 'No trace of his research or working notes can be found in his office, to which he and Rodney Fellows alone had access.'

'Then the way ahead is clear!' announced Pinstripe. 'We urgently need to speak to this man Fellows.'

'That,' stammered Sir John, 'is impossible. Fellows has gone missing.'

Pinstripe drew himself to his full height, and lifted his eyes to the ceiling.

'He must be found without delay. On no account must he be allowed to leave the country. All border controls, ports and airports must be notified. The picture is clear. This Fellows is the culprit. Drakananoff discovers that his research has been stolen. His work and reputation are in tatters. He loses his mind instantly. Information that any country would go to any lengths to acquire cannot be found. Meanwhile, Fellows vanishes into thin air.' Pinstripe turned to Sir John. 'We must find him!' The pinstripes took on a frightening intensity. 'Find him now!'

*

His head was pounding.

When he opened his eyes, for a moment it was as if he'd just awoken from a deep sleep. It must be night, because his bedroom was pitch black, blacker than he had ever known it, even when there was no moon. And someone had played a trick on him, made an apple pie bed in which his legs were trapped.

It was only when he tried to move his arms that he felt the cold steel of the handcuffs. Still barely conscious, he wasn't unduly alarmed; his legs would take him beyond the bedroom, into the bathroom where he could freshen up, and into the kitchen where he could slake the thirst that scratched at his throat. But when he couldn't move his legs, he knew something had happened.

The piercingly damp cold gripped his body. He waited for the black to diminish, but there wasn't a chink of light, although a little way from where he was imprisoned – yes, that was the word for it – he thought he could make out the outline of a door.

'Hello,' he called. And waited. And then called 'Hello' again.

From the first, he didn't expect an answer. He strained to hear any sign of life going on beyond this place, but it was as if he were the sole survivor of a science fiction invasion. He began to breathe more regularly, and calmed, reminding himself that he was Rodney Fellows, renowned for the clarity of his scientific mind.

He rasped the shackles that chained him to the wall, and knew at once that only a Superman could break free of them. He must wait on developments, hope until something, or someone, turned up. And just as he sometimes struggled to remember dreams immediately after waking, he knew he had to piece together what he remembered before waking up in this prison.

The day had started well (had it been yesterday?). Janet had brought him a cup of tea in bed. Beautiful, caring Janet. She had been looking forward to their holiday. He'd been sleeping badly for weeks. Not because things were going wrong, but because they were going so right. And this Saturday was the day when he and the professor completed their task. Drakananoff had never been an easy colleague, but easy didn't come naturally to geniuses. This particular morning, Drakananoff was greatly excited and – a very rare thing – had arrived at the laboratory long before Rodney.

Drakananoff knew as well as he that this was a momentous day. The very last tweak, the mere matter of implanting a simple component into the weapon that they had been developing with such fervour, was to be slotted into its atomic body.

When Rodney walked into the laboratory, he was startled to find the professor already at work. He had the crucial component, their very own 'missing link' between the countless months of research and the finished project, in his hand.

Rodney felt an immediate unease. Drakananoff and he had signed the security agreement in which they had sworn that such material could only be brought into the laboratory when both men were present. Somehow, on this last day of the project, it didn't seem to matter so much; it was only natural that the professor should be so keen at the very moment when his greatest achievement was about to be fulfilled, and yet...

Rodney tried to fit together what happened next. He had said good morning (in Russian, of course) to the professor, but instead of giving his usual cordial response, Drakananoff violently switched round as if he had been found with bloodied hands standing over a corpse. Then, he moved swiftly to one of the control panels and typed in a command with frenzied fingers. Rodney thought he must be dreaming. The information flashing excitedly up and across the command research screen was unlike anything Rodney recognised. He knew at once that the fulfilment of their dream – a weapon that would do good instead of bad to the world's population – was turning into a nightmare. He had shouted at Drakananoff, words he now couldn't remember, and suddenly the two men were struggling with one another, Rodney desperately trying to reach the controls, in a frantic effort to see what Drakananoff had fed into the very mind of the terrible weapon.

Drakananoff was quite mad. He snarled and hissed. He knocked Rodney to the floor, and started on a systematic destruction of all the documents, phials, instruments and scientific paraphernalia in the room. Rodney felt the warm trickle of blood at the corner of his mouth, and began to lift his head from the floor.

It was then that the door leading to the Fantasy Express swung open. A figure, its face masked by a scarf, filled the space. Help had arrived! But the figure moved with a slow swagger across the room, as if unaware of the terrible scene. Ignoring the groaning Drakananoff, its eerie shape leaned menacingly over Rodney, who put out his arm imploringly. If only the stranger would lift him up and lead him to safety, but the shadow overcame him, and Rodney's descent into blackness began.

*

There was an uncomfortable atmosphere in Sir John's Bentley as it took Janet Smedley and Francis and Gordon away from Northcrack Hall back to Branlingham.

'I've told them nothing,' she said.

'Was that wise?' asked Francis.

'They'll only twist things, and use Rodney as a scapegoat. That will be how they deal with it.'

'They have to find him first,' said Gordon. 'Have you any idea what can have happened to him? They think he's responsible for Professor Drakananoff's madness, and that he's stolen the formula to give to our enemies.'

'That's nonsense,' cried Janet. 'There must be another explanation.'

'As we've all three of us signed the security document, we can talk freely among ourselves,' said Francis, making sure that the glass panel between the driver and the Bentley's passengers was securely closed. 'There must be something that Rodney said to you that alerted you to something unusual going on.'

'Well…' Janet stammered. 'He woke up shouting the other night, as if he was coming round from a horrid dream. I calmed him and settled him back to sleep.'

'Could you make out the words?' asked Francis.

'Oh yes. He said "The Differentiator".'

'What?'

'Just that: "The Differentiator". He shouted it three or four times, as if a flaming monster with fangs were coming towards him. When he awoke, he was agitated and sweating. He pleaded with me to tell him what he had been saying in his sleep. I told him, and… it was extraordinary… he slid back inside the bed and pulled the covers over his head, and didn't say another thing.'

'This… Differentiator?' asked Francis. 'What did it mean to you?'

'Nothing,' said Janet. 'Why should it? I presumed it might be to do with his work, but beyond that…'

'And you have absolutely no idea where he might be now?'

'No. Why would he want to vanish? If he were in any trouble he would have come directly to me. He was so looking forward to our going away together.'

'What were your plans?'

'Well… neither of us have much money. It wasn't going to be the South of France. We'd rented a cottage on the Norfolk coast. Rodney lived by the sea when he was a boy, and he so seldom gets the chance to revisit.'

'What about his family? Is there a chance he could be with them?'

'I don't think he had much family of his own. I tried asking him, but… I don't know… he'd change the subject. There was someone he was hoping to look up when we were away, though.'

Francis couldn't see how this had anything to do with finding Rodney Fellows, but all the same…

'He mentioned a Mrs Ainsworth. All he knew was that she was in a residential home, somewhere in Yarmouth. But I don't suppose it matters now… Oh please, please,' cried Janet, 'find him.'

Gordon made a mental note to track down the residential home. It was a long shot, but there seemed no other connections, and as he and Francis were not involved in the official search for Rodney Fellows, they might as well follow this up.

*

When Gordon arrived at the branch library the following morning, Blodwyn was unwrapping her early morning Wagon Wheel, and writing in a notebook.

'Hullo, Miss Williams.'

'Morning, Gordon,' replied Blodwyn. 'You look flushed.' She tucked the Wagon Wheel out of sight and slid the notebook underneath a newspaper.

'It's rather urgent. I was hoping you might lend me a telephone directory.'

'Oh. Another game's afoot, is it?'

'Until tomorrow, if possible,' said Gordon, not wanting to be drawn into details. 'If Mr Quantock would be so kind.'

Blodwyn pulled herself heavily off her stool and walked to the office door. She put out her hand to open it, and pulled back suddenly.

'Silly me,' she said. 'I quite forgot. Mr Quantock is in a meeting at the moment. But as it's for the Boy Detectives, I'm sure he won't mind. The directories are over there. We have flags of all nations.'

'Very good of you, Miss Williams.'

'My sister Glenda used to tear them in half.'

'Sorry?'

'Telephone directories. It was her party piece, like. Glenda the Bender they called her. There's a knack to it, see. Leave them in the airing cupboard for a few months and the warm air sucks all the glue out of them, and breaking the spines is no more than ripping a piece of tissue paper. A kitten could do it.'

'That's very interesting. Thanks so much.'

'Make sure you bring it back in one piece,' Blodwyn called. 'Of course what Glenda the Bender used to…'

But Gordon had already mounted his bicycle. He drove

past the row of Nissen huts that were linked to the library, the last two of which had been boarded up and unused for years.

Back at Red Cherry House, he and Francis pored over the directory before hurrying off to the telephone box.

Two hours later, a thin drizzle was misting the windows of the Norwich train as it shuddered to a halt in Great Yarmouth Railway Station. It was a short walk through the ancient 'rows' of the town close to the market place before the boys found the building. The lazy rain, encouraged by the north wind, did nothing to enhance the appeal of 'Ever Glade', subtitled on a creaking sign above its porch 'Rest Home for the Elderly and Infirm'. The chipped paint, broken brickwork, missing slates and concreted forecourt spelled neglect. A black silhouette of a lady in Victorian dress with a lamp dominated the wall, and must have darkened the heart of those unfortunates arriving on the doorstep. Dingy net curtains hid the interior from view, but promised to keep up the external air of depression. It was a surprise when the door was opened by a young redheaded woman in a pretty cretonne dress of emerald green. She had a bright, open face.

'Good morning. May I help you?'

'Do you by any chance have a Mrs Ainsworth here?'

'Well… who are you?' The smile grew fainter as she looked the boys up and down.

'I'm Francis Jones, and this is my cousin Gordon. We've come from Norwich, in the hope of seeing Mrs Ainsworth.'

'Francis and Gordon?' After another quick thoughtful stare, the young woman's smile broke out as friendly as before. 'Of course! The Boy Detectives! Come in.'

Francis, despite a general dampness, had retained his composure. Gordon, on the other hand, was impersonating a drowned rat. Wet weather played havoc with his unruly red hair, and his spectacles had steamed up, but being recognised by strangers always made the boys feel better.

'What a pleasure to meet you. And yes, we do have a Mrs Ainsworth here. Of course, she may not be the Mrs Ainsworth you are looking for. Come into the office.'

From the street, 'Ever Glade' had all the allure of a workhouse, but inside there was a warmth about the place, and from the office the boys noticed the chintzy comforts, the plump cushions, the walls painted in pastel shades, and a solid Victorian oil of Yarmouth harbour in its original gold frame.

'You must be on the track of something,' said the young woman. 'I'm Mary Drew. I took over the home last year. It's been allowed to fall into very bad repair. We are making improvements. Slow but sure. Old Black Bertha – you must have seen her on the side of the house – she's being painted over next week. But you've come to see Mermaid.'

Francis and Gordon looked puzzled.

'A mermaid?' said Francis. 'It might just be possible to find one in Yarmouth Aquarium, but…'

'Oh!' laughed Mary Drew. 'That's how we know Mrs Ainsworth. She's one of Ever Glade's oldest residents. Ever Glade: that's something else that needs changing. It sounds too much like a Los Angeles cemetery. Are you related to her?'

'No,' said Gordon, thinking how interesting it might be to have a mermaid in the family. 'But we are working on a case, and she may be able to help us with our enquiries.'

'I hope you won't be disappointed. Her memory is poor, and she's got rather out of the way of having visitors.'

'Has she no family?' asked Francis.

'Having a family doesn't ensure visits,' said Mary Drew. 'But not that I know of. She was married. Her husband was Ernie. You'll probably hear Ernie's life story before you leave. Of course, at 93 many of her friends have gone to that great bingo hall in the sky. She'll enjoy having two young men call on her. She's had a hard life... things rather went wrong for her.'

They saw at once why Mrs Ainsworth was known as Mermaid. A veil of perfectly silver, lustrous hair cascaded from her head, draping her shoulders and falling down her back, until it seemed as if she were sitting on a throne of it. Her room was small but neat and welcoming.

'Well,' she said, looking up at the boys. 'Gentlemen callers. Things are looking up.'

Mary Drew gently put her hand on the old woman's shoulder.

'This is Francis and Gordon, Mermaid. Don't wear them out. They've come all the way from Norwich especially to see you.' She winked at the boys. 'I'll bring some tea and cakes. A vanilla slice for you, Mermaid.'

'Last woman we had was a proper old cow,' said Mermaid, as Mary left the room. 'Vanilla slices!' She looked from Francis to Gordon and back again. 'You from the Welfare?'

'No,' said Francis. It was an uncomfortable moment. After all, they couldn't offer any real reason for making the visit except that it might lead to some information about Rodney Fellows. Francis felt weak and silly.

'This is a very pleasant room,' he said, vaguely aware that he sounded like a member of the Royal Family.

'My snaps,' said Mermaid, indicating her bedside table. 'All ghosts. This is Ernie.'

She put out a bony hand and took up a framed picture. A brilliantined young man in a shabby suit and a collarless shirt, leaning on a spade, smiling somewhere from an untidy garden of long ago.

'I was lucky,' said Mermaid. 'Ernie never lifted a finger to me. Gave me his money end of every week.'

'He was very handsome,' said Francis, and passed the photograph to Gordon. 'Mermaid... is it all right to call you Mermaid?'

'Mermaid...' The old woman moved her eyes around the room, as if just such a creature might have floated into view.

'Never looked at another man,' she said, 'not till Ernie went. But we lived near the docks, see... and the Welfare came round, and the kids were taken away.'

She looked up sharply.

'You're not from the Welfare?'

'Certainly not,' said Francis. 'How many children did you and Ernie have?'

'Never had any. Who told you we did?'

Mermaid's eyes gleamed so brightly that for a moment Gordon could have sworn he saw the sea in them.

'Had men in the palm of my hand.'

She glanced up at Gordon, who thought he should probably have been blushing.

'My gentlemen... My Tuesday afternoon regular... regular as clockwork... used to dress up as a baby.'

'Now then, Mermaid!' Mary Drew brought in the tea and cakes. 'You're not telling these young men naughty things, are you?'

'Nappies. Every Tuesday afternoon, there he'd be, dressed

159

up like a great big baby. And one day I opened a newspaper and there he was opening a motorway.'

'I think Mermaid was friendly with a Minister of Transport,' said Mary. 'Tea?'

'I was telling Mrs Ainsworth that we heard about someone who knew her when he was a child,' said Francis.

'They're the Welfare,' explained Mermaid.

'His name was Rodney. Rodney Fellows.'

'They were all fellas,' said Mermaid. 'That was what did for me.'

Mary paused from pouring the tea. 'This Rodney... could he have been one of Mermaid's children?'

'I thought Mrs Ainsworth said she never had any children,' said Gordon.

'I don't think you had any of your own, you and Ernie, did you, Mermaid? You were foster parents, weren't you? Looked after lots of children. I bet you were a wonderful mum and dad to them.'

'I let them down,' said Mermaid, and the sea in her eyes went dark. 'Let them all down.' She set about trying to cut through her vanilla slice. Mary took the fork and helped.

'Do you remember a Rodney?' asked Gordon.

'Would that have been Roddy?' Mary sat beside the old woman and cupped her hand. 'You remember Roddy, Mermaid... You've told me lots about him. Rodney Fellows. You were expecting two boys to arrive from the Welfare, weren't you, because they said you'd be getting fellows, but when the car came it was just Roddy.'

'Lovely Roddy,' said Mermaid. 'They used to come in cars.'

'Roddy was one of your great successes, wasn't he?' Mary warmed Mermaid's hand, and proudly turned to Francis and Gordon.

'She and Ernie looked after him right until he went to university. Cambridge, wasn't it, Mermaid? I mean, that was quite something, because he'd come from a very unstable home. And you helped him achieve all that, Mermaid, you and your lovely Ernie. You were the mum and dad he'd always wanted, and you looked after him all those years.'

Mermaid smiled and tucked a sliver of cream into her mouth. 'They weren't all good. That other one...'

'I know what you mean,' said Mary. 'Ernie and Mermaid took on another young boy around the same time as Roddy arrived, but you didn't like him so much, did you? He was another very bright boy, but he wasn't so likeable as Roddy.'

'No. Didn't like him,' said Mermaid. 'Hills... Mendips... We got bored... He liked games.'

'What was his name, Mermaid?' asked Mary, but as if she were about to descend into the depths of the ocean the old woman closed her eyes, and her head drooped.

'I think it's time for mermaid's to take their afternoon doze,' said Mary.

'I hope we haven't tired her,' said Francis.

'Not at all... I'm trying to think of anything else she may have told me that might be helpful to you. There is one little thing, but...'

'Oh?' said Francis.

'Nothing, really. It's about that other boy. He wasn't simply unlikeable. From what she's told me about him, I think Mermaid was quite frightened of him. A jealous streak, she said, and when jealousy infects a highly intelligent person the result can be quite disastrous, can't it? But in a way that boy was as much a success for Ernie and Mermaid as Roddy was. I think he did quite well in later life.'

'What happened to him?' asked Francis.

'I've no idea, and I don't suppose Mermaid would remember. She doesn't like talking about that other boy. Doesn't even mention his name, although she's probably forgotten it anyway. It's Roddy she thinks about still.'

'He hasn't by any chance been here in the last few days?' asked Gordon.

'No.'

'When did he last visit?' asked Gordon.

'He never has. From what I can gather, she and Ernie only saw him once after he left for university. He's never come here. She never has letters. Nobody telephones. She never hears from any of the other children they fostered. Not so much as a Christmas card. It wouldn't be much to ask, would it? After all she's done for them.'

Francis and Gordon were silent on the return journey to Norwich. From the train window, it was glorious to see the spring sunshine flooding the marshes with light, the cattle looking as if they were waiting for a Victorian painter to immortalise them on canvas. There was a real sense of time stood still, but too soon the train was chugging into the light industrial suburbs of Norwich.

Uncle Billy was waiting at Thorpe Station to pick them up in his car. After dropping Francis off at Red Cherry House, Billy and Gordon set off for Bundler's Cottage.

'They've got no further with that terrible business at Northcrack,' said Uncle Billy.

In the confines of the little car, there was an extraordinary atmosphere of confidentiality.

'No trace of that Mr Fellows, and no one can make sense of the professor. As for where the weapon is…'

'What do you know about the weapon, Uncle Billy?' asked Gordon.

'About as much as you do, lad, and that's not much. Only that everyone knew something very hush-hush was going on. The trouble is, only that Professor Drakananoff and young Rodney Fellows had access to the laboratory, with their own entrance, and their own codes to get in and out.'

'That's interesting,' exclaimed Gordon. 'So Rodney could have got out of the building without anyone knowing?'

'Exactly. And that's why nothing was discovered till Saturday morning, when you and Francis were taken round the facility. If you and Sir John hadn't gone there that morning the professor wouldn't have been discovered until Monday morning, by which time…'

Gordon shuddered.

'My goodness! It doesn't bear thinking about. And the professor lives alone, doesn't he?'

'Yes. He left any family he had behind in Russia, and he's not exactly a talkative or very sociable cove. Mind you, he was always friendly enough to me.'

'I didn't think you'd have come across him at the station,' said Gordon, his ears pricking up.

'Well, what I'm going to tell you really *is* top secret.' Uncle Billy chortled. 'When I was in the Navy I got to know some Russian sailors, and picked up a good bit of the lingo. Enough to get by. Howdy do and "'orrible weather we're having for the time of year" and so forth. So when I did see the professor we used to say good day to one another.'

'You're a dark horse, Uncle Billy' laughed Gordon. 'But you never met him outside of the station? Or knew anything more about his life and the people he knew?'

'No,' said Uncle Billy. 'But I know he liked playing chess. He'd got a prize for it in Russia. You have to be seriously brainy to get prizes for chess. And I said one day what a pity it was he couldn't go on playing it here. And he said, Yes, yes he did play it here. He told me he'd got a friend who he played chess with.'

'*It's* been a tiring day in Yarmouth,' said Gordon. He had met up with Francis later that evening. 'I wanted to get on with reading *The Children's Newspaper*. Can't it wait till the morning?'

'Do it while you think of it,' said Francis. 'Never put off until tomorrow what you can do today.'

Gordon almost threw something at Francis. Why did he come out with such pompous statements?

'The sooner you take the telephone directory back to Blodwyn the better,' argued Francis. 'After all, other things may turn up tomorrow and then you'll regret not having got it out of the way.'

As usual, Gordon reluctantly knew that Francis was giving sound advice. It would only take half an hour or so to pedal there and back to the library, and would be – what was another of Francis's pompous expressions? – 'another job jobbed'!

When Gordon walked into the library he was struck at once by the quiet. Of course, he was the only person there, except… yes, there was a faint noise… surely it couldn't be… someone was crying. He moved towards the source of the sound, and there was Blodwyn, crumpled on a chair behind a book stack, whimpering into a handkerchief.

'Oh, Miss Williams!' said Gordon. 'Is something wrong?'

Blodwyn started, made a quick dab at her eyes and stuffed the handkerchief into the sleeve of her baggy cardigan.

'Oh! Gordon! Didn't see you there... No, nothing wrong. Hay fever.'

He was unconvinced, but knew he shouldn't enquire further.

'I'm returning the telephone directory I borrowed.'

'Oh yes. The directory... was it a help?'

'Yes, thank you. Shall I leave it on the counter?'

'Put it back on the shelf in the reference library, would you? I'll be there in a jiffy.'

'The reference library' was a grand description of what was little more than an alcove, with a glass partition along its back wall that looked out into Mr Quantock's office. That sanctum was immensely tidy, as per Mr Quantock's reputation, and the books that had been left on the shelf in front of the glass partition had been lined up precisely, with their spines facing the glass. Gordon glanced at the titles, thinking that Mr Quantock was, as Blodwyn was forever telling everyone, a well-read man. There were books on Quantock's desk, too, and a tearaway day calendar.

Gordon was still staring into the office when suddenly Blodwyn was standing next to him, her face rigid and white as snow.

'Closing time,' she said.

Her eyes were red, but the tears had gone, and Gordon thought he saw a sort of steeliness in them.

Whatever else, he had to keep his mind sharp. The pattern of the curtains in his bedroom, the layout of his garden, numerating the clothes in his wardrobe, the number of days before Janet's birthday... if only he could keep remembering the details of the life he had left behind. The world outside, and Janet, and what he would do when he escaped from this hell-hole.

He thought of too many things he had left undone, that his life had been filled up with work, and how, since meeting Drakananoff, the Differentiator had taken over his, and Drakananoff's, life. When – *if* – he escaped this prison and got back to the outside world, he would make changes. He would make the effort to find his foster mother, realised at last that he had waited too long to meet her again.

Time had taken on a new meaning. He had his watch to go by, but had forgotten to wind it up at some stage since his incarceration, so didn't know if it was night or day. Not that it mattered. It was always night here. At least food and drink were brought in, and a chink of light (perhaps it was only a chink because it was night when his jailer arrived) showed beyond the door. And the figure would be standing there in the room, a few inches from him, silently putting out dishes and water, slices of orange, a hunk of bread.

On his second visit, the figure had pointed to a recess where a working lavatory was hidden, and had changed the chains that bound him to allow him to reach it. Rodney had tried to reason with his captor, wanted to know why he had been brought here, what had happened to Drakananoff, what his captor wanted from him. The hooded figure, carefully keeping to the shadows, never spoke, only moved stealthily, as if in a silent film that flickered through Rodney's mind, around the dismal space.

Now, he strained to listen. Nothing, except the delicate scratch of what might be an inquisitive rat. But another sound, a grating sound, took over. Yes, the door to his prison was being prised open. How wonderful if this were Janet come to take him home, to say 'You're safe, darling, and everything is going to be all right for ever and ever.' But the door closed on the world, cutting out the hint of sunlight that for a brief moment had promised to flourish, and the hooded and masked figure was back in the room with him. The man's breath, sharp and ragged, seemed almost deafening in that otherwise total silence.

'I regret to tell you that you have become a problem,' said the figure.

The distorted words so shocked Rodney that for a moment he didn't know if it were a man or a woman. Footsteps came closer.

'I have to decide what to do with you,' the muffled voice went on. 'They are looking for you. You are the one they will blame. We cannot continue in this way. You must not be allowed to interfere with my plan.'

Rodney shivered.

'What plan might that be?'

'Don't insult me by pretending you don't know. Detonation, of course. What else? At last I can rid the world of certain elements… certain… unwanted elements.'

'You fiend!' said Rodney, straining at his chains. 'You despicable creature! It was you who drove Professor Drakananoff to distraction. What the authorities never realised is that he and I were intent on making a weapon that would benefit the world, not obliterate it. It was a revolutionary concept that we were about to reveal to mankind. We made the one thing mankind had never contemplated… a kind bomb.'

'Kind?'

The voice snarled and broke into hysterical cackles.

'A kind bomb! What rubbish you talk. What place has

kindness in this world? It never showed kindness to me. As for Drakananoff, he was a fool! A foreign fool! I appealed to his vanity, and won his confidence. I even beat him at chess. Beat him until he felt himself totally under my control. In such a weakened state he was easily persuaded to change the course of history for ever.'

'Have you any idea what you are dealing with?' shouted Rodney. 'The Differentiator! What did you do to it?'

'I did nothing' said the voice, and a slow, menacing laugh worked its way through the scarf.

'You and the professor are solely responsible for what will happen to the world. Your names will go down in infamy. It is you they will blame. When they find your body, they will assume that you realised the hopelessness of your situation, with the British government hot on your heels, and did what every self-respecting British gentleman does in such circumstances.'

'You must be stark raving mad!' cried Rodney. 'You'll never get away with it!'

But even in that overpowering darkness he was aware of the figure putting his hand into his coat pocket with ominous determination. The voice moved closer, and Rodney could just make out the shape of a gun.

'From this angle, I think,' said the voice, 'it will appear to be a clear case of suicide.' A cruel laugh cracked his mouth. 'Don't worry, Rodney. Dear little Rodney. Such a nice little boy. Everybody's favourite. I won't leave you here. I will take you to a pleasant woodland, where your body will be discovered. Unfortunately, it will be too late to do you any good. And you always liked being good, didn't you Roddy? Mr Goody Two Shoes! Never read a decent novel in your life! Never read the novels of E F Benson! I should have been the one to go to

Cambridge instead of that awful crammer I got sent to. They never realised that it was *me* that taught you everything you knew about biology and physics and chemistry! Never knew that it was *me* who should have had all the love and support that was showered on you. And now the world will never know!'

Rodney felt the cold steel of the revolver against his skin. His heart was beating with tremendous speed. He pulled in his breath and braced himself for what was to come, when a blinding flash of light slanted across the room.

'I wouldn't if I were you,' said Pinstripe.

A week later, the Bentley slid exquisitely to a halt outside Red Cherry House. Standing at the living room window, Doris Jones watched the passengers disembarking: Sir John Richardson with the Chief Constable of Norfolk Constabulary accompanying a tall gentleman in a pinstripe suit. Then there was poor Mr Fellows whose name had been all over the papers, and a very pretty young woman whom Mrs Jones immediately took a liking to. Their voices soon filled the house, for Francis and Gordon were at the door to greet them. After much laughter and hand shaking, they moved into the living room.

It warmed the cockles of Mrs Jones's heart to know that Rodney Fellows and the young woman were such a happy couple, sitting side by side on her sofa with their hands intertwined and gazing at each other with misty eyes. Mr Jones could see her getting broody. Mrs Jones told him to go into the kitchen and watch the oven.

'What a thoroughly pleasant occasion!' exclaimed Sir John. 'And very good to see you so recovered, Fellows.'

'Thank you, sir. I'm quite well now,' said Rodney. He gazed

at Janet, and squeezed her hand gently. 'What news of Professor Drakananoff?'

'Most encouraging' replied Sir John. 'He is sitting up and has taken a little broth, and the doctors tell me he will regain complete lucidity.'

'That's wonderful news!' said Rodney. 'Hopefully we will be able to work together again. This time, with no interruptions!'

'The laboratory is being reconstructed as we speak,' Sir John assured him, 'and new security measures are being put in place to prevent a reoccurrence of these appalling events. I think that's correct, Ponsonby?'

The man in the pinstripe suit gave a stiff bow.

'That is so,' he said, 'although I believe I am now better known in some quarters as Pinstripe.'

He winked at Francis and Gordon, and general laughter broke out.

'We owe an inestimable debt to you boys,' Pinstripe continued. 'But I think we are due for an explanation. We were still scratching our heads at M15 when you solved this affair.'

'Yes,' said Janet. 'How on earth did you boys do it?'

'Well,' Francis began, 'it was teamwork, as always. Some of it was me and some of it was Gordon. We were helped by being on the spot, so to speak, and could notice things that much more intelligent and skilled people from London might not realise the significance of.'

'Such as?' asked the Chief Constable.

'Little things. Jigsaw pieces that you have to look at from a different angle. Gordon and I knew nothing about the work Mr Fellows and the professor were doing, and nothing about their lives, so when the professor went mad and Mr Fellows went missing, we were as much in the dark as anyone. It was Miss Smedley who gave us our first real lead.'

'What was that?' asked Janet.

'About you and Mr Fellows planning to visit someone in Yarmouth, someone who had known him as a child. That took us to Mrs Ainsworth…'

'Oh yes. The lovely Mermaid,' said Gordon.

'You consulted a mermaid?' The Chief Constable blinked. 'You boys have the most extraordinary contacts!'

'She was my foster mother,' said Rodney sadly. 'A wonderful woman. And I felt terrible that I'd lost touch with her.'

'Francis and I went to see her,' Gordon continued. 'She told us about you, and about another little boy she'd looked after. She tried to think of his name. She said something like Hills… Mendips… I mean, her speech could be a bit muddled up. I thought she was thinking of places where she'd been. It was only yesterday that I realised she might have been trying to think of a similar sort of word… Hills… Mendips… what she was trying to think of was Quantock, another geographical word…'

'Yes,' Francis chipped in, 'those hills in Somerset, the Quantocks…'

'She was trying to think of the name of another boy she had fostered. The boy who was so jealous of Mr Fellows.'

'And don't forget,' interjected Francis, 'she also said something about being bored… and then said something about games… that was when she was speaking about that other boy. At the time it didn't mean much, they seemed two very different things that had come into her head, but it occurred to me later… we thought she said "bored" as in "not interested", but I think she was trying to say "board"'.

'Yes!' cried Gordon, 'she was trying to say "board games", and eventually we linked that up with the fact that Professor Drakananoff was a Grandmaster at chess. It made a connection between that other boy she had fostered and the professor.'

'Well, well,' said the Chief Constable. 'As we now know, Quantock had been going to Drakananoff's flat to play chess. It must have been through these meetings that Quantock was able to begin convincing Drakananoff that he needed to change the character of the weapon the professor was working on.'

'It's a terrible thought,' said Rodney. 'Of course I can't even now tell you the full facts, but I can reveal that the weapon is called the Differentiator.'

'Yes,' said Janet, 'that's what you used to wake up screaming…'

'I knew how important a weapon it would be, darling. The future of the world depended on it. But I never dreamed it would be put to so warped a use as Quantock intended. He had always been insanely jealous of me when we lived with Mrs Ainsworth… with *Mum*. He had a brilliant mind, in many ways much more brilliant than mine, and he was always teaching me things about science that I don't think I would ever have known if it hadn't been for him. The truth is, it was he who should have gone to Cambridge, not me.'

'Instead of which he went to library school,' said Francis. 'I checked his qualifications.'

'When I took the telephone directory back to the library, I happened to look into his office,' said Gordon. 'There were two piles of books, so neatly arranged that I realised at once that Mr Quantock was obsessive in his behaviour. The odd thing was, one pile of books was on atomic science – what use had a branch librarian or his readers for those? – and the others a very much thumbed collection of novels by E F Benson.'

'Of course,' exclaimed Rodney. 'I remember now. When he left to go to library school – we both left our foster home around the same time – he was already besotted by E F Benson's novels, especially the "Mapp and Lucia" books, all about a group of frightfully snobby people. He was always saying that anybody who was worth anything must have read those books, that people who hadn't read them or couldn't appreciate them belonged to some sort of sub-species... Now, of course, I realise he was quite unhinged. I didn't take it seriously at the time when he said such people shouldn't be allowed to exist.'

'Monstrous arrogance! Such high falutin' concepts,' said the Chief Constable. 'Really, these artistic types…!'

'And that was what has consumed him through the years,' said Rodney. 'When he discovered the top secret work being done on the Differentiator at Northcrack Staithe, he wormed his way into Drakananoff's life through their mutual love of chess, and persuaded him that he must make one crucial alteration to the weapon…'

'Exactly,' Francis said. 'The weapon would be programmed to *only destroy those who had never read or heard of the novels of E F Benson.*'

A tremendous intake of breath went through the room. It was no less cataclysmic from Mrs Jones, who hadn't the slightest idea of what the others were talking about.

'Well,' sighed Pinstripe. 'One cannot deny the brilliance of Quantock's brain. His conception of an intellectual bomb… appalling but fascinating. I think that is something quite new in atomic science.'

'I can't help feeling sorry for that poor girl at the library,' said Janet. 'She was obviously in love with the man.'

'Yes, poor Blodwyn,' said Gordon. 'But I think she'll get

over it. She has… well, let's just say she has other things to occupy her…'

'Presumably charges could be brought against her for aiding and abetting Quantock?' asked Sir John. 'She was covering for his actions, wasn't she?'

'Well… she didn't know what was going on,' Gordon explained, 'only that he was missing from work. She kept up the pretence that he was in his office when he must have been plotting and keeping Mr Fellows in captivity. I realised that Mr Quantock was missing when the date on his tearaway calendar was three days in arrears. He was such a fussy man. He would never have neglected such a thing, so I knew he was missing and that Blodwyn had been pretending he was in his office as usual… and that something was very wrong.'

'And then, to find me as you did!' said Rodney.

'That wasn't difficult,' said Francis. 'Some of those Nissen huts that had originally been part of the library complex had been closed up and neglected for years. They seemed the perfect solution to Mr Quantock. It meant he didn't have far to go to check on his prisoner, and he was the only person who knew how to access them.'

'And so ends the affair of the Bensonian Differentiator!' said the Chief Constable. 'As always, Francis and Gordon have taught the constabulary something… there's nothing so dastardly as a frustrated librarian!'

It was a perfect moment to break up the explanation with festivity. Mr Jones appeared bearing a tray with glasses of sherry, while Mrs Jones took time off from tackling one of Verdi's trickier arias to offer a plate of drop scones.

*

Next day, the sun was radiant, dismissing the early morning mist in the clear air. Branlingham Branch Library, despite having been revealed as the nest of a treacherous villain, was as quiet as a library should be. Blodwyn Williams counted out the day's ration of Wagon Wheels, opened her notebook and unwound the top of her fountain pen. The world was always waiting for yet another Mabel Mayfield romantic novel. This one would resolve the problems of that frustrated sheikh…

Francis and Gordon were up early. Rodney Fellows and Janet Smedley were collecting them at ten o'clock.

'Nice day for it,' said Mrs Jones. 'Doing something special?'

'Very special indeed,' said Francis. 'We're taking a mermaid for a ride along the prom.'

BEST BOYS

1903

' *It's* a trick. A trick of the light. That's all it is.'

Laura could barely make out her husband's words for the rackety noise around them. Hunks of painted canvas were being hammered onto a rudimentary wooden frame the size of a greenhouse at Kew, inside a glass greenhouse that might itself have been at Kew, except that this one was on rails, a greenhouse that could be extended to catch as much natural light as possible. That was why they were in Hove, because there was so much light to catch.

The workmen blew gusts of hot air into the cold November morning; they might have been dragons, breathing fire. Standing in St Ann's Well Gardens outside the studio, Laura felt her feet dampen. If it hadn't been for the prop carpet she huddled herself in she would still be shivering.

'What is it today?' she asked, her teeth almost chattering.

'Today,' said George Albert Smith, 'a role that encompasses the iron resolution of Desdemona, the mischievousness of one of the Merry Wives of Windsor, and the tragedy of Ophelia. In short, a feeble-minded parlourmaid who gets blown up the chimney.'

'Thank you, George. Will it take long?'

'Well, the film should last about four minutes.'

Laura frowned. 'Don't you think you're overstretching yourself?' she asked, but George didn't answer. 'And there's that black cat again.'

'Where?'

'There. He's always moping about somewhere. He must be on a day's outing from Brighton.'

'I think we're ready. Bring him in with you.'

'Is there a cat in the film?'

'There is now,' said George.

1958

The Jones family would not have described themselves as filmgoers, but as filmgoers go, they went. Only last week Doris Jones had been to see *Island in the Sun*. The climate had done Harry Belafonte no end of good, and the cinema sweltered in tropical heat. One of the usherettes, with whom Mrs Jones was on nodding terms, told her the film had broken the Regal's record for ice-cream sales. She wasn't hopeful about next week. It was *Ice Cold in Alex* and the cinema manager was having the heat turned off.

At the Gaumont, Mr Jones sat through *Naughty Mamselles from Marseilles*, only to find it was about an unmanageable French poodle. Hoping to combine enjoyment with cultural improvement, Mr and Mrs Jones joined forces to see *Hamlet* and *Seven Brides for Seven Brothers*. Mrs Jones thought *Seven Brides for Seven Brothers* would have been better with Laurence Olivier, and Mr Jones thought chorus girls would have perked up *Hamlet*.

Francis and Gordon dipped their toes in the world of film at the Saturday morning childrens' matinees, so named by someone who didn't know much French. Today, the serial was *The Voodoo Mystery*. All week, the boys had eagerly looked forward to Part Four, *The Terrifying Abyss*, to see how the hero would cope with having fallen headlong into the terrifying abyss filled with writhing snakes. Last week's episode had ended with him screaming as he plunged to certain death. This morning's instalment had a change of heart. At the last moment, just as he reached the edge of the terrifying abyss, his companions pulled him to safety. Such, Gordon whispered to Francis, was the magic of film.

On reaching Branlingham, the boys were surprised to see Lady Darting's Rolls Royce outside Red Cherry House. Her chauffeur, Dimple, hid the nub end of a Woodbine behind his back, but waved a hand when he saw them approaching.

'Afternoon, lads,' he called. 'Been to the pics?'

'Yes, Mr Dimple,' replied Gordon. 'Are you a fan?'

'Well, I wouldn't say no to a couple of hours in the dark with Jayne Mansfield. But wait till you hear her ladyship's news. I think you'll be interested!'

Certainly, everyone at Red Cherry House glowed. Lady Darting was enthroned in the best armchair, balancing a slice of Mrs Jones's ginger cake and a steaming cup of tea, while Francis's parents looked on, obviously in a state of disbelief. No wonder: the film world was coming to Branlingham!

'On location,' screamed Lady Darting, scattering volumes of ginger crumbs in her excitement. 'For one whole week!'

'A most charming American gentleman, a Mr Rockefeller or some such name, such a fat cigar, has hired the Hall for the whole week, beginning next month. His lordship has already been cast in a non-speaking role, as an… oh, what is that word?'

'Extra?' suggested Mr Jones, hinting at an encyclopaedic knowledge of cinematic terms.

'They wanted him to play a bartender in a night club scene, but he persuaded them he would be more convincing as a gypsy woman.'

'He's supplying his own costume, then?' asked Mr Jones.

'With castanets,' replied Lady Darting. 'To think that the Hall will soon be seen on screen all over the world!'

'It's amazing,' said Francis. 'Who's starring in the film?'

'Mr Guggenfeller informs me that contracts have yet to be finalised, but it seems certain that Stewart Granger and Merle Oberon have been cast. Dear Merle! How I look forward to entertaining her for dinner at the Hall.'

Mrs Jones was thinking she wouldn't mind having Stewart Granger for any meal, preferably breakfast.

'Who's the director?' asked Gordon.

'Mr… how difficult it is to remember these names… did say. Now, what was the name of the director? Very distinguished, I know.'

'Otto Preminger?' suggested Mr Jones.

'Ah… yes, it could well have been. Now I think, I'm sure that was the name. We shall give him the best room at the Hall. The Purple Room, but since the sun has faded everything in it, we'll rename it the Pink Room. Then, of course, there will be the film premiere in London, with all the publicity that will involve. Vulgar, but it can't be helped. And I shall need a new evening gown for the occasion. I'll telephone Norm directly I get back to the Hall.'

'Norm?' enquired Mrs Jones.

'Norman Hartnell, although speaking to him on the telephone is very difficult. His mouth is always full of pins. Then, I shall require careful corseting, Mrs Jones. Naturally, I place that commission in your hands.'

Anxiously weighing up Lady Darting's sharp-boned torso, Mrs Jones made a mental note to order another supply of stockinette-lined rubber.

At last, Lady Darting turned to Francis and Gordon.

'And of course I shall arrange with the headmaster at St Basil's for you both to have the week off.'

The boys were puzzled. 'The week off?' asked Francis.

'Certainly. You are to be… oh, what is that expression, Mr Jones?'

'Best boys?'

'Precisely. Best boys.'

'Well, there's a first time for everything,' said Mrs Jones.

No one in the village was more excited about the filming than Blodwyn Williams, the Welsh assistant at the branch library. It wasn't only that she was an avid fan of *Picturegoer*; she haunted the local cinemas. She was the obvious person for Francis to turn to when he wanted to know more about what might be happening in Branlingham.

'Well,' said Blodwyn, setting aside her now crescent-shaped Wagon Wheel with reluctance, 'I know I'm from the valleys and all that, but let's not get too excited.' She had taken advantage of a quiet morning at the library to rootle out a few facts.

'I mean, let's face it, we're not actually talking Twentieth Century Fox here. Important Films? Well, not sure about that one. There are a lot of these minor companies, Eros and Butcher's and such, who produce "B" films.'

'"B" as distinct from?' asked Francis.

'As distinct from "A". "B" films are the ones you see by accident. It's the "A" films, often American, that have the big stars and get all the attention. The "B"'s just happen to be on at the cinema when you go to see something else. They're there to fill up the programme, and there's quite a thriving industry in them.'

'But they are not really important?'

'Oh, no. You'd be wrong to think that. I mean, I know people around here think I'm odd because I come from the valleys and all that, but me, I go to "B" films. I mean, I go out of my way to see them. I don't rightly know why. Perhaps because they are less pretentious, more fun. Perhaps because they're not perfect, and nobody has spent enough money on them, or because I always hope to find something unexpected and good in them. And if they're bad, it's a good laugh, like.'

'What you're saying is that there's pleasure to be had from a lack of perfection?'

Blodwyn laughed. 'Goodness, Francis, that's an essential you'll have to learn if you want to get the best out of life. Always be wary of perfection. For starters, it won't come your way very often, and when it does it can be really boring. Speaking for myself, and I know I'm from the valleys and all that, I'd rather a mistake than a masterpiece.'

'Right. So, what do you know about this set-up, Important Films?'

'They've been on the scene for a few years. Owned by a wealthy American, Theodore Banksum. They usually film at the Regina Studios in Hendon. Sounds grand, like Elstree, but it's really a big converted garage. They've made a few comedies. The one I saw was shockingly bad. Their stuff is mostly for the northern market, so I'm surprised they've come to Norfolk. They work at the really cheap end of the business. They specialise – if you can call it special – in crime films, murder stories.'

'But no stars?'

'That depends on your definition of a star. The biggest name involved in the making of *Blonde Warning* is in the director's chair. Bromley Marchmont. Thirty years ago he was the great white hope of British cinema.'

'That would be, what, in the 1920s?'

'The late 1920s, yes. Bromley Marchmont directed some of the most successful films of the period. Silents, you see, before sound. Different altogether from how films are made now. It all started in Hove with the first filmmakers, George Albert Smith and the like, back at the turn of the century. Smith made lots of little films, often with his wife Laura as the leading lady.'

'What were the films like?'

'They'd seem really crude now, but in their day, audiences were amazed. Smith invented all sorts of cinematic tricks. There's one where this parlourmaid can't light a fire so she uses paraffin and blows herself up. Smith managed to show her shooting out of the chimney top, and then had her rising from her grave in search of her paraffin can. When she finds it, her ghostly form sinks back into her grave. There's a black cat in it, too, probably Smith's cat, just happened to be in the studio at the time.'

'So, this George Smith, he was there at the beginning of it all?'

'Yes. Writer, director, technician, actor, everything. Now, everything's much more specialised. Bromley Marchmont only has to concentrate on directing his pictures, although he edits them as well, I believe. He made some decent films in his time. *Unlikely Encounter*, that was one of his best. And' (she looked down at an open book on her desk) '*Poisoned Promise*. The critics really loved that one. For a time, Marchmont was mentioned in the same breath as Alfred Hitchcock.'

'So, he's famous?'

'Was. It's just that time has moved on. Other names, and Hollywood has taken over. It's his silent films that are considered his best, but who's seen any of them for the last thirty years? No, he's really remembered for something else. He gave the world Veronica Chasen.'

A heavenly glow lit up Blodwyn's face. Francis wished he didn't look quite so blankly at her. She understood.

'Of course, you wouldn't know. She's forgotten now. I doubt if her films still exist. So many of them were lost when sound came in, and silent films were on nitrate stock, highly inflammable. One of the most famous couples in British silents, Henry Edwards and Chrissie White, kept cans of all their old films in the loft. When someone told them the stock might burst into flames at any moment, they took the lot into the garden and made a bonfire of their life's work.'

'So, was Veronica Chasen a big name?'

'One of the biggest, and it was Marchmont who invented her. She was up there with Theda Bara, Gloria Swanson, Mary Pickford. Audiences idolised her. Her face was on every hoarding. That's what it was all about when films were silent. No words to say; they expressed everything on screen through emotion, so that audiences could stare up at them and think "I know that feeling… this has happened to me!"'

Francis waited. Blodwyn was in a state of reverie, as if she had transported herself back to that lost, soundless world.

'It was all so long ago,' she said. 'When Veronica Chasen

was known to be passing through a town, the local newspaper would print the expected time of her arrival, and crowds would gather just to catch a glimpse of her. She endorsed bedtime beverages and feminine hygiene products. When she married, it was headline news. And when she divorced. She did both several times, of course. And then, it ended, just like that.'

'But why?'

'She spoke. In 1930 she made her first sound film, *Make it Happy*. Marchmont directed her, as he'd directed all her earlier movies. There was so much expectation around hearing her speak for the first time. At last, that angel would be able to communicate directly with her adoring fans.'

Blodwyn sighed, dropped her head and slowly closed the book.

'She wasn't the only casualty when sound arrived. Several of the biggest silent stars couldn't make the transition. Mabel Poulton was another. Mabel was such a pert little thing on screen, refined and pretty beyond words. But that was just the trouble. When it came to the words, what came out was this hard Cockney squawk. It made a nonsense of her public image, and her career was over. Lillian Hall-Davis was another. She couldn't manage the change. She killed herself.'

'But that's terrible,' said Francis. 'Surely the fact that she was no longer in the public eye didn't justify her doing that? What a waste of her life.'

'There's danger in success, Francis. That's what's held me back,' said Blodwyn enigmatically.

'And did Veronica Chasen have a Cockney squawk too?'

'Her voice didn't come over well. They said it didn't match up with her face. Remember, the early studio microphones were crude. They weren't flattering. She only made two more pictures after *Make it Happy*, both with Marchmont directing, but both were flops. Some of the critics put the blame on him. And just as Veronica Chasen vanished, so Bromley Marchmont's career went into the sidings and – well, I know I'm Welsh and all that – but I think he left his glory days behind three decades ago.'

When the time came, the film crew came, one misty evening in November. Of Otto Preminger, Merle Oberon or Stewart Granger there was no sign. Branlingham had worked itself into a fever of anticipation, ready for a quick shot of Hollywood glamour. Lady Darting had even begun spelling the word 'glamour' without a 'u' to get into the transatlantic groove. Some of the party were being put up at the Hall, others at the Wedded Stoat and in various dwellings around the village. Dimple had been instructed to move the Rolls Royce from its usual ostentatious post at the entrance to the Hall, where visitors more or less had to trip over it to get to the great iron pull, as space had to be made for the luxurious limousines in which the film people would be arriving. At four thirty, as daylight dwindled, the Darting's butler, Fetch, was summoned to the Hall's massive oak door. On opening it, he could just make out the shape of a dishevelled elderly man in a soiled trench coat. Behind him, a potato lorry noisily spurted fumes.

'G'night, mate,' called a voice from the cabin of the lorry that explosively shuddered back into the street.

'I appreciate that the sign for the Workman's Entrance is not illuminated during twilight hours,' said Fetch, 'but it's round the back.'

He was closing the door when the visitor wedged his foot in it as if he were a vacuum salesman.

'Not so fast, old chap. I'm Bromley Marchmont.'

Lured by the disturbance, Lady Darting, dressed in an extravagant gown with a six-foot train made from several ostriches calculated to receive movie personalities, appeared behind Fetch.

'Mr…?' she faltered.

'Bromley Marchmont. Important Films. This is Farthing Hall, isn't it?'

'*Darting*,' corrected her ladyship with acerbity.

'Well! What a good job there's an "h" in Farthing, eh?'

The interloper laughed atrociously, and plumped a sack of King Edwards into Lady Darting's arms. He cut a dispiriting figure. Short, thick-set, balding, with pebble-glassed spectacles and topped with a skewed trilby, the man peered obliquely at Fetch, and then at the creature standing beside him in the porch. Peering at Lady Darting, Bromley Marchmont could just about make out what he thought was a phenomenally tall vulture in fancy dress.

As Fetch stooped to pick up Marchmont's battered suitcase, so heavy that he wondered if the man was an anvil salesman, and so dilapidated that it looked as if it been around the world and back via many hedges, another voice broke through the mist.

A trim female figure in a mink coat came into sight, tottering on high heels and balancing an attaché case, vanity case and hat-box. Fetch's heart melted.

'Hello, luv,' she said in a thick northern brogue. 'Eee, it's colder than Oldham. Where's yer loo?'

Bromley Marchmont turned to the newcomer and squinted.

'Who are *you*?' he asked.

'This is the right place, chuck?' she said, looking into the door for confirmation. 'Important Films? I'm in the film they're making. Gloria Devine. Miss.'

Bromley almost visibly blenched at the sound of her voice.

'Miss Devine? Oh dear. I think there may have been a misunderstanding. Your agent led me to believe…'

'Ah, you shouldn't believe anything an agent tells you, luv.'

'Your agent told me that you had won the Gold Medal at the RADA.'

'That's right, luv. I won cups, too.'

Bromley squinted his eyes harder. 'At the Royal Academy of Dramatic Art?'

'No. The Rochdale Amateur Darts Association.'

'Oh dear. This is not a good start. Well, it won't be the first time I've had to model from rough clay.'

'Beg pardon? It's not that difficult, is it, this film acting? That agent said I'd fill the screen.'

'Well, that can hardly be doubted,' said Bromley, his eyes drawn to her magnificent chest. He waved a hand before her. 'After you, Miss Devine.'

Bromley and Gloria Devine had crossed the threshold and were being fulsomely welcomed by Lady Darting when a snappy little red sports car fizzed to a standstill outside the Hall's entrance.

'Wait for me!'

Gloria Devine's eyes switched to the tall, leggy young man who leaped from the car onto the gravel.

'Evening all! Room for one more? Leonard Whiteside. Romantic lead.'

Admiring his proportions, Lady Darting saw at once that here was a Stewart Granger of the future, and indeed was convinced that had Mr Granger at that moment been standing in her porch she would have been deeply disappointed. Fetch was piling up the various suitcases and bags as the introductions continued, and the door was closed against the clammy evening.

As her ladyship directed Bromley Marchmont to his room, Gloria Devine and Leonard Whiteside were taken to the library where Fetch was instructed to bring tea. Gloria perched on an ancient sofa while Leonard stood with his back to the roaring fire, and with infinite grace lit a long filtered cigarette.

'I've been touring with Wolfit,' he said, pushing out the smoke.

'Oh,' said Gloria. 'That must have been nice for you.' She looked about for a moment. 'Wolfit *who*?'

Leonard almost choked. 'Wolfit! Sir Donald. I don't usually do this sort of rubbish, I can assure you.'

Gloria supposed he was referring to the film they were due to start shooting the next morning.

'Shakespeare,' he said.

'Oh. What were you in that, then?'

'First attendant to King Lear. Tricky work. The sword was very heavy, for cardboard. Everything was hunky dory so long as you didn't get in Sir Donald's light.'

'New to this game, then? Films?'

'Goodness, no. I've done a couple of Old Mother Riley's. I helped Fabia Drake out of a taxi in a film last year, and last month I handed a champagne glass to Jean Kent in a frightfully swish night club.'

'Oh. What did you say?'

'I said nothing. Jean Kent said "How delightful. Thank you so much, young man". I suggested to the director that I should reply "Not at all. Any time. Would you like a cherry in that?", but they would have had to pay me more if I spoke. So I didn't.'

'Sounds like a funny sort of business, this film lark,' said Gloria. 'So, are you famous, then?'

He flicked his cigarette dramatically into the fire and slid with the smoothness of a sleepy panther onto the sofa, moving so close to her that she could feel his breath on her face.

'I'm your leading man,' he said, 'and I'm looking forward to page 58 of the script. Our romantic scene, where we kiss passionately and cling to one another against the darkness of the unthinking world. I fancy we're going to need a good many rehearsals to make it look like the real thing.'

'Oh, yes?'

Gloria turned to where Bromley had appeared in the doorway.

'Here, Bromley. What's this about page 58? I'm a convent girl, me!'

1903

It had always seemed to Laura extraordinarily lucky that George, as well as being a genius, was so good looking. His hair, black and abundant with curls, gave him the look of a tousled god. His eyes had a constantly questioning quality that she found totally reassuring; his lusciously wayward moustache had been a source of illicit delight all their married life. Since taking over St Ann's Well Gardens in Hove, George had been more exasperating than ever, but she thrived on his restlessness, his forever looking beyond the next thing. Not that it surprised her. He had always been ambitious, with too many talents that he tried to balance. She'd seen it in the early days when he'd been a stage hypnotist – fake, of course, although he always denied it. He'd left all that behind, even if part of him would always be showman and charlatan. Now, it was film, film, film. It filled his life. Each morning his moustache bristled with it, his head bursting with ideas that might have come from Mars. There were days when Laura felt she couldn't keep pace with him, and that in some way this might see them drift apart.

'I've made a list,' she said.

'What sort of list?' asked George.

'An acting list. When you're shouting out directions, there are times when it isn't really clear what you want me to do.'

'I've never been that good with words. Pictures, that's the thing.'

'Well, this might help. It's a sort of system.' But she was doubting her idea already. 'Here.' She put the paper in front of him. He stretched out his legs under the table, pushed the paper under a table-lamp and read.

'It's easy,' said Laura. 'Against each number, there's an emotion. So, Number 1 is Happy, Number 2 is Hopeful, Number 5 is Deliriously Happy, Number 6 is Sad, and so on. Twenty numbers and twenty emotions.'

George was casting a dubious eye over the paper. 'So, how does it work?'

'You call out "2" when I go to the door to fetch a letter, then as I open the door you call out "6".'

'Why "6"?'

'I don't know. Perhaps because it's a letter from an old aunt who's passed away.'

'But you'll have come into all her money so I'd call out "5".'

'Well, you see how it works. I've kept the list down to twenty to keep it manageable, although there's another I thought of yesterday: "So absolutely livid that I begin jumping up and down".'

George laughed, kicked his legs up, made the paper into an aeroplane and sent it flying towards her.

'Darling, your mastery of the art of acting never ceases to amaze me. Anyway, today you have a film all of your own, apart from a black cat and a few extra people.'

'Oh!' said Laura, flouncing her head. 'A leading lady at last.'

'Yes. Almost like a star shining in the sky... what you might call a film star.'

'That sounds good. Where's the cat?'

'Don't worry about the cat. I thought you preferred dogs.'

He had hidden the puppy behind a bit of the fireplace. It was her birthday, and he never forgot. The little creature was so small, so vulnerable, so warm to the touch.

'He's lovely. How beautiful he is! Oh, George!'

She kissed him, his moustache getting in the way as usual. 'What shall we call him?'

'How about Oscar?' said George.

1958

On the first day of the shoot for *Blonde Warning* the actors and crew assembled at Darting Hall. Bromley Marchmont introduced Francis and Gordon to the company as the film's best boys. An unsmiling Doreen Clissold, the continuity 'girl', interrupted to say that Bromley didn't know the meaning of 'best boy'. She redefined the boys' tasks on *Blonde Warning* as helping out whenever wanted, fetching and carrying, helping the actors go through their lines, and making the tea. 'But we'll call you best boys if it makes you feel any better,' she said, still unsmiling.

Even Bromley took notice when Doreen spoke. It was Doreen who could be relied on to keep a gimlet eye on every aspect of the filming, especially crucial when time was so short and the director so short-sighted.

'Thank you, Doreen,' he said. 'I've never had the pleasure of working with you before, but of course I know of your reputation for being a calm vessel patrolling troubled waters.'

That didn't elicit a smile from her, either. Sharp-featured, with mousy hair and thin lips that suggested they had never seen lipstick, her eyes looked out behind crimson-tipped butterfly spectacles. Even at first glance, the boys knew that she would wear variations of the same clothes each day: a well-pressed beige blouse, thin wool cardigan tightly buttoned, tartan skirt and sensible shoes. Her clipboard was always in place, held between herself and the world like a portable drawbridge.

'So, you're the best boys?' asked Des Drew the cameraman, who was trying to remember the name of the film they were making. His sight wasn't too good either. He saw four boys but had been told there were only two.

'From what I've heard, these lads are local heroes,' announced Bromley.

'Too darned right,' said Leonard Whiteside, languorously draped over one of the Darting's armchairs. 'They're more famous in these parts than any of us!'

'I don't care if they're Rawicz and Landauer,' snapped Doreen, turning to the boys. 'Don't get under people's feet. Things will be muddling enough without.'

Within minutes Francis was going over lines for Denier

V Warren, an elderly actor whose starring role in *The Bells* decades before had left him with an insatiable urge to work some of that play's dialogue into everything he did. Still, Francis took an immediate liking to the old boy with his stories of Henry Irving, while across the room Gordon was wool-winding for the octogenarian actress Marie Brewer who was playing the heroine's mother and smelled of lavender water and kippers.

'Oh my dear,' she told Gordon, 'poor old Bromley must be one of the most disorganised directors I've ever worked with, and I've worked with a few. That girl' (and she lifted an eye in the direction of Gloria Devine) 'is green as a gooseberry, and as for that leading man, Mr Whiteside, I've seen more charm in an umbrella stand. I recall once, and oddly enough it was at the Oldham Coliseum, that I played opposite an extraordinary young man who had no talent at all, and went on to stardom on some appalling quiz programme on the television.'

'Oh, don't talk to me about Oldham,' said Doreen dismissively.

'Mr Whiteside has played with Wolfit!' said Gordon.

'Oh my dear!' cried Marie Brewer. 'So have all the worst actors you could hope to meet at the Labour Exchange. Goodness knows how Miss Devine will get on with him. She seems a nice enough gal in her way, but…'

'No experience,' said Doreen out of the corner of her mouth. 'Poor kid. She's got a romantic scene with that creeping Casanova tomorrow. I hope Bromley realises we're aiming for a "U" certificate.'

'I don't think these young boys should be on set when that is shot,' said Marie Brewer. 'Standards have slipped since my day.'

'Not to worry,' said Doreen. 'It'll be about as sexually alluring as creosoting a shed.'

'Have you worked on many films, Miss Clissold?' asked Francis.

Doreen gave him a cold stare. 'Enough. I've worked with the best, not that it's done me much good. Continuity is way down the pecking order but, yes, David Lean, Thorold Dickinson, they always ask for dependable old Doreen.'

Knowing how much these movie people loved talking about themselves, Gordon asked 'What are you doing next, Miss Clissold?'

Doreen frowned at her clipboard and said 'Retiring.'

The ineptitude involved in the making of *Blonde Warning* was obvious to Francis and Gordon from the first day of shooting. Having surveyed all the rooms and locations around Darting Hall, Bromley decided there was nowhere suitable for the scene when the blonde heroine returned to her shabby suburban flat after a night out at a sophisticated night-club.

'If we use this place as the back-shot, it'll look like she's living in Buckingham Palace,' shouted Bromley. He usually shouted, often through a megaphone, even in a confined space. The studio's carpenter couldn't be got from Hendon, so the crew did the best they could, and knocked up a fake façade outside the stables. As this was to be the very first scene to be filmed, it set everyone's nerves on edge. Francis and Gordon had already overheard whispers of discontent. Leonard Whiteside complained that Bromley was so short-sighted that he had been giving acting directions to Des Drew for the bedroom scene.

'Just make sure you keep one foot on the floor and all will

be well,' Bromley told him, before being informed that he was talking to the cameraman, not to the leading man.

'Think nothing of it, Bromley,' Des answered, 'I've got double vision.' Leonard remarked that the portents for the film were quite bad enough without its cameraman seeing two of everything.

Riffling through the costumes sent down from the Regina Studios, the cast looked with dismay at the ill-matched garments they were expected to wear.

'Just as I expected,' said Denier V Warren. 'It comes as no surprise to any of us who have worked on an Important Film production before. The woman who does the costumes is colour-blind.'

Shooting began at ten o'clock on Monday morning outside the stables. Gloria arrived with Doreen. For a moment, Leonard didn't recognise his leading lady. She wore a blonde wig. Of course, he thought, the film is called *Blonde Warning*. She seemed a decent sort. He felt he got on rather well with her. Her lack of airs had made him think he might have too many of them, but somehow, he saw now that nothing about Gloria worked. The wig didn't suit her. The awful clothes didn't look right on her. The colours jarred, but perhaps in black and white it wouldn't really matter. He thought that might be the perfect motto for Important Films: 'It Doesn't Really Matter'. Bromley made a brief speech to the assembled company about how they were all embarking on making a work of art, then gave Gloria some instructions about the first scene. The very tone of his voice told the company he didn't have much hope of getting anything like a performance out of her.

She was portraying a beautiful young woman returning to her humble abode after spending the evening at an exclusive

London night-club with her wealthy boyfriend. Looking on, Leonard suppressed a snigger. Gloria should have been wearing a shimmering gown or Paris-cut cocktail dress, not the frowsy, badly constructed frock with its absurd butterfly bow stuck on its rump. It made her look like a chorus girl from a third rate production of *Rose Marie*.

'You go up to the door and open it,' announced Bromley. 'Roll cameras!'

Gloria had a slight tussle with the door, but got it open.

'Cut and print!' shouted Bromley.

'The wall shook, Bromley,' said Doreen. 'Didn't you notice? Should we do another take?'

'Put something about subsidence in the next scene,' said Bromley. 'What's next?'

'Golly,' said Francis, under his breath. 'I suppose it will get sorted out by the film editor. Norman Reeve, isn't it?'

'Yes,' said Gordon. 'Except that Norman Reeve's just another name for Bromley Marchmont. He always edits his own films. That man needs new glasses.'

It was eight o'clock that night when they shot Scene 14, in which the heroine visited the stately home of her boyfriend's family. The sky was moonless, and a chill wind was sweeping autumn leaves into a slight frenzy around the crew's feet. Gloria sat in a canvas chair on the edge of the set at the entrance to Darting Hall, a blanket over her legs.

'Gordon, luv,' she called. 'You couldn't get us a cup o' tea, could you? I'm perished, me.'

Gordon couldn't have been more delighted. From the first moment he had seen Gloria, he had been her willing slave. He hurried to the kitchen where Leonard Whiteside was propping up Lady Darting's Aga. Leonard looked down at his legs, twisting his feet about.

'Doreen!' he called. 'Shouldn't have flannels on now, should I? Shouldn't they be the pin-stripe trousers for this take?'

Doreen was passing, and said there wasn't a problem. Gordon made haste with the kettle and was soon at Gloria's side with a beaker and biscuits.

'What a malarkey this is,' said Gloria, almost whispering in his ear. 'I wish I was 'ome.'

'Home?'

'In Oldham. I like Oldham. There's no place like 'ome, Gordon. You'll find that out if you don't know already.'

Gordon knew he knew already. Uncle Billy had made a perfect home for him at Bundler's Cottage. He couldn't imagine being happier anywhere else.

'Me mam's not been too well,' said Gloria. 'I were just tellin' Doreen. Mam's gettin' on, you see, and they put her out o' the mill. She loved working there. They don't want the old women now, they can't work quick enough, can't keep up with the fancy new machines. She's been right down, me mam.'

'Oh, that's tough,' said Gordon. Just to think that he was speaking to a film star gave him a warm feeling inside.

'I were safe in Oldham,' said Gloria, looking around and lowering her voice even more. 'I don't know why I'm 'ere. Now, that Leonard, he's a real actor and all. Me, I've done sweet Fanny Adams. I don't know 'ow I got into all this. There's Bromley thinking I'm a real actress from that RADA place, but I told him, all I ever was is Miss New Brighton of 1955.'

'Well, they must have cast you for a reason,' suggested Gordon. 'I can think of several.'

She lifted a quizzical eyebrow at him.

'I mean, you are very beautiful,' Gordon said, and blushed as he said it. 'And you seem like a really nice person.'

Doreen Clissold bustled into the room. Gloria was examining herself in the mirror in readiness for the next scene, half of which they had shot earlier.

'I'm sure this isn't the right hat, Doreen' said Gloria. 'I wore a different one for this scene, didn't I?'

Doreen said no, it was fine. By now, Gloria was thinking of being somewhere else. 'I wish I could telephone me mam, let her know I'm all right.'

'Why don't you?' said Gordon. 'Lady Darting'll let you use her telephone.'

'Not much good. We haven't got a telephone at 'ome. We don't know anyone in Oldham who 'as. Anyway, you know how to cheer a girl up, Gordon. Some girl's goin' to get lucky one day. You make a lovely cuppa.' She shivered. 'It's a bit spooky around here when it gets dark.' She shifted the fox fur that had been hung over her shoulders, and sniffed at it. 'It smells horrible.' She looked at a label that had been fixed to the fur. 'No wonder. According to this, it's been poisoned.'

'You'd smell bad if you'd been in a damp studio wardrobe since 1928,' said Doreen. She took the fur and gave it a vigorous shake.

Bromley was announcing the next scene through his megaphone.

Gloria sighed, 'I can't remember the words, Bromley.'

'Just as well. There aren't any. You come into frame walking up to the porch from the drive. You have arrived at this stately home by taxi.'

Gloria looked around. 'Where's the taxi?'

'Unnecessary expense,' said Bromley. 'There'll be the sound of a departing taxi on the soundtrack as you come into view. You feel in your evening bag for the key, fumble about a bit. Then you hear the owl hooting.'

'Where's the owl?'

'On a gramophone record. You look up, startled. You catch your breath – "too wit too woo" – and you're just about to bring the key out of the bag when you hear a twig snapping. You switch around, alarmed, and back up the steps to the porch as you see this man coming towards you out of the pitch-black night. Then just keep looking straight into the camera. Sheer terror.'

'You mean, as if the camera is the man?'

'That's it. Press yourself against the door, as if you want to melt through it.'

'She's got two fox furs on,' shouted Des from behind the camera.

'You really must get your eyes sorted out,' said Bromley. 'Roll!'

The arc light swung into play as the star of *Blonde Warning* approached the porch of Darting Hall. Everything considered, the rest of the day's shooting hadn't gone too badly. People remembered their lines (or an approximation of them), stood in the right place, gave performances that wouldn't have disgraced the Bridlington Weekly Repertory Company. Until this moment, it was nothing but a job. Now, just as Bromley shouted 'Roll!', Gordon felt something in the air, something that cancelled out optically challenged Des, the self-centred leading man, the hideous costumes, the shaking artificial walls, Bromley stumbling through scene after scene. Only Doreen seemed efficient, alert to every nuance, forever referring to her clipboard and making notes. Now, even she was still.

The place fell quiet. Gloria walked slowly from the imaginary taxi, heard the hoot of the (to be added later) owl, fished in her bag for the key, turned her face as the twig snapped, then switched to look directly into the camera as the imaginary man approached her, coming closer and closer. It was then that her body seemed to become another being. Her face almost lurched into the canopy of the porch, as her eyes blazed into the eye of the camera. It wasn't a beautiful face, as Gordon had imagined. In repose, it was brassy, too made-up, the features too angular, the cheekbones slightly out of sequence, but in the intense blackness of that night, with the arc light burning into her face, even the hardened cameraman Des, with over sixty films to his credit despite his double vision, tingled.

Something in the air changed. The old actors acted (not in front of the camera) differently. Respect hung in the air; conversation was quieter. The following morning as the company assembled for the first shoot of the day there was a calm on the set that Doreen had never known before. It was soon shattered. Bromley was the last to arrive. He rushed in, his face flushed, looking about the place as if searching for something.

'She's gone! Gone!'

'Who's gone?' asked Doreen.

'Gloria. Vanished. Early this morning she got a telegram from her mother. Gloria just telephoned me from the train station. She's on her way back to Oldham because her mother needs her. She says she'll be back at the end of the week to finish her scenes.'

'Well,' said Denier V Warren, 'she's cooked her goose and no mistake. Irving would have had her hanged and quartered.'

'What is happening to our profession?' cried Marie Brewer. 'The girl's a complete amateur! She'll never work again.'

'She's a funny kid,' said Leonard Whiteside. 'I've got to like her. In a strange way, I trust her. She isn't like us.'

'What on earth do you mean?' asked Marie Brewer.

'She's more real than any of us. There's something else going on inside her.'

The others turned to stare at him. Doreen Clissold couldn't waste time wondering why the girl had messed up so badly. The shooting schedule would have to be reworked in the hope that Gloria would return. There seemed no way of getting in touch with her. She hadn't left an address in Oldham, and her agent knew nothing.

'Of course,' said Denier V Warren, 'she could be replaced.'

'Dash it all,' said Leonard. 'Let's face it. I don't think this film's worth a twopenny ticket without that girl.'

Then, there was nothing else to do than to get back to work. Doreen was looking in her handbag for a handkerchief when some keys fell out of it. Leonard stooped to retrieve them, and looked down to where the handkerchief had got entangled with some jewellery. He pulled a bracelet free and held it to the light.

'This is a lovely thing, Doreen.' The bracelet had been engraved. He looked at it closely. 'Whose initials are these?'

Doreen almost snatched the bracelet and other baubles from him and stuffed the trophies back into her bag.

'Very impressive initials, anyway,' laughed Leonard. 'Did you distinguish yourself on the battlefield, Doreen?'

'Don't be ridiculous. I'm very proud of it. It was my grandmother's. And don't waste time on fripperies. This film is a mess,' said Doreen, turning to Francis and Gordon. 'And I don't want you two boys hanging around all the time! There's enough to worry about without that. If you want to stay, you can take it in turn by working shifts, one boy at a time.'

To everyone's surprise, Gloria came back two days later. Her journey had been a waste of time. There was nothing wrong with her mother. The mill-owner had taken her on again. Gloria couldn't understand the telegram at all; her mother had never sent it. Bromley was relieved to have his leading lady back on the set. Des Drew said it was as if the weather had suddenly got out. She faltered over some of her lines but everyone laughed it off and the scenes were shot again. It was Gordon's turn to be working on the set that morning. He noticed how the others looked at her, heard Marie Brewer say to Denier V Warren 'Sometimes, you know, Denier, it's a once in a lifetime thing. It's given to very few to have greatness thrust upon them. Of course, I worked with Marie Tempest so I know what I'm talking about.'

Gordon didn't understand, only felt something he couldn't explain.

The boys had all but forgotten about their association with *Blonde Warning* by the time it was released in cinemas. The Jones's family returned to Red Cherry House from their outing to the Gaumont. Doris Jones said she had never seen anything like it. George Jones had laughed most of the way through (except during the bits that Gloria was in), while Uncle Billy couldn't stop thinking of how proud he was that Gordon was now part of the film world. While the adults continued their discussion, Gordon and Francis went up to Francis's bedroom, and for a while they remained silent, Francis propped on the pillows of his bed with his hands behind his head, Gordon crumpling himself inside Francis's roomy old armchair.

'As we got to the end of that first day,' Francis began, 'do you remember Gloria looking into the dressing-room mirror and saying "I'm sure that's not the hat for this scene"? She thought she'd worn a different hat in the bit of the scene she'd done earlier, but Doreen said it wasn't the wrong hat. Gloria just accepted it, and carried on.'

'Yes,' said Gordon. 'And I caught Leonard Whiteside looking at himself in the mirror...'

'Nothing unusual there,' laughed Francis.

'... looking himself up and down, and he said something like "Are these flannels OK, Doreen? I think I wore the pin-stripe trousers, if we're doing the other half of that scene we did this morning." Doreen gave him one of her school ma'am looks, consulted her clipboard and assured him that the flannels were correct.'

'Well, no one would have the cheek to question Doreen. She was renowned for her tight grasp on continuity, so no one dared question her, and the rest of the crew were either too short-sighted or disinterested or wrapped entirely up in themselves to notice.'

'Part of the problem being that a film set is so confusing, doing bits and pieces of the script out of sequence, and people always coming and going.'

'Exactly,' agreed Francis. 'It was bedlam. Which just goes to show how vital a really good continuity person is.'

'Then, there was the telegram that Gloria was sent,' said Gordon, 'asking her to go back home to Oldham at once. Gloria didn't even stop to consider: she had to go. That's the sort of home-loving girl she is. Even though walking out on the film would probably ruin her reputation, she didn't hesitate. But her mother had never sent that message, although it had come from Oldham.'

'Wait a bit. During one of the tea breaks I remember someone, I think it was the lovely old Miss Brewer, laughing about having played in something dreadful at the Oldham Coliseum, and Doreen said "Don't talk to me about the Oldham Coliseum!" The way she said it suggested she might have worked there herself at sometime, so it's quite possible that she knew people in Oldham.'

'Yes, and telephoned them to ask a special favour. Knowing what sort of person Doreen was, they would almost certainly have agreed to send that message from an Oldham post office, as if it had come from Gloria's mum.'

'And it was on that second morning, the morning Gloria vanished, that Doreen told us we were no longer both required on set at the same time.'

'So, why did she do that?'

'For the same reason she had got Gloria out of the way by sending her back to Oldham. Gloria had her head screwed on the right way. She was far from being the silly, dizzy person that Leonard Whiteside first imagined, although he really came to respect her later. Doreen knew that Gloria would soon have worked out what was going on, as would we.'

'So, what you're saying is…?'

'*Sabotage*,' announced Francis. 'Doreen had no interest in *Blonde Warning* beyond doing a professional job on the continuity; she knew the film would play a handful of cinemas as the supporting feature, and be quickly forgotten. But almost at once, as soon as the camera looked at Gloria, Doreen could see something special, something that didn't come out of a make-up box or could be taught at RADA or anywhere else. Doreen thought she was watching a sort of miracle.'

'I don't understand,' said Gordon. 'Why wasn't it

Bromley or Leonard or Des or any of the others who recognised it?'

'Well, I think they probably did. But Doreen's reaction was more intense.'

'Why?'

'She knew what it meant.'

'Oh, come on, Francis, less of the riddles! What are you *saying*?'

'Remember when Leonard picked up that bracelet that fell out of Doreen's handbag?'

'I think so. So what?'

'He held it close up and said something about it being engraved with initials. He laughed and said "You haven't distinguished yourself on the battlefield, have you, Doreen?" and Doreen said, "It was my grandmother's. I'm very proud of it."'

'I still don't get it,' said Gordon.

'I think the letters engraved on the bracelet were V.C.! Victoria Cross! That's what Leonard *thought* the initials stood for, that's why he made that crack about her having been on a battlefield, and Doreen played along. She made out it had been her grandmother's bracelet, and sort of left the suggestion, although no one spelled it out, that her grandmother had won the Victoria Cross, and it had been commemorated in the bracelet.'

'So what?' shouted Gordon. 'I'm no wiser.'

'Well, for a start, *no woman has ever been awarded the Victoria Cross*.'

'Then…?'

'Come on, Gordon… don't you see? V. C. stood for something quite different,' said Francis. 'It stood for Veronica Chasen.'

'*Doreen Clissold* was *Veronica Chasen*?'

Gordon was certain that an agape face didn't suit him, but quickly recovered. 'Apart from anything else, Bromley Marchmont would surely have recognised her? After all, he had *made* Veronica Chasen the star she was.'

'Yes, thirty years earlier. Now, she was a totally different person. People do change, you know, and the image perpetuated by those early silent films of hers had long vanished. Blodwyn Williams thinks that the films themselves probably no longer exist. And Doreen Clissold wasn't beautifully made up. That hair is probably a home perm, and she could have bought her clothes off a market stall. And those butterfly shaped glasses disguised eyes that had once bewitched a nation!'

'You have got a way with words,' said Gordon, 'but that still doesn't explain why. Mind you, you'd already told me about that Veronica Chasen film Blodwyn Williams had talked about, *Poisoned Promise*. Of course I didn't connect it at the time, but the day Gloria complained about that smelly old fox fur she had to wear for one of the scenes, she yanked it off her shoulders and saw there was a label attached to it. She just glanced at the label and said she wasn't surprised the fur was smelly because it was poisoned. I suppose the fur had a label that said '*Poisoned Promise*' as it had once been part of the film's wardrobe, and Doreen said something about she wasn't surprised either, because if Gloria had been hidden away since 1928, she'd be pretty smelly too.'

'Yes! Doreen recognised it as the fox fur she'd worn all those years before.'

'That's all very well,' said Gordon, 'but it still doesn't add up…'

'Can't you see? Doreen must have thought she was coming to the end of her working life. She hadn't planned ever to meet

Bromley again after they drifted apart. Their relationship had been professional, not personal. And then Important Films hired her for *Blonde Warning*. She knew that Bromley's reputation had dwindled after he slipped into making "B" films. She wasn't surprised when she started work on it that it was just as second-rate and shoddily put together as she'd expected. She steeled herself to get through it and then she'd fade away.'

'So, what changed?'

'She saw Gloria. It was immediate, from her very first scene, I think. All of us were aware of something different having happened. By the end of that first day Doreen knew that the camera loved Gloria, and Gloria, in some magically inexplicable way, gave herself to it. And then the idea came to her. Gloria might be the leading lady but she had relatively few scenes, and half of them were in the can by the end of the first day. Doreen arranged for her friend in Oldham to send the telegram that lured Gloria away.'

Gordon was no less mystified. 'But why go to all that trouble?'

'Simple. She knew that *Blonde Warning* would suffer the fate of almost every "B". It would sink without trace, an absolutely average little film with a starless cast and washed-up director. Doreen, or Veronica, had seen something in Gloria that she felt she couldn't let slide into oblivion. So she sent Gloria to Oldham, and made sure, with careful timetables on that clipboard of hers, that neither of us ever worked on various bits of the shooting. She was free to carry out her plan; to make the film as ridiculously bad as she could, so that attention would be drawn to it. People would read about how laughably terrible it was, and go to see it, and there would be Gloria, and they would leave the cinema walking on air.'

Gordon got it at last.

'So, that's why that vase on the table changed three times in the same scene. That's why one minute it was dark night outside the window, and when the character moved around the table, the next shot of the window showed a brilliantly sunny day. That's why those pictures on the wall kept switching, one second a painting of cows in a field, the next a red-faced clown. And the scene with the policeman, one second he was clean-shaven, the next shot he had a beard, and the third he was clean-shaven again, all in the space of thirty seconds.'

'That's it,' said Francis, 'and Doreen knew that Bromley would be doing his own editing, and he wouldn't notice the discrepancies. It was an act of huge generosity on Doreen, or Veronica's, part.'

'I should say it was,' agreed Gordon. 'Now, the public can't wait for her next film.'

'Ah, well, the public may have to be patient.'

'Why?'

'I'm not sure Gloria is even aware of what she did. There was something utterly natural about her, something so rare and genuine that she's left people speechless. For the moment, she's quite happy back in Oldham.'

'And Doreen? I mean, is she still Doreen Clissold or is she Veronica Chasen?'

'There's to be a major retrospective of her films in London. And you needn't worry about poor old Bromley either. According to some of the critics he's invented a whole new genre of film. He's famous all over again; the oldest cinematic *enfant terrible* of all time. People go to mock *Blonde Warning* and they leave with their lives changed forever. Gloria's soul opened for them. She reached out beyond the screen. She'll be one of the greats.'

1903

'It's like a great big box of delights,' said George. 'A great big glass box of delights.'

Laura looked on as he locked the door of the studio, his very own Crystal Palace, where he daily worked wonders, dissolving, inventing close-ups, superimposing images and screen wipes. Tonight in the laboratory he would work into the dawn on the ghostly apparition of that parlourmaid arising from her grave in search of her can of paraffin.

She was holding Oscar, the gifted dog, who couldn't bear being away from her. 'You look tired, George,' she said.

'Only exhausted.'

It was seven o'clock in the evening, and already the dark was smudging the landscape of St Ann's Well Gardens.

'What are you calling the film?' she asked.

'I thought *Mary Jane's Mishap*.'

'Hmm. Good title. It'll bring them in.'

It was good to snuggle into the fur of Oscar, like burying herself in a heart-beating muff. She dandled the puppy close to her face so that their eyes met. For the briefest moment, she had the sense that the animal looked directly into her soul. She couldn't tell what he saw there. Perhaps he was the only creature to see that despite being the first leading lady of British films, Laura Bayley would die forgotten. She couldn't tell, but a faint shiver, a tiny electrical shock, broke the link between the woman and the animal.

George was already walking away from the studio towards the house, his shoulders a little more hunched, his step a little slower, his moustache a little wilder. She often worried about him, although she needn't have bothered. He would die at 95. For all his cleverness, it was still the showman and charlatan about him that Laura loved best.

How could it be otherwise?

After all, he had immortalised her.

First and Last

The first shall be last and the last shall be first. Time and its tricks, thought Francis Jones.

He had never imagined he might return, but here he was, watching fields and lanes and half remembered patches of woodland scudding past the car window, and then the signpost, *Blackton 8 miles*, pointing him back twenty years.

'I'm pleased you came, Francis,' said the driver. 'Pleased we met.'

It happened by chance. Edward Pember had travelled north from London the previous day, booking in at the County Hotel in readiness for his aunt's funeral the following morning. Two days earlier, a friend of Francis had remembered to ask 'Did you see that obit in the *Telegraph*? I thought of you. Didn't you know her? Alicia Ackington?'

Then, it hadn't occurred to him that he might be at the final farewell, but that evening, sitting in his garden as the late summer night's gloom deepened, he made up his mind, telephoned the County Hotel and booked a room. He and Edward had literally bumped into one another in a corridor, and discovered over a drink in the deserted bar that they were on the same mission. Francis didn't drive, but Edward had come by car, and offered Francis a lift to St Benedict's.

'Aunts can be very time consuming,' said Edward, breaking a silence as the car took another corner.

'Sorry?'

'Aunts. You were telling me about your aunt. Winifred, wasn't it?'

'Oh, yes. Auntie Winn. A jovial soul. There was always an abundance of aunts when I was growing up.'

'In Norfolk?'

'Yes. Branlingham. Do you know it?'

'No, but it sounds very Norfolk.'

'Auntie Winn was Norfolk born, but tended to be a bit of a rebel, married a northerner and moved up here. Every summer I was packed off to spend some of the school holidays with her and her husband.'

'So, you know Blackton well?'

'I think I must have, once,' said Francis, but as the green approach to the town gave way to the first dribble of ramshackle houses, he wasn't sure. It wasn't the physicality of the place he remembered, but the atmosphere, the feelings that even now, twenty years later, he could summon up.

'And I can't get used to calling it Blackton,' he said.

'No,' said Edward. 'It's not often that a town changes its name.'

Since winning a painting competition in the *Eagle*, Gordon Jones had become something of a personality in its pages, having been featured in 'Hobbies Corner' as a collector of cheese labels. He was now a proud member of the Fromologists' Circle, and had just swopped a surplus-to-requirements label for Caerphilly Minor for an elusive label for Double Gloucester Minor. His suggestions for new plotlines for the *Eagle*'s resident policeman P.C.49 had also borne fruit, for 'The Case of the Bruised Avocado' (one of 49's most baffling problems) had been based on Gordon's plotline.

The end of the summer holidays promised to be exciting, too, for Gordon was to be a special guest, as an '*Eagle* Friend to All', at Hulton's Boys and Girls' Exhibition at Olympia. The one disappointment of the summer was that he couldn't join his cousin Francis at his Auntie Winn's house up north. Auntie Winn had assured Gordon that as he was now famous, he owed it to his admirers not to abandon them, and if (which was most unlikely) he should not be so famous next year he was very welcome to come to stay then.

Much as Francis enjoyed living with his mother and father at Red Cherry House, there was a different sort of pleasure awaiting him at Auntie Winn's, the little house perched on a hill above the dirty town somehow keeping itself above the fray, and smelling of Lurpak and furniture polish.

Uncle Eric, Auntie Winn's husband, was a college lecturer, and always treated Francis as if he were a long lost friend, ready for a walk through the woods, or an excursion to the yachting pool, or playing a gramophone record that he particularly wanted Francis to hear. On this particular day Uncle Eric had to go to London on business. It was a spanking bright morning licked by a warm breeze, and Francis was surprised by how homesick he felt. His spirits hardly lifted when Auntie Winn's daughter-in-law, Ivy, called in for a cup of tea.

Auntie Winn had tuned in to Francis's doubtful mood. 'Lovely day for it,' she said, whatever 'it' was. 'Too nice to sit about indoors.'

As if under instruction, the sun strode across the back

garden that sloped down the hill, giving the lolloping tulips a Technicolor gleam.

'Dad's old bicycle is rusting in the shed,' said Auntie Winn, 'just waiting for a run out.'

'It's a death trap, that bike,' said Ivy. 'Why don't you come out with me? I'm off to The Vale. Francis would enjoy that, wouldn't he, Mum?'

As the years passed, Auntie Winn grew increasingly unsure of what a growing boy might or might not like, but she thought it best to sound encouraging.

'Oh, The Vale. You'd love it, Francis. It's a lovely drive, and the garden's out of this world.'

'We can stop off on the way back and have a grand tea somewhere,' Ivy added, and five minutes later Francis was sitting beside her in her green Morris Minor.

'What's The Vale?' he asked.

'One of the oldest houses around these parts. I work there as a part-time companion to Miss Ackington. The Vale's a special place.'

It must have been, compared to the dreary rows of terraces that surrounded it. Like a shy old lady who had gathered her skirts around her and retreated into a world of her own, the house was hidden from the road by high brick walls and abundant laurel that spilled out over them, so green that it was almost black. Turning into the drive between the stone pillared gates, it seemed to Francis that the very air he was breathing had changed. It was absurd. The distance from the gates to the house was only two hundred yards or so, but it wound its way, each bend accentuating the separateness of the building that waited at the end of the twisting journey.

The little car might have been a vehicle from outer

space, from which this place appeared as something distinct. Although the sun shone here, just as it did at Auntie Winn's, a quiet coolness enveloped him as he got out of the car and stood looking up (for it had a tallness, like an imposing person standing over him) at the house. So, this was The Vale.

'You'll enjoy the garden,' said Ivy, wrenching back the hand brake. 'Miss Ackington doesn't like visitors in the house, but she'll be delighted for you to explore the grounds. I'll be about an hour.'

Francis tried to smile but felt angry, as if he'd been sent to the Tradesman's Entrance, although according to Ivy he wasn't even going to get as far as that.

'Rose will look after you,' said Ivy.

'Who's Rose?' Francis was trying not to sound surly.

'Miss Ackington's housekeeper. She'll be on the outlook for you. There's plenty to see. Don't go too near the stream at the bottom of the garden. There's a rat run there, and they're such horrid things. Now, let's synchronize.'

Ivy pulled back Francis's cuff to reveal the Ingersoll *Eagle* issue wristwatch that Gordon had bought him for his last birthday.

'I'll be finished at half past three. Have a good time.'

Ivy chucked him under the chin and went into the house. Francis made up his mind he'd never come to the place again.

'You were privileged to get to know my aunt,' said Edward Pember. 'Few people did.'

A signpost told them it was five miles to Blackton.

'But not that first day,' said Francis. 'Ivy made it quite clear that I wouldn't get beyond the kitchen.'

'And a cup of Rose's tea?'

'Exactly. I suppose I felt miffed at being so ignored, but the garden… well, it sort of overcame me. It was the first garden to have that effect on me. It wasn't that it was spectacular, or had magnificent waterfalls. Thinking of it now, I suppose it was quite neglected, but the wildness had got into the heart of it. It seemed to welcome me. Do you know what I mean?'

'I think I do.'

'I was glad that I'd been dumped there, and, sorry to use such a tired phrase, but it really seemed as if… well, as if time stood still. Something changed in me that day, and it began in the garden at The Vale. It's difficult to explain.'

'No, go on.'

'Naturally, the first thing I did was the forbidden thing. Never mind Ivy's warning. I had to find the stream. Sure enough, it was only a moment or so before I saw the first plump rat, sleek and nimble, skidding into the water. The stream was overhung with willows and trees. It was an intensely private place, where the sun had blotted out, and the liquid sound of the water trickling in from wherever it was sourced. It was as if there could be no other sound in the world, but I was to find out later that everything about The Vale seemed only to belong there, different from everything that was happening outside its walls.

'When I'd had enough of the shade and the rats, I wandered through the grounds, the greenhouses filled with decaying fruit because nobody had bothered to collect it, the walled garden where most of the plants had run to seed. The path across the lawn led me back towards the terrace that ran off the back of the house, and that's when I heard the voice. At first I thought it might be the cry of an old animal.

'It was Rose. "Boy!" she called, and I caught sight of her.

She reminded me of an elderly blackbird I'd once seen waiting on the railing of a church. "You, boy! Tea!"

'She had gone from the window when I got up to the house. Being a polite boy, of course I knocked at the nearest door. It must have been on the latch, because it swung open and there she was, standing against the ancient stove of the kitchen, wiping her hands on a towel. It wasn't only her head that was bird-like. She wore a long black dress that finished just above her ankles, and she was short, with tiny feet tucked into flat black shoes that fastened across the top with a button, and small hands. Her grey hair scraped the top of her head. She told me to come in and sit down. "What's your name?" she asked. She didn't take much notice when I told her. "It makes no odds to me," she said, "but *she'll* want to know. Would you like a lump of cake?"

'She pointed to a shelf, and to a tin that had 'Cake' helpfully embossed on its side. I took down the tin. She prised it open and cut a thick slice of sultana loaf.

'"You can pass me the tea caddy as you're up," she said, nodding at another shelf.

'I picked up a caddy and was handing it to her when she almost shouted, "No, not that one."

'She snatched it from me and set it back on the shelf. "The one with flowers on it."

'I'm not sure what else she said at that first meeting. Nothing much more, as I recall. I just sat and ate the cake and drank the tea with her sitting there across the table. It should have made me feel uncomfortable, but it didn't.'

'Well,' Edward laughed, 'Rose wasn't exactly known for her scintillating conversation.'

'When I'd finished the tea, she looked at me quite strongly

and said "Francis, isn't it? She'll want to know. You'd best go back to the garden now, until Mrs Bannister collects you."

'It must have been another half hour before Ivy – Mrs Bannister – collected me. I suppose I did feel as if I were a parcel. It was pretty obvious that Rose hadn't spent much time around sixteen-year-old boys. I think perhaps her curt manner came from a shyness.

'I wandered through the grounds, cut through to the stream, watched a rat or two going about its business. It began to grow dark. I made my way back up to the house. I'd made up my mind to knock on the door and jolly well let Ivy know that I was fed up with being kept in the garden like a mongrel let off the lead. Even so, I was too timid to march up to the front door, and I certainly didn't intend finding that Tradesman's Entrance.

'Just as I reached the side steps onto the terrace, I heard music. Nothing unusual in that. Mum and Dad always had the wireless on when I was a boy, and Uncle Eric never thought a day complete unless he'd sat me down to listen to something, Elgar or Delius or one of those. But this music was different. It was the first time music *stopped* me: I can only put it like that. Just stopped me, as if it had taken me over.

'It was a piano I could hear, and a melody that made me shiver. Not those frightening shivers you get when it's suddenly cold as if an icy finger has trickled along your backbone; this was quite different. The music waved over me, soft as a breeze. I breathed it in. For a moment or two I couldn't see for the ecstasy. It was only when I heard the melody hesitate, then stop and start again, that I knew it couldn't be the wireless or a gramophone. No. Someone in the house was playing the piano. I crept a little down the steps, standing with my back against the rhododendrons, just to listen and keep out of sight.

'And then Ivy came out and called that it was time to go. Just as she started the car, Rose ran up and presented me with a little parcel of goodies: some home-baked ginger snaps, I seem to remember. We drove off, and I don't suppose I'd have given The Vale a second thought. After all, I'd been treated as a nuisance and a nonentity, which of course in itself can be a useful lesson in life. But the next day Rose telephoned Auntie Winn and told her that Miss Ackington wanted to meet me.'

'So, that's how it began,' said Edward.

'That's how it began,' said Francis.

'You've achieved something that no one else in Ackington has managed,' said Uncle Eric. 'You must have a magic touch. I've got something somewhere…' It took him a while to find the recording.

'Ackington's Second', he proclaimed, waving the shellac records in the air. 'She was a great composer. Twenty, oh, thirty years ago she was considered one of the best of her generation. Two symphonies, three string quartets, a tone poem, chamber music, some piano pieces considered progressive in their day. And then she stopped composing. The music dried up.'

Through the fierce crackle of the gramophone records, Francis detected something of the feeling he had experienced that day in the garden, listening to the piano being played at The Vale.

'Alicia Ackington is as mysterious as the Sphinx,' said his uncle through the sucking of his pipe. 'We've had newspaper journalists and people from the radio and television making pilgrimages up here just to catch a glimpse of her, let alone meet her, but they've never succeeded. Some people think it's selfish of her. In her parents' day, The Vale was the centre of this place, the moon around which lesser planets revolved. Writers, painters, film stars, composers, there was always someone staying up there. There's a painting in Blackton Museum of the family on the terrace at The Vale, with Sir Edward Elgar and Alicia Ackington as a child sitting on his knee. All that's gone now, of course. There's just her and that miserable housekeeper.'

Francis wasn't sure that miserable was the right word for Rose, but wanted to learn more from Uncle Eric about the mistress of The Vale. The facts themselves seemed to belong to a forgotten history. Alicia Ackington had been born in India of wealthy parents before being brought back to England. Her father, Sir George Clausby Ackington, had broken away from the family business in the north. There had been a time when no British home was complete without a bottle of Ackington's Remedy to safeguard against all known ills, but George hadn't the will to carry on the quack chemistry on which his forefathers had thrived, and advancing science was steadily undermining the business.

George Ackington wanted the artistic life. He became a famous painter, immortalising the most successful people in society, and set up his family in South Kensington and a villa in the South of France, as well as the ancestral Ackington family home, The Vale. His daughter Alicia was educated at home, and, after studying at a famous London musical academy, revealed her talent to a grateful world.

'*She* is easily tired,' Rose said as she took Francis through the hall to the drawing-room on his second visit. As her hand touched the handle of the door, she turned and said 'She liked the look of you. She watched you from the window.' For a moment, Francis could have sworn the housekeeper was suppressing a smile, but she almost fiercely turned away from him, stepped into the room and announced 'Francis Jones', as if he were arriving at a ball.

Alicia Ackington was standing by the open French windows in what Francis instinctively recognised as a pose she had adopted for effect. The late afternoon light was stark enough to turn her figure into a silhouette. When she turned to face him, he saw her face, old, with a powdered, mask-like quality.

'So you are the boy I saw in the garden,' she said, making no attempt to come closer, and not seeming to ask a question.

'Yes. I'm Francis.'

'I,' she said, 'am the last of the Ackingtons.'

She moved carefully to a wing-backed chair, sat, and indicated a large portrait above the fireplace.

'My father,' she said, waving a hand in its direction, but not looking at it. 'Sir George Ackington. He would have liked to marry me off to some poor young man, but I could not let that happen. What a very disappointed poor young man he would have been. My mother taught me by example. When she could no longer put up with Sir George, she took to her bed and died of something that was never adequately explained, death being the less scandalous alternative to divorce. My father went into what in those days was delicately referred to as a decline. Childhood beckoned him back. He had never been an easy man, or a good father, and was slow to make friends. A friend or two in life is never a bad idea. You would do well to remember that. Forgive me; I've forgotten your name.'

'Francis.'

'Francis.'

She pondered this for a moment.

'My father suffered a terrible fate; the worst that can befall an artist. He became unfashionable. I think he'd lost count of the number of royals and aristocrats who sat for him in his studio. The younger generation called him "The Cadet" – in the line of Constable and Sargent, you understand – and his paintings were regarded as being behind the times. He was not without fault. He despised what they call modern art. He was quite wrong, of course. You should keep your mind open, Francis. After all, what is a work of art? I suspect that each of us is one. It was arrogant of him to paint only what he saw and what he thought others wished to see. He became more of a reporter than a painter. His work is largely discredited today. He would have been furious. Even the gallery that he founded has taken his works from its walls. The sad thing is that my father thought he was painting the truth.'

'What was it like being the daughter of a great painter?' asked Francis. 'Did he ever paint you?'

'I forget.'

She turned away from him.

'The years play such tricks. My father lived long enough to see the town that his forefathers had created from nothing grow shabby and lifeless. It must have been difficult for him.'

'And for you,' suggested Francis.

She stared hard at him for a moment.

'Well, perhaps. No matter what happened, I knew that I would stay here, although The Vale is far too big a house to be rattling about in.'

'You had your music to sustain you,' said Francis, eager to find out everything about it, but, as he was to discover throughout his later visits to the house, any reference to her career met with a blank response. Perhaps it seemed to her to belong to a different time: it had ended, after all, decades before, since when all had more or less been silence.

'When Sir George died, we still had staff to run the house, but his will was unhelpful. There was a queue of creditors, and it was impossible to keep them on. I always think of what Saki wrote: "The cook was a good cook, as cooks go; and as good cooks go, she went."'

'At least you have Rose,' said Francis.

'Ah,' said Alicia Ackington. 'Rose… Dear Rose.'

When it was time to leave, Miss Ackington said 'Make sure to see Rose before you go. She'll be annoyed if you escape without her parting gifts,' and sure enough as he was crossing the hall to the front door Rose came bustling up with a paper bag filled with good loose tea. Even during these acts of kindness, Rose had a habit of arching her eyebrows as if she had just enjoyed some displeasure. Her mouth would move about, but never settle into a smile. She never waved him off, but scuttled into the back of the house as soon as she pressed her leave-taking present into his hand.

That night, as they were getting into bed, Auntie Winn told her husband 'I don't know what that old woman sees in him.'

'That's not very complimentary, Winn. I can't think why anyone wouldn't like Francis around them. He's a thoroughly nice young man.'

'Don't be daft,' said Winn. 'Of course he is. And I think Doris has done a brilliant job bringing him up.'

'Well, it's a change to hear you say something good about that sister of yours.'

'Well, she has. And I love Doris, of course I do.'

'It's not as if he's anything like either Doris or George, is it?' said Eric. 'Francis seems to get on superbly with them, and they think the world of him. He's as intelligent as they come, too. He must be a breath of fresh air up at The Vale with those two crabby old women.'

'But is it good for *him*?' asked Winn.

They need not have worried. When Francis left for home at the end of the two week's summer holiday, he took away with him a copy of the complete works of Shakespeare and a manicure set, both presents given to him by Miss Ackington, but almost at once his Norfolk life took over. At first, there was no time to think of The Vale or Alicia Ackington, and certainly not Rose. There was so much to catch up on with Gordon, and the few remaining days before the new school term were filled with a blitz of brass-rubbing. Like an enchanted castle that vanishes into the mist from which it mysteriously emerged, The Vale faded from his mind.

That was how it seemed, but it was not so. As summer segued into autumn, Francis began to be aware of changes in his life, almost imperceptible at first, as if something was gently tugging at him. It was unsettling. He thought it might be hormones. Sometimes, when he heard music, it was as if his nerve ends came alive and took control of him, but control was what he felt he was in danger of losing, so powerfully could a piece of music threaten to overcome him. Bit by bit, he remembered the day when Ivy had left him in the garden, the afternoon he'd been left to wander aimlessly about. He was taken back to how he had felt when, hidden from view, he heard the piano being played in the house. Then, of course, he hadn't known that Alicia Ackington was a composer. Now, he thought 'Why on earth didn't I ask her what she was playing?'

Perhaps he didn't want her to think he was snooping.

Perhaps she was a witch, a white one, of course, for her playing had awakened something in him that would never leave him. He knew instinctively that whatever music he heard that day had been her own. From nowhere, the melody came back to him.

'*So* you went back to The Vale?' asked Edward.

'Yes, the following summer. When I got to Auntie Winn's there was a letter waiting for me, so my visits began again. In a funny way, it was as if they had never stopped.'

'You know, I think over all the time I knew Aunt Alicia I can't have been to the house more than two or three times. And you were going, what, every day?'

'During those holidays, pretty much, yes.'

'My aunt never mentioned you,' said Edward, but he didn't sound accusing. He could sense what she might have seen in the boy.

'Come to think of it, I never mentioned *her*,' Francis replied, as if that were explanation enough. 'Our friendship – for that was what it was – was something that concerned no one else. A boy of, what was I? Sixteen? And an elderly woman. Me wanting to find out everything about the world, and she trying to keep it at bay. And that's how it went on that second summer, just the two of us, and Rose of course. And, once, your aunt's lawyer.'

'Oh!' said Edward, and he turned his head to Francis and laughed quickly. 'You met Jonathan?'

'I'd forgotten his name.'

'Jonathan Bothwell.'

'I was invited for tea one afternoon, and arrived early. Rose was looking out for me from the window as I came up the drive. She told me to wander about the garden because "she" had an important visitor with her.'

'Back to wandering about the garden? It must have been quite like old times!'

'Yes, back where I had started. It was a lovely day, and I thought I might as well make the best of it. I decided to try to retrace the route I'd taken the very first time I went to The Vale, so I made for the stream. The rats hadn't moved house. I counted a few, and then made for the greenhouses, and wasted some time in the walled garden. I kicked my heels for a bit and got fed up eventually, and remembered that the next thing I should do was wind back to the house and stand at the side of the terrace and do some eavesdropping. It was a spiteful and silly thing to think, and of course I had no idea that there would be anything to overhear, but just as I got halfway along the steps up to the drawing-room I heard a man's voice from within the house.

'"A mere formality," the voice said. It was velvet smooth, quite soft and immaculately enunciated. Only those three words, "a mere formality", but I instinctively thought it was a voice out of place, a voice that didn't belong to the house, that the house wouldn't have been happy with it. And the voice continued, "It will be quite safe with me, I assure you" and then a sound as if a chair was being pulled up to a table. There was another pause, and then the voice: "Here" (then, after another pause) "and here... most satisfactory. And now, Miss Ackington, I think we need speak of the matter no longer."'

Turning towards the windows, the man caught sight of Francis. 'There's a boy in your garden,' he said.

'Ah yes,' said Alicia Ackington. 'That will be Francis. Come in, Francis. This is Mr Bothwell.'

'Jonathan Bothwell,' said the man, offering a hand. 'Bothwell, Bothwell and Staine.'

His mouth widened, revealing a good many teeth.

'Pleased to meet you, sir,' said Francis.

'Of course, I remember now. Miss Ackington has been singing your praises. She sees so few people at The Vale. You seem to have made rather an impression here.'

'It's very kind of her to invite me.'

'Presumably you will soon be returning to school?'

'At the end of the week.'

Bothwell's smile grew even wider.

'Just as well, perhaps. We mustn't tire Miss Ackington.'

'I hope I haven't been a nuisance.'

'Not a bit of it, I'm sure,' said Bothwell.

He smiled and gave a deep sigh at the same time, which seemed to indicate that so far as he was concerned the matter was now closed, and that Francis would never again darken The Vale's doorstep. The sharp crack of the clasp on his attaché case provided a full stop, and Bothwell put out his hand again.

'A pleasure to have met you, young man. A safe journey home.'

Jonathan Bothwell's car was as sleek as the skin he lived in. Instinctively, Francis knew that the engine would never rise above an apologetic murmur. He would remember the softness of the man's handshake and the eyes with no warmth in them. None of that upset him. He was more put out when, just as Bothwell reached his car, Rose ran out to him and pressed a paper bag into his hands. So, she wasn't making a special fuss of Francis with her parting gifts; Jonathan Bothwell was also sent home with freshly made Devonshire

227

scones or a wedge of Victoria sponge or a packet of loose tea. The only consolation was that Rose wasn't smiling at him either.

The day before the funeral, Francis telephoned the Ackington Gallery from the County Hotel. He was referred to a young man who introduced himself as the curator, listened to what Francis had to say, and agreed to see him at three o'clock that afternoon.

Forlorn as the Ackington Gallery looked, across the road from the Job Centre, its sandstone façade was enlivened by a neon sign that read *Nights and Lights: Rural Prospectus*. The rooms of the gallery were grand, tall and wide, the walls painted white, with here and there patches of black text overhung with fluorescent tubes. Traffic noise fed through a multitude of loudspeakers criss-crossed the building. Anxious not to offend a woman in a rag dress (Francis suspected she might be the artist, and didn't want to upset her by appearing disinterested) he feigned interest in the exhibits. It must have been his grammar school training! He was rescued by a bearded young man in cords and a white shirt who walked up to him, his head enquiringly on one side.

'Mr Jones? Hello. I'm Sam Draper. Good to see you. I think I've read your books.'

'Oh, really?' Such recognition embarrassed Francis. His response was always to change the subject as speedily as possible. 'You're one of the few. I'm sorry to have rung you out of the blue.'

'Pleasure. You were asking about our holdings?'

'Yes. I wondered if you still have the Ackington paintings here?'

'Ah.' Draper made a sort of grimace. 'The Ackington paintings. Are you looking for anything in particular?'

'Well, I was hoping you might have some on display.'

'It's a problem. Changing times. Do you know the history of the gallery? It was the gift of Sir George Ackington. I'm sure you know that the Ackington family invented this town. Until a few years ago, when the family quack medicine business collapsed, the town was more generally known by the locals as Ackington. It's only in more recent times that they've got used to calling it by its given name, Blackton.

'And you probably know more about Sir George Ackington than I do. He donated his substantial private collection of works to the gallery, including a great number of his own paintings. Under the terms of the endowment they were to be displayed in turn at frequent intervals.'

'A shrine to Sir George?' suggested Francis.

'Effectively, yes. Up until a couple of years ago anyone coming through our doors would have known exactly what they were going to see. People like the familiar. But changing tastes, you know. New brooms have to do their sweeping. The Ackington collection was taken down and put in store.'

Draper looked over his shoulder and lowered his voice.

'Between you and me, it gets even a little more embarrassing. Some of the Ackington paintings have been sold off on the quiet; you won't sneak on me, will you? That almost certainly went against the terms of the bequest, but we couldn't get any clear answer from the estate. Alicia Ackington. She's the last of the family. She said she didn't much care what we did with her father's work. So, some were sold – at least they've managed to help the gallery stay open – some have been passed on to other galleries, and the rest are in store here.'

'A wasted journey, then.'

'Not necessarily. As I say, we still have a few of Sir George's paintings in store. You're welcome to take a look if you wish.'

Francis expected a basement vault, but the picture store was at the top of the building, reached by an ornate spiral staircase, concealed behind a door that wouldn't have defeated a novice burglar.

'We should have a dozen or so,' said Draper. 'These are the ones we couldn't farm out.'

Francis had seen many Ackingtons over the years. The quality varied, and these were not the best. Not for the first time, he wondered what Sir George had thought of his paintings. Did he look on his own work with a sense of achievement? There was no doubting the professionalism, the man's craftsmanship with paint and brush, but for Francis the paintings had a deadness, a chill, that repulsed him. He admired the man for having broken away from the Ackington family business to strike out as an artist. In his way, Sir George had been a genuine Bohemian, but Francis couldn't identify with what he saw on canvas. He remembered what Alicia had said about her father all those years before: 'He thought he was painting the truth.'

'These are all there are,' said Draper. 'Nothing much to interest you, I suspect.'

They were on the point of leaving the store when Draper reached into the rack and took out a large framed oil.

'This one shouldn't even be here. It's obviously not an Ackington. Too weird!'

He turned the frame towards Francis.

'Its titled on the stretcher,' said Draper.

Francis's heart leapt.

'And it's signed,' he said excitedly. 'Look. Bottom right.'

'So it is. So it is an Ackington! Nothing like his other work. But that's his signature, certainly.'

'You can just make it out,' said Francis, 'beneath the girl's shoulder.'

'You think that's a girl? I would never have thought of Ackington as an abstract artist. I mean', and Sam Draper looked intensely at the canvas and then back at Francis, 'if that is a girl, the poor thing must have been horrified. What was he trying to do? The anger comes out at you, doesn't it?'

'It's safe here, anyway,' said Francis. 'Where no one can see it.'

The day of the funeral was warm. The little church of St Benedict's was pleasantly cool that morning, although the sun was already up, beating against the East Window and through the reds and greens of the stained glass. As Francis and Edward Pember settled into a pew half way down the nave, a small woman in black, a tidy black netted hat perched at one side of her head, walked down the aisle to the front of the church.

'It's Rose,' said Francis, almost to himself.

She turned briefly in their direction as she arranged her dress before sitting. She didn't smile, but made a slight nod. It had been twenty years since she had set eyes on Francis. He didn't suppose she would recognise him.

The vicar tactfully delayed the proceedings a little in the hope that a few more people might make the effort to walk up through the old town to pay a last homage to the last of the family that had made it all possible. As the vicar led the coffin's procession up the aisle, Francis looked over his shoulder, and whispered to Edward 'I don't see Jonathan Bothwell here.'

Edward almost burst out laughing.

'Now, that *would* have enlivened things,' he whispered back. 'They're burying *him* next week.'

The vicar welcomed everyone to the vicarage for refreshment after the service. When Francis and Edward came out of the church, Rose was already getting into a taxi. Francis thought he would probably never see her again, but when they got back to the vicarage Rose was standing in the garden, speaking to some mourners.

'So glad you could come,' said the vicar, who had changed into a casual shirt and slacks. 'I hope the sandwiches hold out. Thank God for Sainsbury's.'

Francis had often thought how much more enjoyable were the parties after funerals; the ones at weddings were much more stressful. He supposed one of the reasons might be that, having seen off the dead, mourners realised that they themselves were alive and kicking. They drew in breath. It was like a new beginning, almost.

He kept watch on Rose, nodding and dipping her bird-like head, as she moved from one group of people to another, until, all at once, he thought she must have gone, but suddenly she was beside him, looking up at him with those arched eyebrows, as if something might be about to make her angry.

'You've grown,' she said. 'But I would have known you anywhere.'

'Rose.'

He balanced his wine glass and plate in one hand and stretched out the other to grasp hers.

'We never lost track of you,' she said. 'She was so proud of all you achieved. She often talked about you, you know. Never forgot.'

Francis wanted to say how often he had talked of Rose, and Alicia, and The Vale, and all they had meant to him, but the vicar was calling from across the lawn.

'Rose. Your taxi is here!'

'I must go,' she said. 'When do you leave for home?'

'Tomorrow.'

'Do you remember the manicure set?'

'Do I? Of course I do.'

She was foraging in her handbag for keys.

'I must get back to The Vale,' she said, and then she was gone. Edward Pember drove Francis back to the hotel, made arrangements to meet the following month for lunch, and left for London.

It was late afternoon by the time Francis walked through the town, up through the shabby streets of Blackton, a place still unsure whether it would be better to be known as Ackington. The iron gates at the entrance to The Vale had rusted. They creaked and stuck when he pushed them aside, resistant against the thick weed of the drive. The sound was a fanfare for his return to that place of childhood enchantment, Ivy bringing him here in her Morris Minor, Auntie Winn and Uncle Eric (both long gone) wide-eyed at what he told them of his visits here, and now on he walked, along the path between the banks of luscious black-green laurel.

Today, he didn't make for the garden but went directly along the side of the house. He hadn't gone far when he stopped to listen.

He knew that sound. The French windows of the drawing-room were open. His skin tingled. He stood, listening and waiting, a stranger in the garden again, just as he had twenty years before, when the music stopped. Rose was facing away from him, seated at the piano. She didn't switch her head, but as he walked into the room she said 'I'm glad you came.' She turned on the piano stool and looked back at him.

'It seems an age ago. That day when you were left to wander in the garden.'

'It was an age ago,' said Francis. 'The first thing I did was to look for the rats I'd been told to avoid.'

'Oh yes,' said Rose, and almost smiled. 'The rats… That might have been the only time you ever came here, and you could have told your grandchildren, "I once was taken to this extraordinary old house and was given a cup of tea by an old housekeeper, and I never realized that the old lady who lived in the house was very famous."'

She touched the piano's keys, stood and walked over to Francis.

'But she liked you. She liked the look of the boy in the garden, and I can't say she was wrong. Alicia had good taste.'

'I've heard that music before,' said Francis.

'I thought you had,' said Rose.

'That very first day. Of course, I've always thought it was Alicia who was playing the piano.'

'And now you know.'

'Yes.'

'How did you find out?'

'It wasn't until a few years ago. I'd had it in the back of my mind that someday I might write about Alicia and you and this house. I wrote to ask if she'd give her consent to my doing some research about her days studying at the Academy.'

'Yes. She told me.'

234

'The rules are quite strict if you want to research that sort of thing. I had to have her written permission before the Academy would let me consult her records. She agreed, on condition that I wrote nothing about her during her lifetime or yours, and of course I said I wouldn't dream of such a thing. The librarian at the Academy terrified me. She made it quite clear that I was only allowed to look at the information that dealt with Alicia's time at the Academy. She sat facing me throughout my visit, to make sure I didn't misbehave, but she was suddenly called away for a telephone call and, of course, still being the boy who went in search of the rats when Ivy had told me not to go anywhere near them, I turned over the pages. One of the reports at the Academy showed that Alicia had arrived there two years after her elder sister, and there was your name, on one of the pages I wasn't meant to be looking at.'

'I hope they said nice things about me,' said Rose.

'Oh yes. Your professors could hardly find the words to express their admiration. They wrote that you had a brilliant career ahead of you, that your qualities were something quite out of the ordinary. That your studies in composition suggested you would go on to write music that would be significant.'

'I see.'

'And when I turned back to read Alicia's reports, I could only find polite encouragement, and her teachers' doubts as to the extent of her talents, and the worry that arriving at the Academy where her elder sister had already established a reputation as a composer of promise would profoundly affect her progress. And yesterday... yesterday I saw your father's portrait of Alicia.'

'Oh dear,' said Rose. Her face crumpled. 'That horrible,

235

horrible picture. I told Alicia to have it destroyed but she wouldn't. What did you think of it?'

'It was as cruel a thing as I've ever seen,' said Francis.

'Our father was a cruel man. To have immortalized Alicia forever on canvas in such a way. Such a disfigurement.'

'She can't have been very old when he painted it? Sixteen? Seventeen?'

'About that, yes. Alicia had been arguing with him. She had always hated his portraits, and in those days the house was filled with them. You couldn't escape them. She told him that real painting was about telling the truth. The terrible thing is, she couldn't express those feelings herself, couldn't put them into anything she did. The even worse thing was that she had such ambition. It overwhelmed her. She wanted to achieve, but she hadn't any talent. She knew she hadn't.'

'And you were the mirror image,' said Francis. 'You had all the talent, just as the Academy recognized, but you lacked the ambition. No wonder she always declined to speak of her work. Alicia became known as the composer of all the work you had created, and you faded into the background and became Rose the housekeeper.'

Rose sighed.

'It didn't matter to me. I was content to see her lauded, and to know I had done what I had to do. It all meant so much more to Alicia than it would ever have meant to me. In the end, it was my lack of ambition that finished it. For some reason unknown to the public, it seemed that Alicia Ackington just gave up composing. I'd had enough, you see. I'd said all I'd ever wanted to say in music, so far as my ability allowed, and I told her it had to stop.'

'What will you do now?' asked Francis. 'You could become

famous overnight. You deserve to be recognized. Tell the truth. It can't hurt Alicia. The truth is what she believed in, in art if not in life.'

'Oh, Francis.'

She sat beside him, put her hands over his.

'How proud she would be to see you now. What would be the point of it? It would betray Alicia and ruin the rest of my life, and perhaps, in a way, yours too. I know I can depend on you to keep the truth in its box where it belongs.'

'Of course,' said Francis. 'You are a remarkable woman, Rose. I suppose I knew that from our very first meeting. I just didn't know *how* remarkable. And we won't lose touch again.'

'I hoped you would say that,' she said, and poured tea into their cups. A plate of banana loaf sat on the tray.

'But it wasn't only us that knew, was it?' asked Francis.

For a second, Rose's hand faltered, and then she began pouring the tea again.

'No?'

'I must have been almost a professional eavesdropper when I was a boy,' said Francis. 'I happened to be walking up the terrace one day when I heard Jonathan Bothwell speaking to Alicia in the drawing room. He said something like "Our secret is perfectly safe with me"' and then he said something like "Here" – and there was a pause – and then he said "There", and then it sounded as if he was so pleased with himself that he might almost cry out with excitement at any moment, and then he said something like "We don't need to mention it again." It struck me at the time that it was a slightly odd turn of phrase for a lawyer whose firm had looked after the Ackington family for generations. And wouldn't a trustworthy lawyer have said "Your secret is perfectly safe with *us*"? He would have been representing Bothwell, Bothwell and Staine, not himself. It jarred with me. And then there were those words "Here" and "There". Of course, he was pointing to where he wanted Alicia to put her signature to an agreement.'

'You were always an intelligent boy, Francis.'

'Jonathan Bothwell knew, didn't he? He knew the secret, and he made Alicia sign a document revealing the truth.'

'Yes. She didn't want to do it, but Jonathan Bothwell threatened to expose us if she didn't. She signed on the understanding that only at her death would he reveal the truth. And now,' she said, pouring more tea, 'you know it all.'

The rest of their talk was of Francis's career, of how Rose had plans to bring the garden back to its Victorian glory, of everything that might happen at The Vale now that Rose had it to herself. For that time, she seemed a younger woman, vital and interested in everything they spoke of, but as the sun went down she grew visibly tired, and Francis said he must go.

'Wait a moment,' she said, all life and energy again. She left the room and came hurrying back with one of her familiar brown paper parcels, pressing it into his hands.

'Loose tea. I couldn't let you go without your parting gift.'

He looked down at the hallowed parcel.

'You are the last of the Ackingtons now,' said Francis.

She smiled at him.

'Yes. I suppose I am.'

They walked arm in arm, down the terrace steps, along the drive, to the gates that opened out to the street. She waved as he walked off, back through her father's blackened town. At the corner, Francis turned and saw that she was there still, watching him, her hand raised.

He walked on, as happy as he could ever remember being,

clutching Rose's parting gift, as he had that first day. It was probably just such a parcel that she had pressed into Jonathan Bothwell's hands on the day after Alicia's death, when he had come to speak to Rose of the arrangements to follow. Into that parcel of tea, Francis knew that Rose had sprinkled a generous spoonful or two of the poison that for years had proved rather less effective at killing The Vales' families of rats.

Time and its tricks, thought Francis.

The first shall be last and the last shall be first.